Praise for Becky Barker's *Stowaway*

"...the well-developed plot and characters will keep readers turning the pages."

~ *Library Journal*

"Once again Becky Barker delivers a treat for both suspense and romance fans... I love the way she writes. She has a way to make you feel as you are part of the story and keeps you hanging on until the very last word. I loved this book and highly recommend it."

~ *Guilty Pleasures Book Reviews*

"*Stowaway* has it all, from a guy redeeming himself to a woman who's trying to put the past in the past... Through it all, there's hot sexual tension between Nick and Keri and a suspense that will keep you on the edge with tons of action in Stowaway. Loved it."

~ *Fallen Angel Reviews*

"I enjoyed *Stowaway*... their relationship was fun to watch develop, and the author did a good job of keeping up the sexual and other tension."

~ *Night Owl Reviews*

Look for these titles by

Becky Barker

Now Available:

On Wings of Love

Cade's Challenge

Stowaway

Stowaway

Becky Barker

SAMHAIN
PUBLISHING

Samhain Publishing, Ltd.
11821 Mason Montgomery Road, 4B
Cincinnati, OH 45249
www.samhainpublishing.com

Stowaway

Print ISBN: 978-1-60928-817-4
Digital ISBN: 978-1-60928-684-2

Editing by Sue Ellen Gower
Cover by Kendra Egert

First Samhain Publishing, Ltd. electronic publication: December 2011
First Samhain Publishing, Ltd. print publication: November 2012

Dedication

For Buzz, my better half in so many ways for so many years. I love you beyond words.

With special thanks to Christina Brashear for leading me into the future.

Chapter One

Desperation clawed through Nick Lamanto's body as he cautiously surveyed his surroundings. He realized, with a grim twist of his mouth, he didn't like feeling desperate. Not one damn bit. Normally, he thrived on danger and adrenaline highs, but this time the thrill seeped from his body as steadily as the blood from his gunshot wound.

Cloaked in darkness, he pressed himself against the trunk of a tree, and then sucked in a ragged breath as pain exploded in his left shoulder. His head spun, consciousness wavering, but he fought it with a strength born of innate stubbornness.

The bullet hadn't lodged in his flesh, yet the wound went deep and his constant movement kept it bleeding. Exhausted and getting feverish, he knew the eighteen hours of running and hiding had taken a heavy toll.

He had to get out of this town.

He didn't have a chance in hell of doing it if he stole a vehicle. Which meant hitching a ride. There would be roadblocks and probably an all-points bulletin out for him. The sheriff's department wouldn't leave anything to chance with a possible homicide involved, and he wasn't entrusting himself to the local good-ole-boys law enforcement until he knew how deep the corruption went.

A cloudy sky and the late hour worked in his favor right now. His experience with undercover work had taught him danger stalked like a jilted lover, but he had keen survival instincts. He trained to stay sharp in situations where one wrong move could cost his life. The odds were rarely in his favor, and even less so this time because he didn't have a clue as to what had gone down or who to trust.

A red neon light heralded the emergency room entrance of the county hospital and spotlights added illumination for a few more yards. Clouds obscured any light the moon might have cast, leaving most of the area in shadows.

Only a couple dozen vehicles remained in the parking lot. He had studied them all carefully. One particular black sport vehicle had camping gear piled to the windows. Plenty high enough to hide a man his size.

He recognized the vehicle. It belonged to the sheriff's daughter, Keri Merritt. Her brother, Jack, also worked for the department. Protective types, both of them, and he'd heard grumbling over her vacation plans. Apparently, she planned to leave town by herself and they didn't approve.

Nick knew she worked as a trauma nurse. He'd met her, along with half the other women in the county, at a community picnic. They'd shared a dance, but only because he'd asked her. She hadn't vied for his attention like many women did. His famed Italian good looks hadn't made much of an impression on her. So much for his irresistible charm too. Keri'd resisted pretty convincingly.

He didn't know where she planned to go for vacation, but it didn't matter. The concrete jungle of Miami was his home turf, and he was completely out of his element in Podunk, USA. He needed transportation out of here. Then he could contact his superiors, lay low for a while and take time to heal.

He'd slipped out of the shadows long enough to try the doors of her SUV, but found it locked. Not surprising. For the past hour, he'd waited and watched as the staff of the graveyard shift arrived and those of the earlier shift headed home. Now it had gotten quiet again so he could try to jimmy the lock and hope her vehicle didn't have an alarm system.

The sheriff's daughter would be a perfect escort to safety. He didn't know why it was taking her so long to leave work, but it was to his advantage. Creeping closer to her SUV again, he slipped a thin blade from his knife into the lock.

He'd just begun to play with it when the whirring sound of

automatic doors reached his ears. He swore silently. Voices accompanied the sound, and he ducked behind the vehicle. The swift movement had his limbs trembling and sweat beading his brow. It scared the hell out of him to feel so weak and vulnerable.

"I can't believe you're really gonna leave us, Keri, honey," teased a cheerful soprano. "You know you won't be gone an hour before you'll be missin' us."

Husky laughter responded to the teasing, deep and sexy feminine laughter. It rippled seductively in the night air, shimmying along Nick's nerves and punching him in the gut. The intensity of his reaction caught him off-guard.

"Forget it, Paula. I'm outta here. I don't care how many people have to work double shifts to cover for me!" she called back to her coworker as she approached the SUV.

Nick heard the gentle thump of the automatic lock before she reached the door, and realized she'd used a remote. Keri and her friend continued their banter while she climbed behind the wheel and turned the ignition. The engine purred to life. She slammed her door, lowered her window, and said a final goodbye just before a male voice called to her.

"Keri! Hold up! Telephone!"

Nick willed her not to ignore the summons.

"I am officially on vacation!" she shouted.

"It's your dad. And I already told him I could catch you," came the apologetic reply. "You know if you don't talk to him, he'll sic the whole sheriff's department on you."

Nick heard Keri's loud sigh and held his breath until she shut off the engine, hopped out the door and slammed it shut again. She dashed toward the emergency entrance where she got swallowed by the electronic doors.

Just the break he needed. She'd left her window down far enough for him to reach inside and unlock the back door. About damn time something went his way, thought Nick. He sent up a silent prayer of thanks to any saint who might still be watching over him.

It took only an instant to unlock the back door. It should have been easy to slide his legs under the piles of clothes and shut the door, but his useless arm made his movements sluggish and awkward. He jarred his shoulder, shooting pain over his body and making him so lightheaded he almost lost consciousness.

Get a grip, Lamanto, keep moving!

The mental nagging had gotten him this far, so he didn't cut himself a break. Once he'd finally gotten settled with his head directly behind the driver's seat, he managed to pull the door closed. Gritting his teeth against more pain, he struggled to adjust his length to the uneven space. Then he made sure he'd completely concealed himself before shifting the bulk of his weight onto his wounded left shoulder.

More pain radiated through him. His stomach roiled and threatened to upchuck. He took several deep breaths until the pain became bearable and his struggle for air less harsh. The pressure against the wound would halt the bleeding, and, if he got really lucky, maybe even numb his arm.

He'd barely had time to regulate his breathing before Keri returned. She shouted a final goodbye as she climbed behind the wheel, slammed the door and set the locks. Next he heard the whir of her window being closed. She switched on the radio, and country music blasted at a deafening volume.

Nick offered another silent prayer. With the radio blaring, any noise he made would go unnoticed. He might be able to get some desperately needed rest.

Once the pain in his shoulder had dulled to a slow throb, total exhaustion settled in. It was a relief to be off his feet and safely hidden even in such a cramped position. He didn't know where his unsuspecting hostess planned to go, but he hoped it was far, far from home.

Then, if luck held out a little longer, she'd decide to get a good night's rest before unloading the SUV. Given a little time, he would be long gone. She'd never have to know she'd helped him escape.

His satisfaction with the situation wavered when the vehicle made a sharp right turn, throwing him sideways. He stifled a groan, adjusted his position and braced his foot against the opposite door so it wouldn't happen again.

The sheriff's daughter had a lead foot and had a reckless streak behind the wheel. Her driving habits probably gave everyone in town fits. From what he'd overheard in his short stay, every member of the tight-knit community concerned him or herself with Miss Merritt's welfare.

Her petite stature gave the impression of fragility, but she looked healthy and capable to him. She had big hazel eyes and light brown hair cut in a short, sassy style. Her chin had a stubborn set to it, warning people not to mess with her. Nothing about the lady hinted at weakness or vulnerability.

Having met more than his fair share of trauma nurses, he knew most of them had more stamina than men twice their size. Still, this one seemed to appeal to everyone's protective nature.

Nick felt a change in their motion once they'd cleared the corporation limits and headed down the highway. They made no more stops and starts at intersections or sharply turned corners. The lights of town faded and a more intense darkness settled over him as the SUV picked up speed. He empathized with Keri in her desire to leave Thornsbury, Tennessee and its residents behind her. If he never set foot in the town again, it would be too soon.

Within a few miles, they'd probably be running into the first roadblock. He didn't know how the authorities were dealing with his disappearance, but he'd be considered armed and dangerous. They'd probably labeled him a person of interest in the investigation of Don Monroe's shooting. If Don survived, the charge would be aggravated assault of a law enforcement officer. If he died, suspicion of murder. Nick prayed his old buddy had survived.

When the SUV began a gradual slow down, he tensed again, figuring they'd encountered a roadblock. Who would be at this particular post? The county sheriff's deputies or the state highway patrol?

He didn't have long to wonder. The volume on the radio went low, the power window whirred and Keri called out into the night.

"Hey, big brother, don't you have anything better to do on a Saturday night than stand by the side of the road?"

Nick recognized Deputy Jack Merritt's voice as he approached the vehicle.

"Hey, Sis, I expected you through here an hour ago." When he stepped closer, he added, "You look totally wiped. Are you sure you want to drive up to the cabin after back-to-back shifts? Why don't you go home and get a few hours' sleep first?"

"I don't need sleep, I need distance," she argued. "You know it takes me longer to unwind after working sixteen straight."

"Have a hard time getting away tonight?"

"You'd think I was leaving home for good instead of just going on vacation."

"Everybody had another word of advice to offer?"

"A word or two or a million," she teased. "Including our father who called one last time."

"He worries." Jack excused their dad's behavior.

"Do you have a legitimate reason for delaying me, Deputy, or are you just bored?"

"We still haven't tracked down Lamanto."

"He has to be long gone or the dogs would have caught up with him by now," she said.

"They lost his scent near the stream and cost us valuable time. They picked it back up again near the highway, but I'm guessing he hitched a ride or had an accomplice waiting for him somewhere close. How's Deputy Monroe?"

"Holding his own but critical," Keri explained. "I thought the visiting cop was a friend of Monroe's. What reason would he have to shoot him?"

Nick's pulse raced at the news that Don was still alive. *Live, buddy, live*, he silently chanted while cheering Keri's reasoning. Why would he shoot the friend he'd come to visit?

Then he heard Jack's response.

"There's always a chance Lamanto turned bad. It happens a lot to those vice guys. He could be a front man for organized crime, trying to set up some operation in our area."

Nick clenched his teeth as blood rushed hotly through his veins. Bigoted bastards. Because of his heritage, people always wanted to link him to organized crime. It had worked to his benefit for undercover ops, but it annoyed the hell out of him when he risked his life to fight that sort of crime. Folks in this area would be quick to judge him. To most of them, he was a foreigner from the big, bad city.

"You think Monroe and Lamanto are involved with something illegal?"

"Don't know," said Jack, "but we aim to find out as soon as Monroe recovers or we find Lamanto. You didn't pick up any passengers on the way out of town, did you?"

"Nary a one."

Nick could tell Jack was scanning the contents of the SUV with a high-beam flashlight. He didn't so much as twitch.

"You're welcome to unpack the whole car if you'd like," Keri taunted her brother, "but then you'll have to repack it exactly the way you found it."

Jack groaned. "Nobody could pack the way you do. Don't you know it's unnatural to be so damned organized?"

Soft, feminine laughter floated back to Nick. For the second time in the space of an hour, he felt himself being enchanted by the husky sound. It eased some of the tension from his weary body.

"I'd rather be unnatural than never be able to find a clean pair of underwear when I want them."

Nick knew Keri kept house for her dad and brother. She probably didn't abide clutter or disorganization.

"That's a cheap shot, Sis."

"If the shoe fits..."

"It might be kinda nice to have you gone for three weeks," Jack decided. "You know the code if you run into trouble?"

She made a rude sound and pushed the power window button. Nick heard Jack's orders to drive safely before she shut him out completely. The window closed, the radio volume rose again and they eased around what he assumed to be a collection of patrol cars. Keri tooted the horn in greeting, and then they picked up speed again.

Relief washed over him with a paralyzing effect. He'd begun to think of Thornsbury as his personal Waterloo, not knowing if he'd make it out alive. He'd roamed too far from his home territory and people who trusted him.

He didn't know what the hell was going down, but he needed a clear head to figure it out. Years of working vice had given him a highly developed sense of self-preservation.

That same sixth sense had kept him from going directly to the local authorities after the shooting. Local, county and even state law enforcement around here seemed to be a part of a good-ole-boy network he couldn't fully integrate.

He'd lost his cell phone in the stream, and wasted his lone opportunity to use a public phone trying to reach his lieutenant in Miami. As soon as he was safely out of town, he'd try Alexander again. Right now, he needed time and distance. The sheriff's daughter had just bought him a little of both.

His own guardian angel.

The turn of events also won him a brief respite from the mental and physical stress of being on the run. Exhaustion overpowered his knack to stay focused.

One thing did manage to pierce his lethargy—the sweet, feminine scent clinging to the clothes he'd buried himself under. He found the scent of a woman as captivating as a beautiful smile. Keri's scent filled his lungs now, seeping into his senses and soothing him like a narcotic.

His pain and discomfort began to ease and blessed numbness overtook his body. The humming of the wheels and the gentle rocking motion of the SUV gradually lulled Nick to sleep. He dozed restlessly.

Then he heard the sound of angels singing and it startled him awake. No, he thought, mentally clawing his way through the fog of unconsciousness. It couldn't be angels. He hadn't died, had he? No pearly gates, no choir of angels. Just one angel with an awesome voice. But she wasn't singing Latin hymns, and his heart stopped racing.

Keri Merritt knew the lyrics to every song on the country station, and sang one after another. He didn't recognize many of the tunes and lyrics, yet they reached into his subconscious and struck a chord. Her sexy, Southern accent made each one more stirring.

The sound of her voice echoed around the vehicle, surrounding him, wrapping him in a cocoon of comfort as nothing else could have done. So sexy and sultry and as hypnotically seductive as her laughter.

The longer he listened, the more the music captivated him. Her lovely alto tugged at the depths of his emotions, coaxing like a siren's song. Reality and fantasy merged, and his mind began to play tricks as he faded in and out of consciousness. Keri was close, and then distant again.

He was home in his own bed, rocking on a gentle wave of water. The heat and humidity of South Florida permeated his body in a room steamy with passion. The woman in his arms felt petite yet shapely; tiny but not fragile. She smelled sweetly feminine and alluring. With the voice of an angel, she teased and taunted, and her laughter set his blood on fire.

He wanted her with an amazing ferocity. Every muscle and nerve in his body sang with excitement. He tried to pull her beneath him, but she remained elusive. One minute their naked arms and legs tangled, and the next she had slipped from his grasp.

He groaned in frustration then stifled another groan as he reached for her and pain shot through his body. Very real pain that shattered his dream.

Rudely awakened, Nick stilled his restless thrashing and fought through a haze of confusion until he remembered his situation. Hidden in the backseat of an SUV, heart pounding and pulse racing, he wondered if he'd groaned out loud.

He strained to hear beyond the roar of blood in his ears. The radio still played and Keri still sang. The tension in his body slowly uncoiled, but the remnants of his dream lingered.

His fevered passion turned to spiking fever, burning him up with heat. The piles of clothes and bedding suffocated him. He could hardly breathe. Shoving them from his face, he fought to stay alert, but more feverish thoughts whirred in his mind.

He'd been invited to Thornsbury and welcomed the opportunity to investigate a gun smuggling operation. Last night, he and Don had gotten wind of a meeting to be held at dawn on the outskirts of town. They'd hidden in a copse of trees where several men gathered, but the fog had been thicker than a brick wall. Darkness had shrouded faces. He'd recognized the voice of Russ Carson, a local militia leader, as well as Jack Merritt's. Two other voices had been too muffled to recognize. Then he'd heard gunshots and felt the searing pain.

Sweat poured off him as he relived the shooting. He heard Keri's voice in the distance, but the sound of gunfire reverberating in his head shattered his concentration. He remembered the force of the blast that shook his body and sent pain slicing across his shoulder.

Nick battled his way out of the feverish stupor, trying to avoid the mental replays. He strained to focus on Keri's singing, and let the richness of her voice soothe him again. Once he managed to concentrate solely on the velvety sweetness, he fell into a deep, undisturbed sleep.

Sometime later, somewhere in his sleep, the lilting quality of his angel's voice altered to sharp and commanding. Nick once again struggled for clarity of thought. He opened his eyes to an unexpected light and squinted at the pale light bulb above his head.

Sleep vanished with an awareness of danger. His head still

felt foggy but clear enough to realize the SUV had stopped moving and he wasn't hidden any longer. A narrowed glance toward the door at his feet brought his guardian angel into view. She looked more like an avenging angel considering she was pointing a very lethal weapon at him.

She was little. Her gun was not.

Chapter Two

Keri's expression warned him not to doubt her competency with the .45 caliber semi-automatic pistol leveled at his midsection. Their gazes locked, and he knew his reflected the annoyance in hers.

"Come out of there slowly," she instructed in a tone totally lacking its earlier sweetness. "Don't make any sudden moves and don't try anything stupid."

Nick noticed she stood close, but not close enough for him to kick the gun from her grasp. Smart girl. She couldn't know that kind of action was beyond his capabilities at the moment. It took all his strength to shove aside a few clothes and pull his body into a sitting position.

Once upright, his head swam. The numbness in his arm faded, sending an agony of pain slicing through his body. His breath hitched and grew ragged. He swiftly grasped his left arm to support it with his right hand. It took a few minutes to regain control and a little longer for the nausea to subside. Then he shot a glance at Keri.

"I might need a little help."

"You got in there by yourself. You can get out."

The sheriff's daughter was smart. Irritating as hell, but smart. Nick shifted his legs and carefully eased along the seat to the door, noting she took a slow step backward.

The gun wavered slightly, but she quickly steadied it. She probably didn't feel nearly as bold as she sounded. A woman alone would be a fool to take chances. Even though they'd met on good terms, she wasn't likely to trust him now that he'd been accused of shooting one of her dad's deputies.

Another rush of dizziness hit him when he stepped to the

ground. He held his bad arm tightly and leaned against the SUV until he regained some strength. Their gazes clashed again, and then hers slowly scrutinized the rest of him.

"You're a mess," she declared flatly. "I didn't know you'd been shot too. You'd better get into the cabin so I can see how much damage is done."

Nick took in their surroundings in one brief glance. They'd parked in a small clearing amidst a forest of tall pine trees. Grass or pine needles lay thick beneath his feet, and the SUV was parked in front of a small log cabin.

The pale yellow light on the porch indicated the existence of some kind of power. He couldn't tell if electric lines ran to the place or if it was generated by battery. He wondered about phone lines, the closest neighbors and their isolation.

"Get moving."

He obeyed without argument. His shoulder needed medical attention, so he'd have to worry about everything else later.

The distance from the SUV to the cabin was only a few yards, but they made slow progress. His legs felt too shaky, and his head pounded from lack of food and sleep. Every jarring step sent more pain through his shoulder, so he moved carefully. He sensed Keri's impatience as she followed him, but she kept a safe distance between them.

Negotiating the two steps on to the porch was difficult. He swayed and had to grasp a rail for support, but his gun-toting hostess didn't make a move to help. His estimation of her survival instincts kept improving. He didn't have the strength to overpower her, but she needed to be wary. If he'd had the strength, he'd have taken control of the gun within seconds of having it pointed at him.

He didn't want any more damned guns pointed at him.

Keri followed Lamanto through the door of the cabin, her gaze never wavering from him for an instant. As they moved farther into the lighted room, she noticed the blood stain down the whole left side of his lightweight cotton jacket.

Jack and her dad had wondered if he'd gotten shot too. From the looks of the bloodstains, she wondered how the man could still move. Most people would have collapsed from loss of blood long before now. She'd worked two full shifts since the shooting that had caused such mayhem in their small community.

Lamanto stopped just inside the room, and Keri knew he was mentally cataloging their surroundings. She'd lived too long with law enforcement officers not to recognize the routine.

He'd find the basic, four-room cabin serviceable, but not fashionable. The living room was the largest of the four with a door to the left that lead to a small bedroom and an even smaller bath. A wide archway at the back of the living room opened into the kitchen. Furnishings were mostly rejects from the Merritt home in town.

A thud came from the kitchen area, and Lamanto stiffened. He took a quick step backward and threw out his right arm in a protective fashion. The actions had to be pure reflex as he positioned himself to shield her from the unknown threat.

One tiny half step from him, and she sighed.

He would shield her body with his own, even though he could barely hold himself upright. His action dispelled some of her wariness. Whatever else Nick Lamanto had become, his instincts still leaned toward defending rather than hurting. Given that and his physical condition, she doubted he could fight his way out of a paper bag.

Gut instinct had her lowering the firearm. She hated guns, but her dad had insisted she learn to use them for her own safety. Why didn't it surprise her that even wounded, on the run and burning with fever, her captive cop still reacted in typically male, macho mode?

He was one of them. One of the men she privately labeled as protectors. One of the modern knights who had a penchant for defending the weak and innocent. With or without a badge, they all reacted the same way. She just wished she had fewer of them to contend with in her life.

Until the shooting that had shocked the whole town, she'd heard nothing but praise for the visiting cop. An old buddy of Deputy Don Monroe's, he seemed to have a great sense of humor and got along with everyone. He had a reputation of being a dedicated public servant, and descriptions of him had bordered on celebrity status.

Of course, his dark, striking looks hadn't hurt his public imagine, either. Women could be such fools over a handsome man. She'd met him and felt the pull of attraction, but hadn't been wowed. He came across as too smooth, too self-assured and too much a cop to hold her interest.

She'd didn't much care for errant knights, but this one needed her help. His armor might be a little tarnished. He might be a cop gone bad, yet she didn't consider him much of a physical threat in his current condition.

"I think a bag of groceries fell off the table," she explained the noise. She'd unloaded the back of the car before finding her stowaway. "I haven't unpacked everything."

When his defensive stance relaxed a little, she added, "If you give me your word you won't try to sneak out of here or do anything stupid, I can get rid of the gun and take a look at that wound." Knights, errant or otherwise, always took great pride in keeping their word.

"You're got it," he agreed weakly.

Keri checked the safety on the gun and put it in the first-aid kit where her dad stored it. Carrying the kit, she led her unwanted guest to the kitchen. She couldn't treat his wound and keep a safe distance, so she really didn't have a choice. She'd always been a sucker for wounded animals, of any species, and he barely had enough strength to walk. Besides, being afraid required more energy than she could muster right now.

"Sit down," she said, making room for him on one of the two chairs at the small dinette table. Thankfully, she'd gotten the generator running and unloaded the bulk of her supplies before discovering her unwanted guest.

She gathered clean towels, her first-aid kit and a pair of sharp scissors. When she had everything organized, she pulled on latex gloves and turned back to her patient. He'd managed to get his right arm out of his jacket, and she helped ease it the rest of the way off. Dried blood glued a dark green T-shirt to his muscular torso.

"You really are a mess," she repeated her earlier assessment.

"Yeah."

Despite his weakened, disheveled state, he was one gorgeous man, she thought while snipping through the fabric of his shirt. He'd caused quite a stir in Thornsbury this past week. Every woman within a twenty-mile radius had been raving about the visiting hunk.

His deep, bronze tan suggested health and vitality though he looked a little pale right now. With thick, wavy black hair and dark chocolate eyes, he'd caused a sensation with the ladies in town. He stood about eight inches above her five foot two and oozed sex appeal.

The mostly Caucasian, Protestant community of Thornsbury rarely had attractive visitors, especially one of different ethnic origin. So he'd been watched, analyzed and fantasized about all week. Keri had gotten tired of her friends and neighbors drooling over him.

His profession squashed her curiosity. Good, bad, ugly or handsome, she had no interest. One thing she didn't need in her life was another officer of the law watching over her. The last two things she wanted right now were a cop and a patient. She hadn't taken a vacation in two years, and she badly needed time to herself. She had her own plans and didn't want them jeopardized by some fly-by-night Romeo.

"Lean forward," she told him after tossing the bulk of his shirt toward an empty trash bag. She grabbed a towel, soaked it in water, and draped it over his injured shoulder to loosen the dried blood. "You really should be in the hospital."

He grunted in response.

"Are you allergic to any common drugs?"

"No."

Keri could tell he'd reached the end of what must be considerable strength. She hoped he didn't go into shock. She could give him something for fever and infection, but her emergency medical supplies were limited. She handed him pain pills and antibiotics along with a glass of water.

"If you want me to call the hospital, I can send an SOS. It wouldn't take them too long."

"No."

"You probably need blood."

"Yeah."

"If the bullet is lodged, I don't have any anesthetic to give you while I remove it."

"It's not."

"If you don't need surgery, the very least you'll need is stitches. Do you think you're so tough you can handle that without an anesthetic?"

"Yeah."

Keri supposed he could handle it. At this point, he was barely conscious. He'd probably pass out during the stitching. She hoped he had a high tolerance for pain.

After lifting the towel from his shoulder, she began peeling fabric from his wound, gradually easing closer to him. The chair sat against the wall, and his head dropped back for support.

He watched her through half-closed eyes shadowed by the most incredible lashes she'd ever seen on anyone. The long, thick sweep of lash had just the slightest curl at the ends. His hair had the thick, mussed look of barely controlled waves. A matching pelt of hair covered his chest.

She'd seen plenty of chests—broad, puny, muscled, wimpy, smooth and hairy. She wasn't easily impressed, yet she had to give the visiting cop a ten out of ten.

"Mind telling me why you got shot?" she asked in an effort to keep her mind off her patient's physique.

"Yeah."

Okay. He didn't want to confide in her. No big surprise there. Judging by the heat radiating from him, he'd soon be succumbing to the fever. She could wait for answers.

Keri cleaned his shoulder with water and anti-bacterial solution. The bullet had slashed the flesh, slicing like a knife rather than ripping a ragged hole. He'd been lucky, but it still had to be giving him considerable pain.

She leaned closer and poked the area with forceps, but couldn't see any bone fragment or detached muscle tissue. A sharply indrawn breath reminded her that her patient could feel her probing.

"Sorry." She hated hurting anyone but couldn't avoid it without anesthesia. "It's not torn too badly, but I have to stitch some tissue back together before the outer skin can start healing. It looks like you might be able to get by with six or eight well-placed stitches."

"How many for a faster heal?"

"A dozen or so small stitches would be best," she admitted, "but it'll take me longer and it'll hurt like hell."

"Just do it."

Keri clenched her teeth. Mr. Macho might think he could stand the additional pain, but inflicting it didn't hold much appeal to her. He'd pass out. She just didn't know how much he'd suffer until he did.

"You'll have to lie down in the living room before I start," she explained, knowing she couldn't handle the bulk of his weight once he fell unconscious.

For just an instant, their gazes locked, her eyes bright with annoyance, his piercing as he studied her. Even though Keri knew fever fueled the enervating glitter in his gaze, she felt a ripple of reaction over every inch of her body. It was not a reaction she welcomed or appreciated.

"I'll need some help," he stated flatly.

No please, no polite request for assistance. Just a bald

statement suggesting she should help him. Sometimes she found men, especially the arrogant ones, incredibly irritating.

Correction. She always found them incredibly irritating.

Well-honed muscles flexed as he pressed his good hand against the tabletop to boost himself out of the chair. She slid an arm around his waist for support when he began to waver. He felt like a rock-solid inferno of heat. The press of his flesh against hers seared her skin, inflaming every nerve ending that came in contact with his muscled form.

Then years of professionalism kicked into gear. She allowed him to rest most of his weight on her, but she'd forgotten about piling supplies on the sofa. Fatigue made her careless. Her brain and body would go into total meltdown soon.

"Can you stand on your own?"

"Yeah."

Swiftly, with Lamanto wavering on his feet, she grabbed a fresh sheet from her stack of supplies, spread in over the sofa and moved everything else to the floor. Then she helped him lie down with his injured shoulder toward her.

The small amount of exertion had him sweating and caused the wound to start bleeding again. She soaked a clean cloth with more antibacterial solution and put it on his shoulder while she collected supplies. Then she dropped to her knees beside him. He'd already passed out or fallen asleep so she quickly stitched his wound with small, close sutures.

Her patient wouldn't have time for a slow recovery and rehabilitation. He'd be checked out at the emergency room, interrogated and possibly incarcerated. What a waste, especially if he'd been a good cop at one time.

It didn't make sense to her, but she'd been raised by one of the finest law officers ever born. Her daddy remained her hero even if he sometimes drove her crazy. How often had she heard him say a bad cop could do twice the harm of a good criminal?

Shaking her head, she forced herself to concentrate on the patient and not the situation. Lamanto uttered an occasional low moan of pain but didn't thrash around too much.

After applying a sterile bandage to her handiwork, Keri began cleaning up after herself. She needed to radio her dad about this latest development in her vacation plans, yet she was reluctant to make the call.

First off, she didn't think Lamanto presented much of a threat right now. He was really weak and would probably stay that way for several days. Secondly, she didn't want half of Thornsbury rushing to her rescue.

She knew her family and friends had her best interests at heart. Ever since a car accident had killed her mother and left her badly injured, they'd smothered her with concern. Sometimes she thought she'd go mad if she didn't escape.

Maybe she could help Lamanto recuperate and send him on his way. No one would be the wiser, she thought.

No. Of course not. She couldn't aid and abet a criminal. On the other hand, he hadn't been convicted of anything or even charged with a crime. They just wanted him for questioning. A person of interest, her dad said.

Shaking her head, she reminded herself she didn't want to get involved. She'd had it with men, from the men in her family to the ones who dated her because they wanted free medical advice, some help with a law enforcement problem or just sex.

Keri abruptly decided to go to the rangers for help. She checked Lamanto's vital signs again to assure herself he'd be all right until help arrived.

As soon as she was rid of her unwelcome guest, she could get on with her own plans. Her mother had lost her life on this mountain a little over two years ago. The wreck had been officially declared an accident. Keri had been a passenger. She hadn't remembered anything directly afterward, but over the past year bits and pieces of the memory kept nagging her.

She'd come up here to do some sleuthing, both for the sake of the truth and to help her come to terms with what had happened. Maybe liven up her boring existence. She longed for adventure and excitement. Amateur sleuthing would have to fill the bill for now.

Sighing, she pulled a blanket over Lamanto. Finding him in her car wasn't the sort of excitement she'd expected and exhaustion had dampened her adventurous spirit.

The cabin sat too deep in the forest for any kind of phone service, so she'd have to drive to the ranger station. They could collect Lamanto and then maybe she'd get some much-needed sleep. Snatching up her purse, she shot one last glance at her stowaway and then headed out the door.

An eerie, unnatural stillness engulfed her as soon as she'd stepped off the porch. Cool, damp air and darkness gave her goose bumps. She hadn't been the least bit spooked when she'd arrived earlier. The cabin had always been a second home to her family, but now she felt a shiver of fear. She blamed it on weariness and Lamanto's unexpected appearance.

After climbing in the car and slamming the door, she clicked the locks and pulled on her seatbelt, feeling a little less panicked. The engine revved to life, and she shifted into reverse and started to turn around in the small clearing. When she shifted back into drive again, the engine died. She frowned and repeated the process, pressing the gas pedal to feed the engine. Still, it ignited and died. A red light on the dash flashed a warning. Her fuel gauge read empty.

"No way!" she groaned in frustration. She'd filled the tank at the bottom of the mountain. The cost had given her sticker shock. The gauge had to be faulty.

"Come on, come on," she grumbled, turning the key again, but with the same results. It wouldn't keep running.

Groaning aloud, she dropped her head down on the steering wheel with a thud. How could she be out of gas? She'd had the car thoroughly checked before her trip, and she hadn't run over anything to damage the fuel line. How else could all that incredibly expensive gasoline be drained?

A sudden thought popped into her head. Gas theft. She'd heard her dad mention a rash of gasoline thefts since the price had skyrocketed.

Had someone watched her fill up and followed her to the

cabin? Or had someone at the station alerted someone who lived closer? A shiver raced down her spine. She lifted her head and quickly surveyed the area around her but didn't see anything in the shadowy darkness.

Was someone out there now? Watching her? Thieves hiding or living in the woods? Locals? Cabins stood few and far between up here. Transportation was essential. If they'd steal a basic necessity, what else might they do?

She didn't like the feeling of panic crawling over her, making the hair stand up on her arms. Another quiver coursed down her spine. Feeling like a real wimp, she pulled her cell phone off the dash charger and hit the speed dial for her home phone number.

A *no service* message flashed on the screen, and she let out a long, loud groan. Cell service up here was spotty at best. She'd known that but had actually welcomed being cut off from the constant communication. After punching the button again and receiving the same message, she tossed the phone into her oversized pocketbook and cursed.

How many other glitches could she expect in her carefully planned, long-awaited vacation? Movement in her peripheral vision made her stiffen in renewed alarm. Just some nocturnal creature, she assured herself while holding her breath. When nothing and no one materialized after a couple minutes, she let out a long sigh.

The cabin suddenly looked like a haven from the unknown. She'd have to make a run for it, but first she had to find the nerve. Wimpy wouldn't get it. Adventure and excitement took a certain amount of courage, she argued to herself. She couldn't be balking at imagined threats. She had to look fear in the face and overcome it.

With that thought, she unbuckled her belt, jumped from the car and ran. The nip in the air bit her flesh as she raced toward the porch and its faint beacon of light. Sweating and shivering, she made the dash without being attacked by unknown assailants. As soon as she got inside, she slammed and locked the door behind her.

Breathless from jitters as well as exertion, she leaned against the doorframe, her chest heaving. As she caught her breath, she glanced at Lamanto and relaxed a little. He hadn't moved a muscle and his presence calmed her. Ridiculous! She didn't need a man to make her feel safe, yet...

"Better the devil you know..." she whispered, and then hurried toward the bedroom. The furnishings consisted of a double bed, a dresser and a nightstand. She checked the lock on the window and closed the curtains. Next she went through the bathroom to the kitchen and then into a small utility room off the back porch. After checking more locks, she sat down at the small short-wave radio.

She couldn't contact the sheriff's office in Thornsbury, but she could relay a message to her dad through the ranger station. It took a few minutes to familiarize herself with the controls, and then she started to chant the call letters.

A slight movement to her left caught her attention, and the words got stuck in her throat. Her eyes went wide at the sight of her dad's pistol being leveled on her.

Her pulse had just calmed and it leapt again, then began racing as she looked into Lamanto's dark, deadly gaze.

Chapter Three

"Shut it off."

He issued the command in a tone as threatening as his expression. Keri stared at his frozen features, studying him intently, but saw no evidence of weakness.

Most people in her position would fear for their life. After the initial shock, fear took second place to self-disgust. How could she have been stupid enough to think he was totally incapacitated?

She hoped nobody ever learned she'd carelessly left a weapon within this man's reach. She'd broken the sacred lawmen's rule of never underestimating the enemy. The fact that he held the gun left no doubt about him being the enemy.

"If I don't radio that I arrived safely, my dad will be here before daybreak."

His eyes narrowed. "You radio him directly?"

"I have a message relayed from the ranger station," she explained, keeping her tone low and reasonable even though her nerves felt wired. A slight tremor shook her hand, but she quickly willed away the fear.

"You told them I'm here?"

"Yes, we'll be surrounded by law enforcement officials any minute now," she replied, shifting her gaze to his midsection.

After several long heartbeats, he responded with a challenge. "You're not a very good liar."

"Because I don't make a habit of lying," she snapped right back, annoyed that he'd read her so easily. "Unlike some people who break their word without a qualm."

"Meaning?"

"Meaning you promised not to do anything stupid if I helped with your wound. I thought cops honored their word."

Instead of remorse, the corner of Lamanto's mouth lifted ever so slightly in a wry grin.

"I didn't break my word. I didn't try to run, and I haven't done anything stupid. From my point of view, it would be damned stupid to let you call the authorities right now."

Keri's jaw tightened and she glared at him.

"Make the call," he said, tone sharpening, "but don't try using any codes. Just tell them you arrived and all's well."

Her brows creased in a frown. Leave it to cop to know about a code. If she told anyone she had trouble with the water pump, help would be on its way within minutes.

One look at his pale, drawn features convinced her his show of strength wouldn't last long. Then she'd be in the position of power again, and she'd make sure he didn't get a second chance to intimidate her.

She made the call to the rangers just as he'd instructed.

"Get up," Lamanto commanded when she finished.

Keri eased herself from the small stool by the radio. When he waved the gun to direct her farther from the equipment, she obliged him by carefully moving into the kitchen.

The gun never wavered as it followed her movements. He kept it aimed at her while reaching for a connector wire of the radio, pulling it loose and slipping it into his pocket.

She grimaced but promised herself to collect it later when he'd passed out again.

"What now?" she asked. Beyond tired, short tempered and running low on energy, she felt ready to collapse.

"Now you give me the keys to your car."

At this point, it didn't matter who held the keys. She shouldn't have trusted him when he gave her his word.

"They won't do you any good. Someone stole all my gas."

As soon as the words left her mouth, she clamped it shut, wishing she'd let him find out for himself. Maybe she'd have gained the upper hand in the situation again. Or at least locked him out of the cabin.

"So you already tried to leave," he said. His eyes narrowed. "Did you see anyone outside?"

She shook her head. "I didn't see anything or anyone."

"Then what makes you so sure someone stole the gas?"

"The car won't start, and the fuel light is flashing."

Lamanto heaved a visible sigh. Keri wondered how much longer his strength would hold.

"What now?" she asked. Neither of them had the energy for a trek down the mountain, and she had no desire to face the darkness again. She'd feel braver when she wasn't so beat.

"We get cleaned up and get some sleep. You look wiped. I'll give you ten minutes. Just don't try locking doors."

Keri didn't mention the absence of locks on the inside doors. She didn't feel like making explanations or engaging in arguments. The last burst of adrenaline had zapped her strength. All she wanted to do was lay her weary head down on a pillow. He could go to hell for all she cared.

He followed her to the living room where she grabbed a pile of her clothes and carried them to the bedroom. She chose a dark blue sweat suit and clean underwear before heading to the bathroom. After a quick wash and change of clothes, she returned to make the bed. He leaned against the wall until she'd finished, and then moved directly in front of her.

"Do you sleep on your back or stomach? Right side or left?" he asked.

The unexpected questions had her blinking and staring at him, her mind blank. "Don't even think I'm sharing."

To emphasize her point, she reached out and tapped him on the chest. Too late she realized he'd shifted the gun to his left hand. In his right, he had a pair of old-fashioned handcuffs. A cuff locked on her left wrist with an economy of motion.

Keri stared at the metal shackles in stunned fascination. Her dad stored them in the first-aid kit too, but she'd never imagined them being used on her. After a split second of hesitation, she began to struggle, but Lamanto had anticipated the reaction. He swiftly pulled her left arm behind her back, jerking her body full force against the strength of his own. Her breath hitched at his closeness.

He should be as weak as a kitten, yet the steel of his muscles swiftly squashed any desire for a physical skirmish. She just wasn't sure enough she'd win. She abruptly stopped struggling, tilted her head and glared at him.

"You have a great way of showing your appreciation for my help," she snapped. "I should have held you at gunpoint until my dad could come get you."

"Yeah," he agreed. "You should have."

Keri clenched her teeth in frustration. Another damned man who thought he knew what was best for her.

She glared harder, and he returned her gaze with a steady, unblinking stare. Their hearts pounded frantically in their chests, beating against each other with tension heightened by the strength and heat of his body.

"I'm not going to hurt you," he swore softly, never losing eye contact. "But I'm not going to let you turn me in, either."

"I don't suppose my word is good enough to get this handcuff off?" she tried.

"No." His tone brooked no argument, but his mouth curved in a rakish smile. A glimmer of amusement lit his fevered eyes. Even in their not-too-amiable situation, he oozed charm. He enjoyed provoking her.

Keri's heart tripped again. Damn but the man was handsome. A woman would have to be dead not to appreciate his aesthetic beauty. Up close, she noticed the ebony hair of his eyebrows had the slightest tendency to curl. Deep laughter lines slit the corners of his eyes and softer grooves at his mouth. His mouth was wide, with sensuously full, firm lips. His skin tanned and smooth, pulling tight across high cheekbones.

She stared into his eyes, watching his gaze drop to her lips. His eyelids dropped too, dark lashes sweeping downward. Her pulse fluttered with unexpected and unwelcome excitement. She felt the metal of her father's gun gently pressing against her back, but she felt no fear. In a blink of his fascinating eyes, their battle of wills had become a battle of the sexes.

The air between them electrified, sizzling her nerves. The throbbing of her own pulse nearly deafened her. Keri struggled to shrug off the heavy lethargy invading her body.

Please, no, she mentally begged the gods of desirability. Please don't let this be the fiercest physical attraction she'd experienced in her whole life. Please make her quaking nerves and erratic pulse a result of exhaustion or frustration. She would not accept an attraction for this man.

"You feel good," he murmured as though surprised by the revelation. "And you smell good too."

The arm holding her tightened fractionally. He didn't hurt her, yet he threatened Keri's composure. Her breathing faltered and her breasts swelled against the solid wall of his chest.

She frantically searched her tired brain for a rational explanation. The fruitless search caused an unreasonable spurt of panic in its wake. Defensive and feeling desperate, she pressed her free hand against his chest and shoved.

His low groan reminded her of his wound. Even as she stepped out of his embrace, her gaze searched his face and shoulder to see if she'd done any damage.

"Sorry," she whispered, genuinely stricken to have caused him more pain.

Lamanto gave her a weak smile but kept a firm hold on the cuffs that made her his prisoner.

"No problem. Women always lose their heads when they're in my arms."

The comment didn't sound like a boast as much as a statement of fact. He might have said it jokingly, but her expression hardened.

"Now what?" she grumbled. "I'm going on thirty hours with no sleep, and I'd guess you haven't had much, either. We should both be in bed."

The unwarranted but undeniably seductive gleam in his eyes added to her annoyance. Her frown deepened, and she tugged on the handcuffs to display impatience.

"These are totally unnecessary."

He ignored her grousing. "I need a shower and food."

"You can't get those stitches wet."

"I'll take a bath."

"You're nuts."

"I'm filthy."

"All right, take a bath," grumbled Keri, "but let me get some sleep."

He looked beyond her toward the bed. "I wish the bed had a metal frame so I could fasten you to the headboard or something."

"I don't need to be shackled to the bed. My car's out of gas, the radio's disabled and I'm too damn tired to go anywhere on foot."

He gave her a reproachful glance and gently urged her toward the dresser. "Any clothes I can borrow?"

Her dad and brother kept clothes at the cabin. They were taller men, but she supposed something would fit him. "Jack's sweats will probably work."

"How 'bout some clean underwear?"

"If you'll take this stupid thing off my arm, I'll check the drawers," she retorted, tugging at the metal cuff.

He gave her a wry grin for her efforts but ignored her plea. They had a momentary battle of wills. He didn't flinch. With a deep sigh, she twisted around and opened drawers, collecting socks, briefs, gray sweat pants and an old red flannel shirt. She turned to him again, her expression challenging him.

"Now the bathroom," he said.

She led the way into the small space. It barely had room for two people, but he shifted so she could sit on the toilet seat. Then he reached for the towel rack and gave it a jerk. When it proved sturdy, he clicked the other handcuff around the bar, effectively chaining her in the room.

Keri's mood grew grimmer by the minute and her expression displayed her rising temper. He gave her another half smile and placed the gun on a rack in the shower. Then he began the slow process of filling the tub and stripping.

The sexual tension steadily increased as did the steam enveloping them. Keri tried to maintain her composure, but it started disintegrating when he unfastened his belt and slid down his zipper. The sound rasped along already frayed nerves.

"You can close your eyes if you're shy," he said. Despite the feverish sheen to his eyes, the dark orbs taunted her.

"I'm a nurse. You don't have anything I haven't seen a thousand times," she retorted even though she felt the sting of hot color rising in her cheeks.

"Humor me. I'm modest."

Keri seriously doubted it, but she turned her back as much as the limited space allowed. She heard a muffled groan as he struggled out of his jeans. Every movement had to be hurting him. Then she heard jeans and belt hit the floor followed by the sound of him stepping into the tub.

"Draw the curtain." She couldn't reach it from her tethered position, but she could see his movements in her peripheral vision.

"I'd rather keep you in sight," he replied, shutting off the tap. Next he sank into the water and emitted a deep, heavy sigh.

The sound skittered along her nerves, creating unappreciated and unwelcome havoc on them. She couldn't fully see him, yet she felt his every move. Instead of heeding her stern warning to ignore him, her weary mind recorded every little sound he made as he bathed.

The spicy smell of soap teased her senses as it filled the moisture-laden air. Her imagination conjured images of rich, white lather coating the dark curls on his chest. She could visualize the trickle of water down his hard stomach and into forbidden territory.

Putting an abrupt halt to the uninhibited imaginings, she silently cursed the unexpected curiosity. Her patient deserved respect even if he held the top spot on her personal shit-list right now. She needed to summon professional indifference and halt the increasing sexual awareness. *Think professional decorum,* she told herself, repeating the mantra for the next few minutes. *Professionalism. Professionalism. Professionalism.*

When Lamanto went quiet for too long, she risked another glance in is direction. She peeked but immediately regretted the action. His sleek, wet body reclined the full length of the tub. The water didn't hide an inch of male perfection. The image would stay in her mind for a very long time. More heat suffused her body.

"Don't fall asleep." Her voice held a snap to camouflage a sensory overload.

Another deep sigh acknowledged her warning. Then she heard the water being drained and some awkward movements as he tried to pull himself upright. A low curse had her reacting reflexively.

"Be careful," she said, turning fully toward him.

The sight of him smacked her again and with staggering force. His hard, lean body stole her breath. No way could she ignore the masculine beauty of his glistening nudity.

She mentally catalogued every inch of him from the damp, curling hair on his head, down the broad, muscled chest and flat stomach to his hard thighs and another patch of thick, curly hair.

Her intense, intimate perusal brought a swift reaction from his very male anatomy. She swallowed hard to keep from strangling on the gasp at the back of her throat.

"I'm wounded, not dead," he grumbled, jerking a towel across his abdomen to cover his growing erection.

The action threw him off balance. She quickly recovered her wits and reached out a hand to steady him.

"Thanks," he said gruffly, accepting the support as he stepped from the tub.

"I could be a lot more help if you'd unfasten these stupid handcuffs," she reiterated in an effort to halt the escalating tension in the tiny bathroom.

"I don't need more help. I'll be okay in a minute," he declared, leaning against the wall for support while he dried. "At least if I die, I'll die clean."

Keri stopped arguing. She turned her back on him again and waited impatiently while he went through the laborious process of pulling on clean clothes. She glanced toward the gun.

"Don't even try. You can't reach it, and I don't think either of us is up to another wrestling match right now."

She didn't plan to initiate any physical contact. "All I want is some sleep," she grumbled, facing him again. He'd donned the sweatpants.

"Toothbrush?"

Before she could answer, he'd opened the medicine chest and found what he needed. She helped him get a new brush out of the packaging and spread toothpaste on it. Watching him brush his teeth seemed to intensify the intimacy between them, and she didn't welcome the heightened awareness.

"Now what?" she asked.

"I'm going to get something to eat and a glass of milk, if you have any. Then I'll figure out something."

Keri sat and stewed while he collected the gun and moved into the kitchen. She heard the refrigerator open, milk being poured and thirstily drank. She waited another long few minutes while he helped himself to her groceries.

Leaning against the toilet, she laid her heavy head on her shackled arm. It was a poor substitute for a pillow, but it would do for now. Just about anything would do right now.

The next thing she knew, Lamanto moved close again. The gentle stroke of his finger against her cheek startled her awake. She abruptly straightened and stared at him through sleepy eyes. He fitted the key into the cuff and unchained her from the towel rack, but kept a handcuff around her left wrist. She rubbed it, her eyes searching his.

"Bedtime," he stated softly.

Keri didn't hesitate or even realize he wasn't holding her metal bracelet. She went straight into the bedroom and sprawled on her stomach across the left side of the bed.

Lamanto shook out a blanket and covered her with it. He snapped the handcuff around the bedsprings. She didn't fight him. Exhaustion had pulled her into its depths.

In another minute, the light went out. The mattress dipped as he sat down on the opposite side. She drifted closer to sleep, wondering why she wasn't in fear for her life or at least her virtue, why she felt comforted rather than alarmed by the presence of a man in her bed. A stranger, no less. An unpredictable, fugitive of a stranger.

Maybe because he was incredibly sexy, with the deepest, darkest eyes she'd ever seen. Maybe because he'd never really threatened her. Or maybe just because he was an errant knight. Whatever the case, her weary brain had no logical explanation.

Finally, sleep enfolded her in its blessed embrace.

Nick eased himself onto the bed, routinely slipping the ammunition clip from the pistol before placing it within reach on a bedside stand.

The .45 caliber was a big gun and a familiar one. His own piece was similar, and guaranteed to stop a perp with the first shot. Most times, an officer only got one chance to defend himself. Smaller caliber guns weren't much use against a dope head wielding a sub-machine gun.

He carefully stretched flat on the mattress and turned his head toward Keri. She'd fallen sound asleep within seconds of her head hitting the pillow. He imagined she'd been on the go nearly as long as he had.

The soft, even sound of her breathing was music to his ears. Not as beautiful as her singing but just as pleasing. And he didn't even know why.

She wouldn't be sleeping so peacefully if she feared for her life. Maybe that's what soothed him. He hadn't wanted to involve anyone in his flight from the local law. Despite the fact that her family was the local law, she couldn't be held responsible for their actions.

At this point, he didn't know how deeply her family was involved in whatever was going down in the county. Her brother Jack had been nearby when the shootings took place. Nick needed to figure out what was happening in Thornsbury and if the whole sheriff's department was dirty.

Don Monroe worked for the department too. They'd trained together at the academy, but after graduating, Don had returned to his native Tennessee. He'd issued an open invitation to visit. Last month, Nick had called him to discuss concerns for the area. They'd agreed to let people believe he needed a vacation. It hadn't been far from the truth.

His superiors had given him the okay to spend a couple weeks in Tennessee. While here, they'd hoped he could get a handle on a purported gunrunning operation from Miami to Tennessee. None of them had anticipated a double assassination attempt.

It meant he and Don had gotten too close to tracking down the ringleader of the operation. They'd gotten close enough to spook the bad guys, but now the investigation had to go on hold until his shoulder healed and he regained some strength.

He'd planned to disappear into the night without involving Keri, but her nursing skills had bought him more time. Besides, what better place to hide and recuperate than the sheriff's personal hunting cabin?

He didn't know what to do next. He'd have to work it all out in the morning. Right now, he felt too damn beat to think straight. Thanks to his guardian angel, though, he felt almost human again. He still had some pain and fever, but at least he felt clean, and fed.

Besides all that, he was in bed with a beautiful, intelligent, spirited woman. Just his type. Just where he liked to be. The thought brought a grin in the darkness. His buddies back at the station would say he always landed on his feet. Or flat on his back in bed.

Too bad he couldn't take the opportunity to get to know his nurse a little better.

Wrong time, wrong place. What a waste.

The scent of her gradually wafted closer, enveloping him with its light, heady perfume. The familiarity and sweetness seduced once again. Nick reached toward her in the darkness, letting his fingers relay the satiny-smooth texture of her hair. Then his Braille investigation slid over her shoulder, down her arm and to her hand with its small, ringless fingers.

The contact felt good, surprising him with the depth of contentment he didn't understand or have the energy to analyze. The silky feel of her skin and the melody of her breathing lulled him to sleep.

Chapter Four

Hours later, Keri started dreaming of bathrooms. It was a recurring dream. Trapped in a shopping mall with halls like a rat maze, she searched for a bathroom because she desperately needed to relieve herself. Every stall she found was occupied.

Bordering in a state of half sleep and half wakefulness, she knew she hadn't gotten nearly enough rest. But she knew she wouldn't be able to sleep anymore until she went to the toilet. Rolling out of bed, she tumbled to her knees with a grunt of surprise and irritation. Then dawning realization. She was handcuffed to the bedsprings.

"Hey!" she grumbled sleepily. "I have to pee!" She tugged on the metal links, still barely conscious, until the bed dipped and Lamanto reached over to unlock her restraint.

"Make it fast or I'll come after you with a gun."

She grunted and staggered to the bathroom. In a few minutes, she returned to collapse on the bed again. She went back to sleep while her stowaway snapped the handcuff on her wrist, the right one this time since she'd stretched out on her back.

Feeling like he'd been run over by a truck, Nick staggered to the bathroom and relieved himself too. Stomach rumbling, he wandered into the kitchen to check out the food supply. After eating two peanut butter sandwiches and downing a couple glasses of milk, he searched for the pain killers Keri had given him earlier. His shoulder throbbed like a sonofabitch, so he swallowed a handful.

Midmorning sunshine spilled through the kitchen windows. He should probably make a run for it, but he still felt too damned weak. His legs trembled, so he slowly made his way back to the bedroom. A couple more days, he thought as he settled down on the bed. Just a couple more days and he'd regain enough strength to head to Miami. He'd worry about the details later.

In town, Deputy Jack Merritt paced his father's small, cluttered office. Thornsbury was the county seat of Boone County, with the sheriff's department housed in the east wing of the county courthouse. Both men worked the day shift. It had been a quiet morning, but neither of them felt good about it. They still hadn't found Lamanto.

Sheriff Walt Merritt sat behind his big oak desk and watched his son's restless movements. Tall, broad shouldered and lean of hips, Jack had inherited his stature from the Merritt side of the family. He'd inherited his impatience from his mother's side.

"Stop pacing, Son, you're gonna wear a hole in my carpet," he said, "and you know the budget's too tight to replace it."

His slow, Southern drawl and laid-back attitude had fooled many a man into thinking his mind and instincts functioned with equal slowness. Most wished they hadn't tangled with him. He sighed when his small attempt at humor didn't ease his son's tension.

"What the hell are we going to do about Keri?" demanded Jack.

"Well now, your sister's a grown woman, and, as she's reminded us so much lately, we don't need to worry about what she does with her time."

"You know she went up to the cabin to nose around." Jack ran a hand through straight brown hair. His normally level voice was low and agitated. "She's been really restless lately and asking a lot of questions about the accident."

Walt's weathered features creased in a frown. "It's only natural. She lost her mother, and she's got survivor's guilt."

"Well, I wish to hell she'd deal with her guilt here in town.

She's bound to stir up trouble if she goes sniffing around in the mountains."

Walt's jaw locked in annoyance. Jack was right. Keri had inherited the Merritt ability to stir up trouble and the stubbornness to ignore all his warnings. He didn't want her at the cabin, especially now. It was too close to the activities at the militia camp.

He understood her desire for answers, but she couldn't have picked a worse time to start snooping. He'd hoped her memory of that night would stay blank because he wanted her to be safe. He just hadn't figured out how to protect her from herself without divulging secrets.

"Keri radioed the rangers," said Walt, "so she's safe for the time being. I'll have Dwayne stop by there today."

"She'll get really pissed if we start sending kin to check on her."

"She'll just have to be pissed. The shooting and attempts on Monroe's life shifted everything into high gear. We can't let our worry about her distract us from our ultimate goal."

Jack frowned. "I know. You're right. I just don't like it."

Their discussion halted with a knock at the door. Three men dressed in dark suits, snow-white shirts and ties entered the room without waiting permission. Walt's jaw locked. Two of his uninvited guests were county commissioners Jeff Sturgis and Levi Patterson.

They, and their fellow commissioners, had control of the county's purse strings. They never missed a chance to remind him his annual budget depended on their good will.

The youngest, Sturgis, was third-generation politician. Fit and trim, he stayed perfectly groomed and perfectly behaved. He rarely had an original thought, but the familiarity of his family name kept people voting him into office.

Shorter, balding and rotund, Patterson looked like a man who'd enjoyed far too many official dinners. Most of the time, he acted like a pompous jerk. Walt never did understand how he stayed in office. Probably from kissing a lot of important asses instead of babies.

Terrance Moville, the local funeral director, gave him and Jack a stiff nod of greeting. Everything about the man was stiff, from his spine to his facial expressions. Walt couldn't remember ever hearing him laugh. Considering his profession, maybe he had the right to be grim. The Moville family had served the area for several generations.

"Good day, Sheriff, Jack," said Patterson. "We're just on our way to a Rotary meeting. I'm sure everyone's going to want details about the escaped convict. What can you tell us?"

"First of all, his name is Nick Lamanto. You met him last week at the pancake breakfast. You told him we could use a man like him on our force," Walt reminded and enjoyed the flush of color that crept up Patterson's neck. "And he's not a criminal or an escapee, he hasn't been charged with any crime. He's just a person of interest."

"Person of interest?" demanded Moville. "Isn't that just a politically correct term for a criminal who hasn't been officially charged with a crime?"

"It's just what it sounds like," Walt corrected. "A person we're interested in finding and asking questions."

"What about Deputy Monroe?" asked Patterson. "All the doctors will tell me is he's in critical condition." His tone suggested he felt entitled to privileged information. "Has he regained consciousness? Does he know who shot him and why?"

"Not yet," said Jack. "The doctor said it could be a while."

"A day? A week? A month?" demanded Sturgis. "They have to have some idea if he'll pull through. And what if he doesn't? We can't have a cop killer on the loose in the county. What are you doing to find this Lamanto? To protect our citizens?"

"The same thing I've been doing for more than twenty-five years," said Walt, knowing he'd been a thorn in the side of the commissioners for every one of them. As an elected official, they couldn't fire him. But they sure as hell irritated him.

"We set up road blocks, used the search dogs and put in

some extra man hours, but those new budget cuts have limited our resources. My best guess is he hitched a ride out of state. I've contacted his superiors in Florida. They haven't heard from him either. There's not much more we can do unless he voluntarily comes to us."

Patterson made an annoying, skeptical sound that grated on Walt's last nerve, but he kept his temper. No one spoke as the courthouse clock chimed twelve times.

"Y'all be late for lunch," put in Jack. "Doesn't Rotary start at noon?"

The three men turned and headed out the door. Patterson tossed an order over his shoulder. "Keep us posted."

"You bet," Walt mumbled. He and Jack shared a grin.

"I don't know how you've put up with it for all these years, Dad," said Jack after they'd gone. "I'm so ready to be done with them."

"All in good time, Son," Walt declared softly. "All in good time."

The howling of the wind woke Nick later in the day. The sun had disappeared, but he could tell the darkness stemmed from cloudy skies rather than twilight. His fever had subsided and the room had grown cold. With his good arm, he tugged the blanket more fully over Keri, and then he slowly turned onto his right side. His bad shoulder felt tight and sore, but the fiery pain had subsided to a dull ache.

His nurse-captive looked soft and feminine in sleep. Her hair splayed around her head, framing her face with silken strands streaked in gold. Pale brown lashes rested on the dark circles under her eyes. He frowned at the evidence of her fatigue, holding himself partially responsible for it.

Her short, straight nose seemed a perfect fit for her wide eyes, oval face and nicely shaped lips. As he watched, they parted slightly with each breath. Not quite a snore, but a steady whistling sound escaped and trembled on her lips. Nick found himself smiling.

He wanted to kiss her awake, press his mouth hungrily on hers and demand a response, explore the chemistry they'd experienced last night. His lips tightened to keep from acting on the desire, but his body tightened too. Blood sang through his veins, streamlining toward his groin. His morning erection throbbed with excitement.

"Easy boy," he whispered to himself. He owed the lady a debt of gratitude and she deserved better than randy thoughts or actions. Still, he admired the fullness of her breasts as they rose and fell with each breath. He did love the sight and shape and feel of a woman's breasts.

"What?" Keri's eyelids fluttered and then opened. She squinted at him as though unsure of the situation. Nick could tell the instant she remembered. Her face went all tight and her expression, guarded.

"Lamanto?"

He liked the sound of his name on her lips, liked the soft, southern draw and the way she pronounced each syllable.

"Yeah." He kept his expression bland though he felt more relaxed than he had in weeks. Sharing a bed with an intriguing woman ranked high on his list of favorite things.

"What are you doing in my bed?"

"We slept together last night. Don't tell me you can't remember. What a blow to my ego."

She cocked a brow at him. "I imagine your ego can withstand a couple blows, and I don't remember inviting you to share my bed."

He ignored the part about not being invited to share. "Do you always wake up in such a grumpy mood?"

"Only when I'm chained to the bed," she snapped, tugging her right arm in reminder of the cuffs.

"There's nothing wrong with a little bondage," he said, giving her a lazy smile. "Lots of people enjoy it. Some even pay for it."

He knew it was the wrong thing to say when her eyes

sparkled and her tone hardened.

"I'm sure you have experience to back up that comment, but I'm not interested. I'm not interested in anything before coffee."

"You're more open to sexual experimentation with caffeine in your system?"

"Yes. No!" she stuttered and glared at him. "Stop goading me. It's annoying, and I'm barely awake."

Nick's grin widened as she continued.

"And stop looking at me that way."

"What way?"

"Like I'm a trapped rabbit and you're a hungry fox."

He chuckled softly. "I am a hungry man and you do look delectable, but in case you've forgotten, my movements are seriously restricted. I can't even hold you with both arms."

"I don't want you to hold me," she insisted, her voice going hoarse.

"I promise you'd enjoy it." His eyes met hers and he watched them widen. She held his gaze for a long, breathless minute. Suddenly his heart pounded with excitement and he knew touching her would bring him incredible pleasure too.

What he'd started as innocent teasing blossomed into unexpected longing. Need swelled in him, catching him off-guard and confounding him. He loved to flirt, loved women, but something about this small, sassy one reached right inside him and tugged at his heartstrings.

Not good, especially in their current circumstances.

Before either of them could break the tense silence, they heard the sound of a heavy vehicle nearing the cabin. Nick slowly rolled himself to the edge of the bed and stood. He loaded the clip into the pistol and tossed the handcuff key to Keri. He watched as she unfastened it and rubbed her wrist.

"Whoever it is, get rid of them," he said, morphing into his cop persona.

She flashed him an annoyed glance. "We don't get many

visitors up here and we never send them away without an offer of coffee. It's just not done in these parts, city boy."

"Well, get creative, Miss Congeniality, unless you want to be handcuffed to our uninvited guest for the next few days."

Expression grim, she turned toward the window, pulled back a curtain and looked outside. "Dwayne," she said. "The first of many watchdogs my dad will be sending to check on me."

Nick remembered meeting her cousin, Deputy Dwayne Merritt. He looked a lot like her brother Jack but carried about twenty pounds more weight. He served as an auxiliary officer to the sheriff's department.

When the newcomer laid on the horn, her expression grew more mutinous. After a few long, loud honks, the blaring noise stopped and a truck door slammed. Nick watched from the bedroom window as she threw open the door and stepped onto the porch. Hands on hips, her hair and clothes tousled from hours in bed, she looked and sounded furious.

"What the hell are you doing, Dwayne? Trying to raise the dead with all that racket?" Her demand for answers rang loud and clear.

"Well hell, Ker, I didn't figure you'd be in bed this time of the day."

"I'm on vacation!" she yelled to be heard over the wind. "I came up here for uninterrupted rest and relaxation. If I want to sleep twenty-four hours a day, I'll sleep twenty-four hours a day."

"Well, don't go all ballistic. Your daddy sent me to warn you about some foul weather headin' our way."

Nick could only see the side of Keri's face, but he knew her scowl deepened.

"It's the first of September. Our weather doesn't get that foul in September."

"This is a strange one according to the forecast and it blew up fast. Bad thunderstorms and a couple of tornado warnings.

Your dad said you might get blasted with snow here on the mountain. He wanted to make sure you're prepared."

"I heard warnings on the radio last night," she conceded, lifting her hands to keep her hair out of her eyes.

Nick noted the gusting wind and occasional whirlwind of leaves. Some of the smaller trees bent low while the sky darkened ominously. The temperature continued to drop.

"This cabin's sturdy, I have supplies and plenty of firewood. Go away."

"I could use a refill for my thermos."

"You woke me up," she snapped. "I don't have coffee made."

"Well, don't get your panties in a twist," snapped Dwayne. "Go back to bed. I'll tell your dad you're too damned contrary to listen to warnings. Mother Nature's bad mood ain't nothin' compared to yours."

"Goodbye, Dwayne."

"Yeah, yeah," he said, turning to leave. He'd reached his vehicle when she called out to him.

"Hey, Dwayne?"

Nick tensed, moving closer to the door in case she forced him to show himself and the gun.

"Do you have spare gasoline with you?"

"Sure. Why?" He yelled back at her. "You didn't go and run yourself dry, did you?"

"No, I didn't. I filled up at the bottom of the mountain, but some lousy thief emptied my tank."

"A lot of that goin' on. I'll tell your dad."

"Don't even think about it. I don't want him up here lecturing or hovering. I just want a couple gallons of gas."

"Well, it'll be my hide if he finds out from somebody else." Dwayne moved to the back of his vehicle and lifted out a five gallon gas can. "I'm duty bound to report the theft."

"In that case, I'll be duty bound to tell him how you showed Marla Moville your cruiser last week. You had the windows nice and steamed in the wee hours Tuesday morning."

His response was explosive. "Damn it now, Keri!"

"Damn it now, Dwayne!"

Nick watched as the two faced off with equally belligerent expressions. Stubbornness had to be a genetic Merritt trait, but he knew who'd win this particular battle. Dwayne set the gas can on the porch, grunted a concession to her demand and turned to go. He had nearly returned to the truck when Keri yelled again.

"Hey."

"What?"

"How's Deputy Monroe doing?"

Nick strained to hear the response.

"Okay, I guess, but that friend of his tried to kill him again last night. Some friend. Destroyed some equipment, but the hospital alarms scared him off again."

"You mean Lamanto?"

The only part of Dwayne's response Nick could hear was the word *foreigner.* His jaw locked in irritation.

Keri grabbed a porch pillar to brace against the wind, still yelling to be heard. "Don's okay?"

Thunder prevented Nick from hearing the reply. He watched her wave as her cousin revved the engine of his jacked-up truck. As soon as he headed down the road, she stepped back into the cabin and brought the gas can with her.

"Whew! It's really getting ugly out there," she said, setting the can aside and leaning against the closed door.

Nick lowered the gun as he moved closer. "What'd he say about Don?"

"That you tried to kill him again last night."

He shrugged off her sarcasm. "How is he? How successful was the attack?"

"All Dwayne said was he's still unconscious."

"How the hell could it happen?" he demanded harshly. "Why the hell wasn't someone guarding him?"

She stared, studying him with big, curious eyes. "Are you

angry because you're still under suspicion?"

"I'm angry because Don is an officer of the law. He deserves more respect, some loyalty and a helluva lot better protection."

Her chin rose and her spine stiffened. "Times are tough everywhere," she defended. "Hospital and law enforcement work hours have been slashed. We do the best with what we've got."

"That's an excuse for letting a good man die?"

"He's not dead!" she snapped. "Our trauma team got him stabilized in record time. The gunshot wound was superficial, but he suffered a severe blow to his head. We all do our best. What we can't do is protect the world against lunatics with guns!"

"Can't or won't?" he snapped.

She glared at him. "What are you suggesting?"

"I'm saying it's damned suspicious that someone managed to get to him again."

"They think you're the villain. They probably thought you left the state."

"I'm not, and I didn't."

"Maybe you didn't shoot him but you can't blame them for suspecting you. You disappeared and hid from the search teams. Why not go straight to my dad and tell him you'd been shot too?"

The question surprised him into silence. He clamped his mouth shut and returned her steady gaze. Tension hummed between them as the silence grew. He could see the wheels of her brain spinning until she came up with the answer herself.

"You don't trust my dad?" she said on a gasp of outrage, her body stiffening. "You think he or someone in his department is dirty?" When he still didn't comment, she stepped close and slapped an open hand on his chest. The slap jarred his shoulder a little but the heat of her touch seared him through the thin shirt. That, combined with her flare of temper, stirred him in a totally different way.

"Listen here, city boy! My dad is the best of the best.

There's nobody more honest or trustworthy. He's too smart and too experienced to let anyone pull the wool over his eyes. And he would never condone someone shooting one of his deputies!"

Nick agreed. Her dad was as sharp as they came. Walt Merritt knew everything that happened in his county. So he either had to be quietly collecting evidence or actively participating in illegal activities. When it came to militia movements, you couldn't always tell the good guys from the fanatics. For all he knew, his lovely nurse-captive might be an anti-government militant at heart.

Instead of arguing, he lowered his gaze to where her hand still pressed against him. He puffed out his chest and gave her a come-hither look. She snatched it back and snarled at him.

"Don't try changing the subject with your playboy tactics. If you aren't responsible for the attack on Don, then why did you run?"

"An innate sense of self-preservation?" he suggested. "My gut told me to retreat until I had more answers than questions."

"And if you didn't shoot Don that means someone shot both of you. Why would anyone want to shoot you? What were the two of you doing anyway? Did you bring enemies from Miami?"

When Nick didn't attempt to answer, her scowl deepened and she continued to lecture him. "You should have gone to my dad. If you're an innocent victim, we should head straight back to town, talk to my dad and check you into the hospital."

"So someone can take another shot at me?" he asked tersely.

Keri propped her hands on her hips. "Now you're suggesting I can't be trusted? After I went to the trouble of patching you up last night?"

A thud on the front porch cut off her tirade. Nick glanced out to see an overturned chair and blamed it on the storm. He let out a sigh and raked a hand through his hair. "I'm suggesting we call a truce while we get some food and batten down the hatches."

Keri sighed. "We don't batten down too many hatches in

the mountains," she said in a calmer tone. "I guess if we're gonna be stuck here awhile, I could use some coffee. How's the shoulder?"

"Throbbing like a sonofabitch, but not so feverish or bleeding."

"You need food and then more meds. I'll take a look after breakfast. I hope you're not planning to use the gun or handcuffs anymore. I won't be so easy to intimidate now that I've had some sleep."

He cocked a brow at her. "You were easy last night?"

The little joke didn't sway her. She nodded without losing eye contact or cracking a smile.

"Hmm, I guess I can trust you if you swear you won't—"

"Do anything stupid?" she finished for him.

"Go anywhere, contact anyone or try to use them on me," he finished. "Do we have a deal?"

Chapter Five

Keri agreed to his terms because it suited her for the moment. She didn't welcome the glitch in her vacation plans, but neither did she want the hassle of taking him back to town. She could tolerate him for a couple days if he didn't try changing the rules again. He hadn't shot Don and a punch to his shoulder could quash any funny business. She had no desire to hurt him, but neither did she feel threatened.

"Put the gun and handcuffs back in the first-aid kit while I make coffee," she said.

"Are you always so bossy?" he asked, doing as she suggested and then following her to the kitchen.

"It's how things get done," she replied absently while filling the coffeepot and switching it to brew.

Lamanto leaned against the doorjamb. She gave him a cursory glance. He had a bed head and his skin looked pasty. Dark shadows ringed his eyes, a result of too much blood loss.

"Sit down before you collapse. I need to go to the bathroom and then I'll fix some breakfast."

"I can cook."

"Sit," she commanded, brooking no argument. Her gaze didn't waver until he'd taken a seat at the table.

She grabbed a fresh sweatsuit, went to the bathroom and splashed water on her face. The old, darkened mirror above the sink had a crack down the middle, but it still showed her looking nearly as bad as her patient. Even though she kept her hair in a short, easy style, it still stuck out in every direction after a night's sleep. It helped to run a wet comb through it.

Her face looked pale. She tanned easily, but these past few months she hadn't spent much time in the sun. All work and no play made Keri a dull girl. The refrain ran through her mind as she brushed her teeth, put on clean clothes and headed back to the kitchen.

The smell of freshly brewed coffee energized her as she began collecting bread, eggs and milk. The supplies she'd thought would last at least a week had already been depleted by half a gallon of milk and half a loaf of bread.

"Scrambled eggs and toast is the best I can offer," she said, trying not to feel self-conscious as she moved around the tight confines of the kitchen. Lamanto's close proximity unnerved her more than she cared to admit.

"Sounds great. I think I'll hit the bathroom while you cook," he added, pushing himself to his feet.

Keri let out a small sigh as he left the room. She could breathe easier without him so close. Silly, of course, but a fact. She wasn't used to having her personal space invaded by attractive strangers.

Rain pelted the cabin as they ate breakfast. The old tin roof intensified the sound in the heavy silence. Thunder rolled, lightning flashed and the building shuddered in the force of the wind. The temperature steadily dropped.

When they'd cleaned their plates, Keri cleared the table and lit the wall-mounted space heater. It would keep the chill off the back of the house.

"You have gas out here?"

"A propane storage tank out back. Everything is powered by propane, even the generator for electric."

She poured a second cup of coffee for each of them and sat down again. The sound of the rain on the roof changed. "We're getting some sleet or hail," she commented. "I guess Dwayne could be right about snow."

"Do you get much snow up here?" Lamanto asked.

His strained tone drew Keri's gaze to his face. She'd avoided looking at him while they ate, but now she noticed how drawn and weak he appeared. The nurse in her knew he should be in bed.

"We can get heavy snow, but it doesn't stay on the ground long. Not this early in the season. The temperature can vary as much as thirty degrees in a day." She lifted a brow. "Are you worried about getting snowed in?"

He gave her a lopsided grin. "No, but I need sleep. And as you pointed out, you're in a whole lot better shape right now. I'm wondering how much I can trust you."

"So, you're hoping we'll be snowbound?"

He held her gaze and slowly nodded. "You didn't comment on the trust issue."

"How much can you trust me?" She played along even though she had no intention of stepping a foot outside the cabin. "You're wondering if I'll make a mad dash for home the minute you go to sleep."

He gave her a slow nod.

"We have a truce. I promised. You can take it or leave it. We really don't have any choice but to trust each other, do we?"

Thunder rumbled in the distance but the pounding on the roof lessened. The room grew quiet as their gazes remained locked. When Keri began to feel an unwelcome fascination with the depths of his eyes, she shifted her attention back to her coffee. After swallowing the last drop, she said, "Better let me check your wound and then get back to bed."

Lamanto finished his coffee and pushed his chair from the table. He shrugged off one arm of the flannel shirt and then slowly tugged it off his bad arm. Keri watched as his flat stomach and rippling abs were slowly bared. She scolded herself for the physical reaction, but then reminded herself that any warm-blooded female would feel the same. It was just the chemistry of the human species.

To dispel the sizzle of attraction, she pulled latex gloves from her first-aid kit and moved around the table. He spread his legs and she stepped between them to reach the bandage. She could feel the heat of his thighs brushing against her legs and her pulse quickened. It had been much easier to tend his wound when she'd been too exhausted to react to all the testosterone.

After carefully checking the stitches, she taped fresh gauze over them and pressed it in place. She worked in silence but felt Lamanto's steady gaze on her face. He didn't look toward his shoulder or watch her hands, only her face. She kept her expression and tone bland, but her nerves began to prickle.

"It's healing nicely with minimal seepage. It feels a little hot to the touch, so I'll get you more ibuprofen." Stepping aside, she peeled the gloves off her hands and threw them in the trash. Reaching back into her kit, she realized her hands were trembling. It bruised her professional ego.

"Thanks," he said, taking the pills and washing them down with the glass of water she offered. When he started to pull his shirt back on, Keri realized his good hand wasn't too steady, either. She took the shirt from him, turned it right side out and then helped him get back into it. The shirt was big enough to ease his bad arm into it as well.

"It's getting colder in here. I'll get a fire started, but you should be warm enough in bed."

He frowned. "I can't just go to bed if you need help."

"I don't want help. I have everything I need and plenty of experience doing what needs to be done." Right now, she wanted space so she could breathe without inhaling the scent of him or move without feeling the heat of his gaze. "Go back to bed."

Lamanto slowly nodded and rose from his chair. She followed him into the living room.

"I'll rest on the couch."

"Bed," she insisted tersely.

"Is your nickname Ratchet?"

"I'm a damned good nurse."

Lamanto kept mumbling and grumbling, but he went into the bedroom without more argument. She heard the squeak of the old bedsprings and sighed.

The sound of the storm had lessened. Keri looked out the window to see wildly blowing snow. Giant flakes whirled, creating a blinding curtain of white, obscuring trees still laden with leaves. A chill coursed over her and she realized how much the temperature in the cabin had dropped.

After kindling a flame in the fireplace, she put some logs on to burn and busied herself in the kitchen. First the dishes because she couldn't stand having dirty dishes in the sink. Jack called her obsessive. She preferred order in her life. Trauma nursing led to chaos in her career, so she controlled her personal life as best she could.

Next she braved the weather to finish unloading her SUV. Finding Lamanto amongst her supplies had kept her from collecting everything last night. It took a few trips, but she gathered extra clothes and bedding without getting it all soaked.

Once she'd done that, she moved back to the kitchen. As she started unpacking a box of grocery staples, an image of her mother popped into her mind. A mature version of the image she saw in the mirror each day. Her dear, loving, devoted mother; her empathetic cohort in a testosterone-filled household. Her mother had doubled as a parent, a friend and the sister she'd always wanted.

A sob caught at her throat and tears stung her eyes, but she wouldn't let them fall. "Mom," she whispered quietly. "I miss you so much."

It had been more than two years now, but the grief still ambushed her, the pain as fresh as the day she'd awakened from a coma to learn her mother had died in the crash that nearly killed her too. Her chest tightened as she choked back the tears. It was still hard to think of her mom without hurting.

Elaine Merritt had been a good-natured, generous person who loved cooking and caring for her family. Her mom had insisted on packing baking staples when they came to the cabin, even for a short time. Sugar, flour, shortening, salt, soda, canned milk, dry pasta, beans and rice, she'd had a list of what she considered the basic necessities.

Even though Keri depended more on frozen entrees, she'd still packed her mom's staples. Good thing since she had an unexpected guest with a big appetite. Thoughts of him had her dumping a bag of frozen beef stew into the slow cooker for dinner. Lamanto would wake up hungry, and her cooking skills couldn't compete with her mom's.

She found a tissue, swiped at her eyes and blew her nose. Exhaustion had to be at the root of the melancholy, exhaustion and a return to the cabin. She'd been determined but wary of coming back. That's why she hadn't wanted her dad or brother to witness her return, in case she totally fell apart. She'd hoped it would be emotionally cathartic rather than devastating.

Lamanto had unwittingly eased the return. He'd kept her distracted from the heartache and loss. Not that she ever planned to admit as much to him. Nor did she want anyone to know she planned her own investigation of the accident that had cost her so much.

A glance toward the radio unit had her wondering if she should try to get a message to her dad. Part of her knew it would be the logical thing to do, but a larger part wanted to honor the promise she'd made her stowaway. He'd trusted her enough to go back to bed.

Or had he just trusted the storm would force her to keep her word? Keri supposed she could sneak in there and handcuff his good arm to the bed, but what purpose would it serve? If he hadn't shot Don, that made him a victim rather than a criminal. Who knew?

Shaking her head, she went to the living, put a fat log on the fire and grabbed a book from another box she'd packed. She loved to read but rarely had time, so curling up on the sofa opposite the fire made perfect sense. What could be better than a good book on a stormy afternoon?

A nap? She answered her own question awhile later as she tried to focus on the storyline but failed. Pulling an afghan over her shoulders, she closed her eyes and drifted to sleep.

When she woke, dusk had fallen. The fire flickered and the cabin smelled like beef stew. Her stomach rumbled as she lifted her arms over her head and stretched the stiffness from her limbs.

"Whatever's cooking sure smells good." Lamanto's sleepy voice shattered the stillness as he made his way from the bedroom.

She tossed aside the afghan and sat up straight, her gaze shifting to him as he moved closer. He still looked pale but more rested. They both had a lot of catching up to do on sleep.

"Stew and it's probably ready if you're hungry. I'll put some biscuits in the oven. It won't take more than a half-hour."

"You're going to whip up some homemade biscuits?" he asked, his tone brighter.

"I'm going to open a can," she corrected.

"Oh," he replied, flashing her a grin. "If I had two good arms, I'd whip up some biscuits."

"You're a good cook?"

"Not as good as my dad, but I can hold my own in the kitchen."

"Your dad's a chef?"

"Only for the family. My mama says she wins the bread and Papa bakes it."

Keri smiled. She liked the way he said mama and papa. There was something very old-world respectful and endearing about it.

"Wow," he said, his gaze settling on her face. "You're really beautiful when you smile."

The compliment had her drawing her brows together in a frown. She wanted to chastise him for flirting, yet his words sounded so genuine. The thought brought a blush to her cheeks and warmth to her body. She redirected the conversation.

"Your mother is the bread winner of the family?"

Lamanto nodded but didn't elaborate. He just kept looking at her, making her feel self-conscious about her wrinkled clothes and wild hair. Rising from the sofa, she smoothed both and asked, "What does she do?"

"Who?" he asked, his tone distracted.

She propped her hands on her hips and stared at him. "Your mother. We're talking about your mother."

"She sells candy."

Okay then. Enough with the small talk. Her patient needed to wake up and clear his head. She noticed his right hand was supporting his left arm.

"How's your arm?"

He finally shifted his gaze from her to his shoulder. "Better."

"I should have made you a sling. I'll do that before we eat."

"What can I do to help?"

She didn't really need help, but she told him to add some logs to the fire while she went in search of something to support his injured arm. They met again in the kitchen where she cut a wide strip of fabric from an old pillowcase.

"I think this will work," she said, moving close to him again. She slid the fabric under his forearm and fashioned the support before pulling the edges together. He bent his knees so she could reach behind his head to knot the ends. Eye to eye, they stared at each other as tension sprang between them, as sudden and fierce as the earlier storm. Her breathing stuttered as their bodies brushed.

"Is that good?" she asked, suddenly breathless as she got lost in his deep, dark eyes.

At his slow nod, she secured the knot. Her fingers lingered, her arms around his neck. Then she slid her hands over his shoulders. He straightened and her fingertips skimmed down his chest. It felt deliciously warm. Not feverish, just manly warm. And manly hard.

Lamanto's good hand dropped to her waist, steadying them

both. After another long, tension-filled minute, he took a step backward. His voice sounded rough to her ears.

"That helps, thanks."

Keri studied him. His hair was mussed, his face still chalky. He had a two-day growth of beard. Normally, his dark good looks wouldn't have appealed to her at all. So why did touching him make her heart pound and put her senses on high alert? Was she so desperate for male attention? It had been a long time since she'd allowed any man as close as Lamanto had gotten in less than twenty-four hours.

"What's the verdict?" he asked, studying her just as intently.

"I think you'll live." She dodged the real question and gave him a quick grin before turning to the refrigerator. Better to ignore the sudden raging of hormones. "I'll get some biscuits made."

They shared a quiet dinner, keeping the conversation general. She learned he enjoyed science fiction and action movies while she leaned toward lighthearted romantic comedies. Neither of them had much time for television, but he liked sports and silly sitcoms while she preferred crime-solving dramas. They both found reality shows totally annoying.

"Packaged cookies are the best I can offer for dessert," Keri said as she cleared the table and poured them both a cup of coffee.

"I never met a cookie I didn't like," he said, taking several when she put a bag on the table.

"Can you whip up cookies as well as biscuits?" she asked.

"Not as well as my pop. How 'bout you?"

"Pies happen to be my specialty. My only specialty, I might add."

He moaned around a mouthful of cookie, and then said, "I love pie. All kinds of pie. And pastries. Just about any kind of pastry."

"Me too, unfortunately," she said, patting her hip.

"What's unfortunate about a love of the finer things in life?" he asked.

"Most of the finer foods come with big calories. And they aren't exactly health food."

His gaze traveled over her slowly but not offensively. It caused a little quiver of reaction so she sat down again.

"You don't look like you have a weight issue," he said with just enough sincerity to be believed. "You're not one of those health food nuts, are you?"

"I'm a nurse. I know what's healthy. I eat my fruits and vegetables."

"And pastries?" he teased, his eyes glittering as they locked with hers.

Keri found herself smiling back at him. "I'm especially fond of hot apple pie, and it happens to be among my specialties."

He closed his eyes and groaned again. "Please tell me you brought some apples with you."

Keri couldn't help but laugh at his silliness. "I didn't, but there's a small orchard at the back of the property. If the weather improves, I can go collect enough for a couple pies."

"You have everything else you need?"

Keri's smile faltered a little when she thought of the staples she'd packed. She nodded, feeling another wave of grief. She hadn't baked a pie in more than two years. Taking a big swallow of coffee, she swallowed tears with it. Then a bite of cookie kept her mouth too full to speak.

Lamanto's next question was low and soft. "Want to tell me what brought the sadness into your eyes?"

She swallowed hard and gave him a quick smile. "I lost my mom a couple years ago. It's still hard sometimes."

"Mom and apple pie go together. It's the American way."

She nodded. In her case, they really did.

"I guess me and my pop have done a lot of bonding in the kitchen too," he continued, allowing her time to recover her composure. "He loves to cook. I love to eat."

His tone brought the smile back to her lips. "My mom has a plaque in the kitchen that says, 'The way to a man's heart is through his stomach.' My brother Jack says I'll never find my way since I'm such a lousy cook."

Lamanto gave her a deep, dimpled grin. Her stomach fluttered. She hadn't known her stomach could flutter.

"And what do you say to him?"

"That a scalpel is much more efficient."

He chuckled and the sound warmed her.

"You and your brother are pretty close?"

"You mean despite the sibling rivalry and constant bickering?"

He grinned and nodded.

"We're close, but he's gotten so damned overprotective, it's driving me crazy."

"Since the accident?" he asked.

That he'd heard about the accident shouldn't have surprised her. It remained high on the list of town gossip. The community suffered from a serious lack of newsworthy issues. She wondered if he'd heard a complete rundown on her medical history.

"Yes. He and Dad babied me bad enough before the wreck. Since then, it's gotten ridiculous and suffocating."

"That's the reason for your solitary vacation plans?"

"Mostly," she hedged, not ready to discuss her burning need for answers. "How about you? Any siblings?"

He accepted the change of subject without hesitation. "Four sisters, two older and two younger. Liz and Maria are happily married with a couple rug rats each. The twins, Sonia and Sophie, are seniors in college this year."

"So you're the middle child and only boy. Wow, I'm sure the psychoanalysts would have fun with that."

He gave a long suffering sigh. "Save me from the shrinks."

She hid a grin but teased, "Sounds like a man with experience."

"Department policy. It sucks, but it's part of the regs. Regulations," he clarified.

Keri understood all too well. She'd suffered through endless sessions with the hospital psychologist. They wouldn't let her return to work until her surgeons and therapist had released her.

After a few minutes of silence, Lamanto redirected the conversation. "So you think a man's heart is better accessed with a scalpel than food?"

"You doubt it?"

He rose from the table, carrying his coffee mug to the sink. "I'll wait until I taste the pie before I comment on that one."

"Wise choice." She joined him at the sink and gently nudged him aside. "You're no help with dishes. Go put another log on the fire and check the box of books I brought. You might find something that appeals to you."

She did the dishes and joined him in the living room a few minutes later. He'd propped himself in her dad's favorite recliner and turned the lamp shade for optimal light. He'd started reading a thriller by one of her favorite authors. She picked up the book she'd started earlier and they spent the next couple hours reading in companionable silence.

When her eyes grew tired and her concentration waned, she excused herself and headed to the shower. It felt strange to strip and bathe with a stranger so close, yet she didn't feel threatened. Her instincts rarely failed her and he wasn't the type to accost women. He might charm, sweet-talk and seduce, but he didn't need to take advantage. Despite his misguided suspicions and actions, he seemed a polite, decent guy.

Once she'd finished and dressed in some clean sweats, she found fresh clothes for him in the bedroom and reentered the living room. He'd stopped reading to put logs on the fire again.

"Your turn in the bathroom," she said, handing him clothes. "Do you need help? You shouldn't get that arm wet."

"No. I'll be fine. I'll make do with a quick wash, and I can take the couch tonight."

She started to argue, but he waved off any discussion.

"I slept too much today. I'll probably be restless, so I might as well keep an eye on the fire."

"You're sure?" Bed did sound good to her. She couldn't believe how weary she still felt.

"Positive."

"Then go ahead and get cleaned up so I can check your arm before I go to bed."

When he returned, bare-chested and with sweatpants riding low on his hips, Keri drew a fortifying breath before touching him. He smelled of soap and warm, sexy male. She checked his stitches, pleased to see how well they'd healed.

After helping him into a shirt, she slipped the sling around his neck as he knelt. Her hormones scrambled when they touched. Having him close created a sensory overload in her body. She went to bed to escape it, but the scent of him lingered there too. It should have annoyed her, yet it comforted.

The thought of succumbing to the attraction zinging between them did annoy her. Heat suffused her body and had her kicking off the blanket. She blamed the feminine weakness on fatigue, reminding herself that it would take more than a few hours' sleep to ease the bone-deep tiredness she'd been experiencing lately.

Sometime during the night, she woke, chilled to the bone. She pulled the blankets over her but couldn't stop shivering. Then a masculine arm circled her waist, drawing her flush against a warm male body. Keri snuggled closer to the heat of him, tangling her legs with his and tucking her hands between them. Heat chased away the chills. Warm and safe, she slept.

Chapter Six

The thin bedroom curtains couldn't dim the brilliance of the sunlight the following morning. Keri woke alone in the bed but not chilled. She frowned, trying to decide if the warm male body had been a figment of her imagination or if Lamanto had shared the bed. Either way, it suited her to wake up alone. Neither of them needed the additional temptation.

Her breasts tingled and her nipples puckered against the soft fabric of the sweatshirt. She crossed her arms over her chest and lectured herself about how much safer it was to wake up alone. Her body refused to accept the argument, so she tossed aside the covers and headed to the bathroom. Frigid water on her face quickly doused the lingering arousal.

As she ran a damp comb through her hair, the smell of coffee improved her mood. She followed the smell into the kitchen. Lamanto stood at the sink, awkwardly trying to stir something in a bowl.

"What's that?"

"Pancake batter. I made a mess putting it together, but it's almost ready."

She didn't care about spilled flour or broken egg shells. The thought of homemade pancakes wiped all other thought from her mind. Her stomach growled.

"I love pancakes, but I didn't bring syrup."

"There's butter and brown sugar."

Keri didn't argue. She got a griddle out of the cupboard and lit a fire under it. They worked in harmony, making small talk as they cooked. Lamanto commented on the brilliance of the sun on the snow-covered terrain around the cabin. She told him the sun would likely melt the remaining snow.

"And tomorrow you can gather apples?" he teased, flashing her a smile and a wink.

Laughing, she teased back, "An army travels on its stomach?"

"Something like that."

The day passed in much with same manner as the previous day with less sleeping and more reading. Their meals got a little more interesting with his suggestions and help. Keri found herself laughing more than she'd done in a very long time. She decided to forget everything but enjoying time with an attractive, attentive man. Never mind that circumstances forced him to be attentive.

When it came time for bed, they repeated the previous evening's routine. Tension sizzled as they touched, heat suffused her each time his dark, dangerous eyes locked her in his gaze. Arousal throbbed between them, a strong, sure entity they silently agreed to ignore. She went to bed alone, hot and restless. Much later, when the bed had cooled, a hot male body drove away the chill. Lamanto didn't take any liberties. He just pulled her close and drove away the cold.

The next morning, she woke alone again but totally aroused. Every inch of her body yearned for masculine attention. Her skin tingled, toes curled and a low ache settled in the pit of her stomach. She hadn't felt this way since before the wreck changed her life, so it wasn't a bad thing. Just bad timing and the wrong man.

The day didn't start in as congenial a mood. She assumed Lamanto suffered with a similar malady. Mounting sexual tension made them both a little edgy and withdrawn. It would be a huge mistake to get involved in a more intimate relationship and they both knew it.

They settled for cold cereal, toast and minimal conversation. After breakfast, Keri announced her intention to collect apples for pie.

"Most of the snow's melted," said Lamanto as he moved to the kitchen window, "but it'll be wet and muddy."

"I have boots."

"You think it's safe to go out alone?" he asked, looking across the heavily wooded field behind the cabin.

"Not much in these woods except deer, raccoon and other small critters. They won't bother me if I don't bother them."

"Someone stole the gas from your truck."

"Sneaking around in the dark of night," she said in disgust. "Those type of cowards usually hide in the light of day."

Nick didn't argue with her reasoning, but he followed her when she left the cabin. Armed with the sheriff's gun and cloaked in a dark, hooded sweatshirt, he crept from snow-laden bushes to clusters of small trees in order to stay close yet out of sight. Feeling far from physically fit, he hoped to use the element of surprise should anyone or anything threaten her.

He frowned at the thought of anyone hurting his Keri. His frown deepened as he realized he thought of her as his. That was just stupid. She hadn't done or said anything to suggest she cared about him, yet he found himself caring more for her each day. He enjoyed spending time with her even when neither of them spoke, and he'd didn't get comfortable with many women. He liked her spirited independence and self-sufficiency even though it also irritated him. He enjoyed sparring with her and appreciated her sense of humor.

Most of his life, he'd felt the need to perform for women. The ones he dated expected him to be the macho cop or the charming playboy. Nobody cared much what he wanted. To be fair, he probably owed that to never letting them get close to the person behind the badge and the charm.

Keri saw through both and moved beyond them. Her smiles made him happy. Holding her through the night made him even happier. And hornier, but he needed to get a grip on the sexual stuff or she'd throw him out on his ear.

After ten minutes of brisk walking, he willed her to slow down a little. The need to stay out of sight made it hard to keep pace with her. Not to mention how quickly his strength was waning. Breathing heavily, he stopped to lean against a huge oak tree and catch his breath.

Just ahead of him, he heard Keri yell. He watched as three men dressed in camouflage uniforms surrounded her. They carried semi-automatic assault rifles and wore full combat gear.

"What the hell?" he heard her exclaim as she looked from one to the other.

Nick tried to quickly formulate a rescue plan as a fourth man stepped into the circle. He greeted her in a warm, friendly tone and gestured for the others to lower their guns.

"Hey, Keri, what's up?"

As Nick watched, her body relaxed. He didn't realize he'd stopped breathing until a quick intake of air burned his lungs. The newcomer gave a nod of his head and the others faded back into the woods with professional stealth. Good, but not good.

"Russ? What in the world is going on? They scared ten years off my life." Her voice rose in indignation. "Who are those men and why are they carrying assault rifles? Nobody hunts game with assault rifles."

"Nothing to worry your pretty head about," the other man assured her. "They're not out to hurt anyone."

Nick didn't like the guy's condescending tone, and he didn't suppose Keri tolerated it any better.

"Then what?" The snap in her voice carried on the clear morning air, making his lips curve in a smile.

"Just some militia training maneuvers. We do 'em all the time, but we don't usually come across nobody back here."

"I thought your militia group had all local guys. I didn't recognize any of those men."

Nick flinched as she challenged Russ Carson. He'd met the militia leader in town and thought him a little unstable. He wished she'd be more cautious.

"Jed Coiner's family is local. The rest are from surrounding counties."

"Well, you can tell every one of them they're trespassing

and to keep their maneuvers off my dad's property. I don't like having guns pointed at me."

"Don't be too quick to dismiss 'em, hon," he said, reaching out to pat her arm. "You might welcome their protection one of these days."

Keri snorted derisively. "Well, not today or anytime soon. I keep telling the whole world, I'M ON VACATION!"

"I know, I know," the other man placated. "But what in the world are you doin' out here in the morning chill? It's not a good time for a nature walk."

"I'm headed down to the little orchard for apples. You know the one, near the stream."

Nick saw the soldier boy glance to his right. "I remember. You figurin' on baking a pie?"

"Yes."

"I truly love your apple pie."

The commando warrior sounded enamored of more than Keri's pastries. Nick felt a stab of jealousy and quickly squelched it. He'd never been the jealous type, and he sure didn't need any new issues to deal with right now.

"The storm mighta froze the fruit or blew it half way to Kentuck."

Keri turned back to her original path. "I'm hoping to get a bag or two before it spoils. The apples should still be cold this morning but if the afternoon sun warms them too much, they'll all rot."

"I'll be glad to help," said Carson as he fell into step with her. "You suppose it'll earn me a piece or two of warm apple pie?"

Nick didn't hear Keri's reply. The pair moved out of earshot and then out of his sight. He didn't follow. His feet had frozen and his shoulder throbbed. He'd pushed his body enough for one day.

He remembered Don describing Carson as a longtime friend of the Merritt family. She'd be safe, at least for now, and he needed to get back to the cabin before those troops started maneuvers again. *Local militia, my ass,* he thought. More like mercenaries.

Was it possible he'd landed right in the middle of the operation he'd been sent to investigate? Carson might be a gung-ho country boy, but there had to be more going on in these woods. What better place to develop a covert camp than in the sheriff's backyard? As Keri insisted, not much got by the good sheriff. So how could this escape his notice?

Nick arrived at the cabin and back to square one with his investigation. Was the sheriff involved up to his eyeballs or helpless to do anything with his suspicions?

He'd run into a lot of racist attitudes since coming to Tennessee. Even in the big city, he'd met dedicated officers with supremacist mentalities. There were plenty who thought they knew all the answers when it came to protecting America from outsiders and unpopular government policy.

According to local gossip, Keri hadn't been back to the cabin since her mother died. What about her dad and brother? Russ Carson called himself the leader, but he didn't have the brains or money to organize an operation spanning several states. Were the Merritts the masterminds of a home-grown terrorist organization? If so, he had to figure out their agenda before anyone got hurt.

When Nick got back to the cabin, he cleaned up all traces of his occupancy. He didn't know if soldier boy would come back with Keri, but he didn't want to put her at any more risk. You never knew what to expect from extremists and Russ Carson sounded like one when it came to his militia. He might have a soft spot for Ms. Merritt, but who knew what he'd do if he considered her a traitor?

When Keri returned to the cabin, its warmth enveloped her. Despite the bright sunshine, the temperature hadn't risen much and she'd gotten chilled to the bone. Kicking off her boots on the back porch, she shrugged out of her jacket and carried the bags of apples into the kitchen.

The absolute quiet gave her a minute of panic. Glancing around, she looked for signs of Lamanto but found none. She took a quick walk through the cabin without seeing a hint of his having spent time there. Had he broken his promise as soon as she'd left him alone? Had he taken off with her car?

Moving to the front room window, she pulled back the curtain and looked outside. Her SUV sat right where she'd left it. Surely he wouldn't have left on foot.

"Lamanto?" she called loudly.

"Right here," he said as he came through the bedroom doorway. "I hid in the shower in case your boyfriend insisted on coming back with you."

Relief washed through Keri. Silly of her to care, but she did. They'd made a pact. She'd honored it, and she wanted him to honor it too.

Giving him a slight smile, she said, "He's not my boyfriend. He offered to carry the apples but got a radio message calling him back to camp."

"Did you happen to get a look at the camp?"

She turned and headed to the kitchen, wondering how much she should tell him. She didn't really know what was happening on the neighboring property. Calling it alarming would be a major understatement.

"Don't bother sugarcoating the details," he said as he followed her. "I saw those troops he called local militia. They aren't poorly organized, poorly financed, weekend warriors."

She glanced toward the window and knew he couldn't have seen the encounter. Not even with binoculars.

"You followed me?"

"I had your back, that's all."

Propping her hands on her hips, she glared at him. "You had my back?" She shot a glance from his head to his toes. "With a bum shoulder and bare feet? What were you thinking? Are you totally lacking in common sense?"

Instead of taking offense, he gave her a grin. "Not totally. I put on shoes and took a gun. I thought I might have to shoot a bear, but I didn't expect you to run into heavily armed mercenaries."

Her frown deepened. She dropped her hands to her sides. "You really think they're mercenaries?"

"I don't know what they are. I know what they aren't and that's good-ole-boys out hunting rabbits."

Keri agreed, but she needed more pieces of the puzzle. "Maybe it's time you told me why someone wanted to shoot you and Don. Everyone was so sure you'd shot him that nobody considered you both being targets. So who felt threatened by the two of you?"

"I wish I knew."

A dodge but truthful, she thought. "Your visit in Thornsbury wasn't spurred by a desire to share time with an old academy buddy, was it?"

Keri could tell he didn't want to lie to her but he didn't want to tell the whole truth. She'd seen the expression on her dad's and brother's faces too many times. It annoyed the hell out of her. While Lamanto took a chair and formulated a reply, she started cleaning and peeling apples.

"Well?" she prodded when he took too long to reply.

"Did Russ Carson say anything unusual or suspicious while you went picking apples?"

"Since I don't know what you'd consider suspicious, I have no idea if anything he said is important."

"He seemed more than a little friendly," Lamanto shot back at her.

"He's been in love with me since kindergarten, despite years of efforts to redirect his affections," she declared matter-of-factly. "And my brother calls me a dog with a bone if I don't get answers, so don't try changing the subject."

"Carson is the subject," he grumbled. "I just don't know what he's involved in or how dangerous his operation might be."

"But Don was suspicious enough to involve an outsider? That would mean he didn't completely trust my dad. I don't buy that."

"Don didn't involve me directly," he explained, snatching a wedge of apple as she quartered them.

Keri let out an exasperated sigh. "Are you always so close-mouthed about your work? It's really irritating."

"Sorry," he said. "It comes from working undercover too many years. The wrong word can cost a man his life."

"If I don't hear some right words soon, I might slice you up with this knife," she threatened, waving the paring knife in his direction.

He gave her a cheeky grin. "You'd just have to stitch me back up, so you might as well spare yourself the extra work."

True enough. She continued peeling and he kept munching. After a long silence, he finally spoke again.

"How about we make another little bargain?"

She arched a brow at him. "I'm listening."

"Why don't you tell me why you really came up here for vacation, and I'll tell you why I chose Thornsbury for mine."

She didn't look at him when she replied. "That's easy. I came up here to get away from everyone down there."

"That's it? You just wanted privacy? No other agenda?"

Keri hesitated. She glanced at him and found his dark eyes steadily regarding her. Jack said her face always mirrored her emotions. Did Lamanto suspect she had a secret agenda or was he just fishing?

"You first," she insisted.

"I came for a couple reasons." He held her gaze while he explained. "My lieutenant wanted me to leave Miami until the department had time to round up all the suspects in a case I'd been working."

"He thought someone might want revenge against you?"

"Yeah, but it's not likely. No more so than any other case I've worked. When I left Miami, the rats were all abandoning ship, either lawyering-up or trying to sneak out of the country."

She knew the risks in law enforcement, but she didn't like it and never would. No good man should suffer from doing the right thing. "From your lips to God's ears", her mother used to say. Justice might not be blind, but she often turned a blind eye. Good men and their families suffered.

"And your second reason?"

He turned his attention toward the bowl of sliced apples and grabbed another piece. "There's rumor about a buildup of munitions in this area. Some of the weapons are stolen in Miami and transferred through Florida. The trail leads to Tennessee."

"A lot of people are really antsy about proposed gun legislation," she argued. "They've started buying and hoarding all types of weapons."

"The munitions include large amounts of fertilizer. It's high on Homeland Security's watch list."

He didn't have to explain further. She shuddered at the thought of homegrown terrorists. Surely no one she'd known all her life could be involved.

As if reading her mind, he continued. "Those men out there today aren't guarding a small militia camp. You don't need assault rifles for that. Did Carson say anything to you regarding the camp?"

She shook her head. "He's a total chauvinist and wouldn't share anything like that with a mere woman."

"Even though he's hot for your bod?"

Keri chose not to address that issue. She didn't want to discuss hot bods with the hottest one she'd ever met.

"The orchard is near a stream about half a mile from the cabin," she said. "Did you follow us that far?"

He shook his head. "I turned back once you had an escort."

"The orchard is in the far east corner of my dad's property. It intersects with my Uncle Ned's land. Dwayne's branch of the family."

"You saw something, didn't you?" he asked, sitting straighter in his chair.

"Not much really. I noticed a new fence and a couple buildings where an old wooden shack used to stand. The militia used it for meetings. Mostly they drank beer and played poker, but Russ called it training maneuvers."

"Training for what?"

"He's always been a little wacko. He believes we'll have another revolution in this country, so he's spent his life preparing for it. His dream is a reincarnation of the Tennessee Minutemen."

"How does he support himself? How's the militia financed?"

"He's an engine mechanic, but I don't think he earns much. I never thought of the militia needing funds. They just bought their own weapons, ammunition and beer. I suppose Uncle Ned still pays taxes on the land. He's a lot older than Dad, has emphysema and doesn't get out much."

"So how does Russ fit into the equation?"

"Russ and Dwayne were really tight in high school. They hunted and fished up here a lot, and set up their militia. More like a man-cave back then. I don't think Dwayne's very active anymore and I know he never has extra money. Those new buildings look like expensive metal modulars."

"Did you ask him about them?"

"Yes, but he shrugged it off with a comment about the old shack crumbling and needing something more sturdy."

Keri knew what conclusion Lamanto would come to about the camp because she'd come to the same one. And it wasn't good. Someone had to be putting a lot of money into the place and it probably wasn't for altruist reasons. Homegrown terrorists. Groups waging war against American citizens, usually innocent people targeted for no reason other than being in the wrong place at the wrong time. She shuddered, remembering the devastation of past assaults.

"What now?" she asked Lamanto.

"I'd like to get a closer look at the camp, but it'll have to wait until I'm stronger."

"Did you not see those men with rifles?" she asked in exasperation. "I think I heard dogs too."

He grimaced. "That doesn't bode well for covert actions, but we'll have to wait and see."

Keri sprinkled sugar, cinnamon and nutmeg over her apples and began making pastry for two pies. They both got lost in thought and then Lamanto returned to the previous subject.

"I told you what brought me to Thornsbury, but you never told me what brought you to the mountains."

Her pulse accelerated at the thought of sharing so much of herself with him, of opening herself to disillusion. She hesitated, realizing how important his reaction would be. It shouldn't have mattered, but it did. In two short days, she'd come to respect his opinion and trust his judgment. She cared what he thought and didn't want to be disappointed. Except for family, the men in her life always disappointed her. And in this situation, even her family had let her down.

He urged her to confide in him. "It can't be worse than terrorism."

Were the two connected, she wondered. She had a growing suspicion they might be.

"You heard about the accident that killed my mother?"

He nodded and she felt the intensity of his gaze even though she kept hers on the pastry dough.

"I was in a coma for a couple weeks after the wreck. When I finally woke up, I had no memory of the details. I fell asleep in the car and woke up in the hospital. That's all I told investigators."

"You lied?"

"Not then. Not ever, really," she defended.

"But the details are slowly coming back to you?"

"Yes, just snatches over the past few months. My mother and I had come to the cabin a few hours ahead of Dad. He planned to follow after his shift. We both felt exhausted from traveling and getting the cabin aired, so we went down to the truck stop for a quick dinner. On the way back, I fell asleep and Mom missed the turnoff to our road."

"Let me guess," he put in, his tone going grim. "She took the road that leads to the militia camp."

Keri nodded, her throat tightening as the memories flooded back. "I woke up when my mom screamed, realizing she'd veered off the road to avoid something. I still don't know what, but I remember the screech of brakes and then a violent collision. I learned later that she'd plowed through a guard rail."

"Didn't your air bags deploy?"

"They did, nearly suffocating both of us. I remember Mom calling my name in a panic. I told her I was okay, and she warned me to sit still. The car was dangling precariously on the rail above a deep ravine."

Keri swallowed hard as she recalled those last panicked minutes with her mom. Ignoring the tears gathering in her eyes, she continued. "The memories get hazier after that, but I distinctly remember the snick of her seat belt. She pounded on her airbag and tried to free us both."

"Is that what caused you to go over the rail?"

"The accident report faulted the weak structure of the guard rail and the weight of our vehicle. Nobody else knows I'm starting to remember more details."

"Like what?"

"I remember the whir of my mom's window being lowered and the relief in her voice when someone approached the car."

"So whoever she swerved to avoid came to help?"

"Whoever she swerved to avoid, murdered her and tried to murder me."

Chapter Seven

"Murdered? How? He pushed you over the rail?"

"All I remember is the relief in her voice as she greeted someone outside the car. It was pitch-dark. The shoulder harness had me pinned to the seat and the air bag was crushing me. Then the car started rocking, and we went over the embankment."

"Did you share any of this with your dad?"

"You're the first person I've told because everyone else changes the subject when I bring up the accident. I know they think they're protecting me, but it drives me crazy."

Keri shook her head and swiped the tears off her cheek. She turned her back on him, busying herself lighting the oven and collecting pie plates. He stayed quiet a minute, giving her time to regain control of her emotions. Then he grilled her with more questions.

"Your mom greeted someone by name?"

"I think so. It's like a recurring nightmare. Every time I remember something, I feel like there's more missing. I don't know who she spoke to that night. I wish I did. I'd make damned sure he was brought to justice."

"You said the car rolled down a ravine. How long were you there? Who found you?"

"My dad found us. He was on the way to the cabin and got a report of a car going over the guard rail. When he couldn't find Mom and me, he called for emergency equipment and tracked us with the GPS."

"He never found out who made the report?"

"Untraceable."

"It was too late to save your mom?"

Keri couldn't speak for a minute. Her throat closed and she swallowed hard. The pain was too sharp and it hurt to breathe. She finished the pie shell and washed her hands then went to the bathroom and grabbed a handful of tissues. After wiping her eyes and blowing her nose, she answered his last question.

"Mom got thrown from the car." She couldn't bring herself to describe her mother's injuries. "She'd unfastened her belt, probably to help me, and her airbag deflated more quickly than mine."

"But you were trapped."

She responded with a nod followed by a sob. Suddenly weak with emotion, she put hands on the table for support. He stood and gathered her against his chest with his good arm. She didn't resist. His understanding and compassion touched her more deeply than she'd let anything touch her in a long while. Sharing the painful secret brought the whole nightmare into the open like a raw wound.

With her face pressed against his neck, she quietly wept for the first time since the accident. She missed her mom so desperately and guilt lay heavily on her heart. Could she have done more? Why hadn't she driven and let her mom sleep? Who could hate or fear them enough to want them dead? Her mom had never deliberately hurt a soul. She'd been a kind, generous woman, so who would want to snuff out her life?

Lamanto whispered to her soothingly, not offering empty platitudes but unconditional support. Keri wondered if he'd be so tender if he knew how emotionally and physically scarred she'd become since the wreck. For the first time in her life, she wanted to hurt someone rather than heal them. If she knew who'd killed her mom, she'd beat them with her bare hands and stomp them into the ground.

Would the man holding her understand the desire for revenge? Would he think her depraved? Criminal minded? A nurse yet a hypocrite? She couldn't let it matter, and she didn't dare get too comfortable in his arms. As he gently rocked her, she forced herself to get a grip.

Slowly withdrawing from his hold, she wiped her eyes and nose again. Her voice sounded a little shaky. “Sorry for drooling all over you.”

He lifted her chin with his finger and stared into her eyes. “There’s no need to apologize. I’m thinking you’ve been holding all that hurt inside for a long time. Right?”

She managed a sniff of concession. “Maybe. Thanks for the shoulder to cry on.”

A teasing note entered his voice. “Isn’t there an ancient custom that says you saved one shoulder so the other one belongs to you?”

She gave him a watery, grateful smile. “You sure mangled the interpretation, but I appreciate the thought.”

“Besides,” he drawled in his playful, playboy tone, “I told you women always lose their heads in my arms.”

Keri groaned, gave him an admonishing glance and nudged him back into the chair. But his teasing eased her tension. He’d lightened the mood enough for her to feel comfortable again. A rare talent in a man—or anyone, for that matter.

“I’m never going to get these pies made if you don’t quit drilling me with questions.”

“Just one more.”

She gave him a long-suffering look. “What?”

“Does Russ the warrior plan to come after pie?”

“I didn’t invite him, but I guess that’s no guarantee.”

“Now that the weather has cleared, we’ll have to expect more visitors and cover any traces of my being here.”

“Dad will be sending someone to check on me. That’s a given,” she said on a sigh. “I won’t be able to keep everyone out of the cabin.”

“I can hide in the bathtub like I did earlier, but it’s not the best of plans.”

Keri agreed. Anyone who visited might want to use the bathroom before leaving again.

"Can you get the oven for me?" she asked, putting the pies on a cookie sheet. He opened the oven door, she slid in the pan and he closed it again. They didn't say anything else while she tidied the kitchen.

When she'd finished, she looked him in the eyes, her expression intense. "I'm about to swear you in as an official member of the Merritt family, but you have to cross your heart and hope to die, promise on your life and give me your undying pledge that you'll never tell another soul what I'm about to tell you."

"Whew," he whistled softly, "sounds heavy."

"Do you swear?"

"Is it illegal or immoral?"

"Nope, just a family secret passed through several generations of Merritts."

Lamanto rose and returned her steady gaze. "Okay, you have my promise."

Keri nodded in acceptance. "Follow me."

She led him into the bedroom and opened the door to a small closet. Other than a couple shirts, the clothing bar stood bare. A pair of scruffy boots sat on the bare hardwood floor. Keri knelt and reached into the closet, tugging on a loose, hidden board. With one strong pull, she lifted the whole floor, revealing a set of wooden steps.

He whistled again and knelt beside her. "A trap door."

"It's narrow, but the steps lead into a small chamber. Bomb shelters were all the rage when my great-grandfather built this place. There are survival supplies down there and lanterns, but that's not the best part."

"It gets better?" he asked with boyish enthusiasm.

"Follow me," she told him. "A metal spring will close the door behind us once the floor is lowered back into place."

Keri backed down the steps, swatting at spider webs until she found an oil lantern and lit it. He followed more slowly. Once he'd joined her, she shone the light around the small underground hideout.

"It's a concrete bunker," he said in awe.

She held up the lantern. It didn't take much light to illuminate shelves loaded with bottled water, canned goods and medical supplies. The ten-by-ten-foot area housed a rollaway bed sheeted with plastic and a stack of plastic chairs. Dust and cobwebs covered all of it.

"I really should clean this while I'm here," she said. "I don't think anyone has checked it for years."

Lamanto moved around the room, knocking down a few cobwebs and checking out the supplies. "What a great idea. Your great grandpa is a man after my heart."

"There's more," she said, amused by his enthusiasm. She and Jack had shared the same wide-eyed fascination when their dad had shown it to them as grade-schoolers.

"There's a tunnel leading into the woods." Turning back to the stairs, she ducked under them and he followed. The walls narrowed into a tight passageway. "It's about twenty yards long with another hidden trap door. Artificial turf covers the opening and lots of natural vegetation camouflages the turf."

"Cool," he said. "So you have a hideout with an escape hatch. Totally damned awesome."

She took him through the tunnel with its gradual ascent. When they reached the narrow step at the end, she climbed up and tried to push the door open, but it wouldn't budge.

"It hasn't been opened for a very long time," she explained.

"Let me have a go at it."

They tried to trade positions in the tight confines. Keri held the lantern to her side. He shifted his bad arm and moved closer. Their actions managed to wedge her firmly against his chest with his good arm wrapped around her waist for support.

The solid contact of bodies stole their breath for a minute. Sexual energy pulsed between them. She inhaled deeply, but that brought her breasts tighter against the hardness of his chest. Her nipples tingled in arousal. Her legs got a little shaky as he tugged her closer. She stared into his eyes for a long moment, her pulse hitching when his gaze dropped to her mouth. She nervously flicked her tongue over her lips. He made a rough sound and then closed his eyes.

She took a cue from him, stepping down and breaking the contact so he could turn toward the door. With his good hand, he shoved first one side and then the other, prying the opening until they saw a glimmer of daylight. Once he'd loosened the turf, Keri stepped closer again. Her heart skipped a beat, but she ignored it.

After taking a good look outside the door and seeing nothing but dense foliage, they carefully lowered it again. She quickly took a step backward.

"There's a dead bolt to the right side if you come in from the yard and want to lock out intruders." She pointed toward the lock.

He grabbed it, slid it into locked position and then back out again. "It's rusty but functional."

"You've seen the propane tank in the back yard?" she asked him as they made their way back through the tunnel to the chamber.

"Yeah."

"It looks like it's surrounded by bushes, but the trap door is on the far side of it. It's easy to find if you know where to look, even in the dark, but it's not easily seen or identifiable."

"Way cool," he said with awe as he followed her up the narrow stairs to the closet trap door. "You have your own safe room. Not a bad idea with a family of law officers."

"That's the intention. That and protection from atomic bombs," she said, unsure if anything could protect them from a nuclear attack. She pushed up the closet floor board, triggering the spring to open the door. Making a mental note to oil it, she turned and passed the lantern back to Lamanto. Once he'd replaced it, she gave him a hand as he climbed the steps.

"And nobody else knows about the chamber?"

"Just my immediate family. Now Dad, Jack, me and you," she said, brushing dust off her clothes. He closed the closet door and dusted his clothes. "Dad swore us to secrecy when we were younger, and we took our pledges seriously. I told you because emergency situations are the exception, but you can't tell a soul or you'll be cursed for life."

He used his right hand to make a cross over his heart. Then he crossed himself forehead to chest, from shoulder to shoulder. "Your secret is safe with me."

Keri grinned. "Covering all the bases?"

"You betcha," he said, returning her grin.

They stared at each other for a long time, the smiles slowly fading to a more intense study of each other's features. Keri noticed a smudge of dust on his cheek. She reached out to brush it off, but the skin-to-skin contact heightened the tension between them, causing the rest of her body to stir in reaction. She badly wanted to explore the searing attraction. Her eyes widened, her lips parting, and he made a small sound of response.

She knew he felt the same sting of arousal, yet neither wanted to make the first move. Neither wanted to be the one who broke the unspoken decree to keep things platonic. Both knew the temptation should be ignored. Keri reminded herself they only had a few days together. He'd be going back to the city soon, and she didn't need more regrets in her life.

"Smells like the pies are cooking nicely," she whispered, breaking the spell. She drew in a deep breath, inhaling the sweet scent of spicy apples. Her next words sounded more natural. "I'd better check on them so the crusts don't burn."

Lamanto nodded, his voice gruff. "Better check the mirror first. You have cobwebs in your hair."

That brought a smile back to her face. "You too," she teased, turning toward the bathroom.

"You're Catholic?" she asked an hour later as they sat down for lunch.

"You have a problem with that?"

She shook her head. "Why would I?"

"Some people dislike anything they don't understand."

"Well, I'm not one of them."

He gave her a smile. "I'm not a very good Catholic," he admitted. "I don't practice the faith, but our parents raised us in the religion, and I agree with most of the teachings."

"I was raised Baptist because that's the norm for Thornsbury, but I've always been fascinated with the study of different faiths."

They discussed various religions while they ate and then Keri cut them each a piece of warm apple pie. She waited for his reaction after tasting the first bite. He didn't disappoint.

"Mmm...wow...that really is delicious."

Her voice rose to a haughty note. "You had doubts?"

Lamanto chuckled. "I told you my dad's a fantastic cook. I doubted anyone's apple pie could compare to his."

"And?"

"And I can't say another word unless you cross your heart, hope to die, swear you'll never tell a soul."

Laughing, she made a cross over her heart. "I promise. You can trust me with the truth."

He took another huge bite. "I think it might be better than my dad's."

"Might be?"

"It's possible."

"Possible?"

She kept challenging, and he kept eating. When he'd finished the whole slice, he responded. "It's possible that I'll need another piece to be absolutely sure."

"I'm still eating. Help yourself."

He went to the counter and cut himself another generous slice of pie. She finished her first about the same time he finished his second. Then he leaned back in his chair and patted his stomach.

"It's official. That's the best apple pie I've ever eaten."

Her smile widened. She found it hard not to smile in his company. He nurtured her overworked, underappreciated inner self that hungered for an intimacy beyond the physical. She'd prefer a less complicated relationship, but decided to enjoy this one while it lasted. *Live for the moment*, she told herself.

"I'm glad you like it."

He licked his lips. "I don't just like it, I love it. And there's still a pie and a half to eat."

"Unless Russ stops by and demands a piece."

Mention of the militia leader brought a frown to his handsome features. "You think he'll be back today?" He stood and went to the window, surveying the area behind the cabin. "If he makes an appearance, I'll have to hit the safe room."

"If not Russ, someone will be stopping. I just hope he leaves his armed buddies at the camp." Another thought came to mind. "You won't be able to hear what's going on up here, so stay put until I give you the all clear."

"Will do."

At the neighboring camp, a tall, casually dressed man paced the bare concrete floor of the main building. He shot a question at Carson.

"Are you sure Keri's alone at the cabin? The commander isn't going to be happy if anyone's shacking up with her."

"Keri? Hell no. I mean, hell yes, I'm sure. She's not the kind of woman who has cheap affairs. She hasn't even dated anyone since she broke it off with Monroe before the wreck."

"I'm not worried about her love life, but we never found that foreigner."

"He's long gone or we'd have tracked him down. Nobody could outsmart the sheriff's department, the highway patrol and my militia. He must have caught a ride out of state before the alert."

"That doesn't guarantee he didn't double back or he won't be coming back with reinforcements. Monroe is recovering too, and his guard's been doubled. We don't want to do anything to draw more attention at this point. We're almost ready. You know how important it is to stay on schedule. Timing is everything."

"Sure, I know timin' is important. We could start movin' in stages, though."

"He doesn't want to move until we get the last shipment of stuff at the end of next week. Then we can put all aspects of the plan into action at the same time. Until then, you and your men will have to be hyper-vigilant."

"Huh?"

"Extra careful."

"Well, speak American," grumbled Carson, annoyed at the way the other man looked down his nose at him. There were times when he'd been tempted to knock the uppity expression off his comrade's face, but he reminded himself that the operation meant more than personalities. Besides, there wouldn't be an operation without the finances provided by him and his partner.

The partner, who liked to be called Commander, hadn't come near the place since Elaine Merritt caught them all in the beams of her headlights. He'd gone ballistic after one of the arms supplier's crew had taken matters into his own hands and pushed her into the ravine. The gang-banger city boys had called it collateral damage, but the locals had to deal with the fallout.

Russ felt bad for Keri, especially since the wreck had left her barren and unhappy. He was glad she didn't remember anything because he sure wouldn't want to hurt her any more. He had the greater good of the country to consider, he kept reminding himself. All critical military exercises produced collateral damage.

"I still want you to watch out for Keri. If you see anyone sniffing around down there, make sure you put the fear of death in him."

"Roger that, sir." Russ kept his features fixed and stern,

but he smiled inwardly. He liked the idea of keeping a closer watch on Keri. No hardship at all. Spending time with her this morning had reminded him how much he enjoyed her company. He'd sure like to kindle a flame there.

"As a matter of fact, I helped her pick some apples this morning, and she invited me back for apple pie." Her lack of an invitation had irritated him, but she hadn't told him not to come back. He could almost smell her fresh apple pie.

"Women should not be vacationing alone," Russ continued. "I don't care if she did grow up in these woods; she should have a man watching out for her."

"Yeah, you're right about that. Better keep a close eye on her," said the other man.

"Speaking of the devil," said Lamanto, "I think that's your soldier boy marching over here now."

"Disappear!"

Keri quickly gathered all their lunch dishes, dumped them into the sink and started filling it with soapy water. She heard the gentle thunk of the bedroom closet door closing just as Russ pounded on her back door.

Grabbing a dish towel, she wiped her hands as she moved through the small porch to the outer door. "Come on in, Russ," she said after unlatching the lock. "I thought I might see you again today."

"Hope you don't mind. I know you want solitary and all," he said with a grin, "but the thought of that pie has been teasin' me since mornin'." He inhaled deeply. "Ahh...it smells great in here."

Keri couldn't fault his enthusiasm, and he'd never treated her with anything but respect and adoration. Despite her growing concern about the militia camp, she didn't consider him a personal threat. "Would you like some pie?"

"Sure would."

She led the way back to the kitchen then grabbed a plate

and fork. Russ placed his hat on the table and took a seat. "That sure is a lot of dishes for one person."

Keri turned, hands on hips and glared at him. "Do you need yet another reminder that I'm on vacation? I don't have to wash dishes after every meal or at all until I need something clean. There's no dishwasher here, so I do them when I feel like it. Okay?"

He gave her a sheepish smile. "Yes, ma'am."

She stared at him a little longer, studying him for the first time in years. The angular features hadn't softened much, but the boyish freckles had faded and the brightness of his red hair had darkened to auburn. A short, military haircut kept the wiry curls in check. He'd always been tall and thin. Now he carried more weight. More muscle, she'd guess.

"What would you like to drink? I have sweet tea or I can make instant coffee."

"Tea'll be fine," he said.

She served him a generous slice of pie and poured him a glass of tea. Instead of sitting at the table with him, she turned back to the dishes, not wanting him to get too cozy.

"Aren't you gonna join me?" he asked.

"I've already had too much pie."

Keri saw him glance at the two pies on the counter. Nearly three quarters of one was missing.

"It must have tasted good to you too," he commented before taking a huge bite of his piece.

"I skipped breakfast and had pie for lunch," she quickly fabricated as she put dishes in the drainer. "I'm a big girl, and I don't have to eat healthy if I don't want."

"Apples are healthy," he teased, washing down another bite with half a glass of tea. "Besides, you're on vacation."

She threw him a grin over her shoulder. "You're absolutely right. I may eat all the rest of it for supper."

He'd nearly finished his piece. "You think you could save me one more slice?"

Keri wiped her hands again and found a disposable plastic container. She scooped the rest of the pie into it. "I guess I might as well wash this plate while I'm catching up on dishes," she said. "You can take the last of it with you."

Russ's brows met in a frown. "Is that a 'here's your hat, what's your hurry'?"

"Not particularly. I just want to clean the kitchen and get back to the book I'm reading. Did you want the rest of it now?" She turned to him with the container in her hand.

He started to say something when his radio beeped. He shot a glance at it and stood. "I guess not. I'm needed back at the compound."

"Do you want me to refrigerate it until you head home this evening?" she asked.

"I can take it with me," he said. "I have a room at the compound."

"You live there now? I thought you just did occasional maneuvers. What about your house and business in Thornsbury?"

"I spend most of my time at the compound, so my brothers take care of the home place and garage."

"I've heard all three of them are good mechanics, but not as good as their big brother."

His chest puffed out at the flattery. Keri saw a blush color his cheeks. He'd hated the telltale, fair-skinned reaction since grade school. She found it comforting.

Chapter Eight

Five days after their arrival at the cabin, Keri checked Lamanto's wound after their evening baths. "I can't believe how well your arm is healing," she said, gently probing the area around the stitches. She'd stopped bandaging it days ago. "Is it tender?"

"Not too much."

"How about when you move it?"

"It throbs a little."

"I think it's time you stopped using the sling and started doing some therapy."

"You're a physical therapist too?

"No, but I know the basics. If you don't start moving it more, you'll lose your normal range of motion."

"Okay, nurse, I've stretched it some, but what else should I be doing?"

Keri tried to focus on his shoulder and ignore the pure male beauty of the rest of him. Freshly bathed and shaved, he looked good enough to eat. The ebony hair on his head and chest glistened with dampness. He'd insisted on a shower, so his body radiated with warmth. He smelled clean and infinitely appealing. After days of close proximity, she had trouble remembering why they shouldn't get involved.

Putting one hand on his shoulder and the other beneath his elbow she slowly lifted until it pointed straight from his body. She lowered it to his side and repeated the motion several times.

"Can you do it yourself?"

Lamanto managed the motion a few minutes before sweat

popped out on his forehead. She could hear the increased labor of his breathing as he struggled to push his torn muscle back into action.

"Show me how high you can raise it."

He got his arm a little higher each time he lifted it, but not close to a normal range.

"Now try a forward motion. Lift it to my shoulder."

She watched his jaw lock as he brought the arm in front of him and lifted it to shoulder height. When it trembled, she supported his elbow with her hand. He dropped his arm on her shoulder and looked her in the eyes.

"That's about it," he said in self-disgust. "Who'd have thought lifting my arm could bring out a sweat?" He put his other arm around her and drew her to his body. She didn't resist as he held her close, his chest rising and falling against hers. She slid her arms around his waist, enjoying the solid feel of his smooth, firm flesh. Pressing her face against his good shoulder, she absorbed the scent of him while he caught his breath.

"That's fine for now. You just have to start using it more," she said. "The skin has healed, but the muscle tissue needs to be flexed."

They held each other as if it were the most natural thing in the world. Lamanto dropped his head onto hers and nuzzled her hair. He inhaled her scent just as she'd done with him.

"I owe the quick recovery to *la mia infermiera d'angelo.*"

Keri lifted her head and looked at him. Between the two of them, she had the more pronounced accent with her strong southern drawl. But whatever he'd called her sounded beautifully smooth and seductive. "You speak Italian?"

"Fluently. My parents insisted."

"Translation?"

"Angel nurse." His eyes lit with amusement. "When you sang in the car on the way up here, I mistook you for an angel."

"You thought you'd died?"

"Until you woke me with a gun. A really rude awakening, I might add. Then I decided a nurse might be more helpful than an angel."

"Thus the angel nurse?"

He nodded, locking gazes with her. They stared into each other's eyes for another long, searching moment.

"I'd like to kiss *la mia infermiera d'angelo.*"

Without waiting for her response, he dropped his mouth to hers. Keri closed her eyes as their lips met for the first time in a long, slow, searching kiss. They took their time nibbling, licking, exploring, savoring. She welcomed his tongue with hers and softly sucked at the offering.

He made a rough sound, shifting her in his arms to mold her closer to his body. She tightened her grip and kissed him without reservation, opening herself to deeper exploration of her mouth, cheeks and tongue.

They eventually broke off the kiss to drag in air, but he used the time peppering kisses on her cheeks, chin and neck. She shivered when he nibbled the pulse beating wildly there and returned the favor, spreading kisses over his face and neck.

Her unbound breasts plumped against the fabric of her sweatshirt, her nipples tingling as they tightened with arousal. Nick slipped a hand under her shirt, first caressing the skin over her ribs and then cupping a breast in his hand. Keri gasped as pleasure spiraled through her entire body. Days of involuntary yearning sneaked up on her and had her moving against him with catlike sensuality.

He made a needy sound as she pressed closer and captured her lips again. She teased him with her tongue, and he welcomed it into his mouth. When he sucked on it, she felt the pull deep into the pit of her stomach. He rocked his hips, pressing his erection near the throbbing ache between her thighs. The hard evidence of his desire felt wonderful, and she moved against him with matching need.

They moaned in unison, but the proof of their escalating hunger reminded her why she couldn't let nature take its course. Why she had to put an end to it.

Pulling her lips from his, she slowly eased back in his arms and looked into his eyes. The dark, swirling passion she saw made her both reluctant to end the embrace and more determined it needed to be done.

"What's wrong?" he asked, his tone low and deep. He didn't try to hold her when she stepped out of his arms and dropped hers to her sides. "I hurt you? Scared you?"

She shook her head and started to speak, but had to clear the huskiness from her throat. "No. Neither. I'm sorry. I just shouldn't have let things go so far when I have no intention of having sex with you. I'm not a tease."

He studied her for a long moment, his gaze gradually clearing. "Fair enough," he said, "but for the record, I'm not the type of guy who expects sex every time he gets aroused."

His words eased her mind and boosted her respect for him another notch. It edged higher each day spent with him. Her face lit with a relieved smile. "Fair enough," she repeated his husky phrase and searched for a way to dispel the tension.

"I'll help you get into your shirt."

She picked it up from the back of the sofa and eased it over his bad arm. He shrugged into the other arm and she fastened the buttons.

"I need to do laundry tomorrow since you only have two sets of clothes. I'll wash your jeans again and maybe get rid of the rest of the blood stains."

Lamanto nodded and moved around the sofa to toss a log on the fire. She followed him, taking her usual seat on the sofa with her legs curled under her. Some evenings they read and sometimes they spent the evening talking.

They shared a lot of the same views on politics and religion, but had varying opinions on other important issues like healthcare reform and immigration. Not surprising since they lived in two different worlds. Even though they sometimes disagreed and shared some heated debates, they respected each other's right to a differing viewpoint.

Using the poker to stir the ashes of the fire, Lamanto started the conversation by mentioning her vacation status. “Your dad must have decided to give you some space,” he said. “We haven’t had any unexpected visitors for a couple days.”

“I’m sure Russ let him know I’m okay and baking pies. I hadn’t done that since Mom died.”

“So, he’d consider it a good thing? A healing, of sorts?”

“Yes. I’m sure he would. I know Dad didn’t want me to come up here alone, but I think he understands.”

“You think Russ went back to town and reported to your dad? I thought he told you he’s living at the camp?”

“I doubt if he actually went to town. They’d have communicated by CB radio.”

“Citizen band? I don’t know much about ’em. Are the signals strong here in the mountains?” he asked, taking a seat in the recliner.

“I guess it depends on the height of the antennas or towers or whatever. I don’t understand the technology. I just know there’s a huge new tower at Russ’s camp. It’s taller than the highest trees, and I imagine he can send signals across several states.”

“Really high frequency, you think? Is there any way to send private signals?”

“I have no idea. I’d think anybody with the right equipment could hear any message, but I could be wrong.”

“If we turn your radio on, can we listen to what others are saying?”

“Sometimes, but it depends on a lot of factors. Our antenna is old and rusty. The radio equipment isn’t in great repair. Weather is an issue too, especially if the winds are high.”

“Maybe I’ll play with it tomorrow. Will anyone know if we have an open frequency?”

Keri shrugged. “I don’t know, but I don’t want anyone to think I’m in trouble or calling for help. I have my own plans for tomorrow.”

"What's up?"

"I want to go back to the ravine where Mom and I had the wreck. I need to see it." She both dreaded and welcomed the chance to revisit the ravine.

"More of the healing process?"

Keri turned her head, avoiding his probing stare. As she watched the fire dancing in the fireplace, she acknowledged the truth to both of them. "I didn't realize I needed to heal more, but I guess I do."

"And getting some answers is part of the process?"

She nodded. "I hope it jolts my memory. If I go there, maybe I'll remember who she spoke to that night. Whoever it was, she trusted him, and he or someone with him that night didn't hesitate to push her to her death."

"I've dealt with fanatics in the past," he offered tentatively. "They honestly believe anything, including murder, is justifiable when the cause is important enough."

"You're defending my mother's killer?"

"Hell no, I'm just trying to help you make sense of a senseless murder. Considering the violence of the crime, I'm guessing it's someone maniacally devoted to a cause."

"What kind of cause justifies killing a friend?"

"I wish the hell I knew."

"How far is the ravine? Are you walking or driving?" Nick asked the next morning. The sun shone brightly and the temps had risen steadily over the last twenty-four hours. Keri declared the weather back to normal September standards.

"I think I'll walk," she said, pushing her feet into sneakers.

She'd shed her heavy sweats for jeans and a pale yellow T-shirt. The front said *ER Nurse.* On the back, it said *Here to save your ass, not kiss it.* He loved it. The phrase suited his *infermiera d'angelo*, a strong, smart, confident woman who didn't abide fools. She didn't have a pretentious cell in her body. The tough exterior might protect a wounded heart, but she didn't welcome anyone's pity.

Nick really liked the way her jeans and shirt hugged her nicely rounded figure. He'd enjoyed watching her move around the kitchen while she cooked them a mushroom and cheese omelet. Every movement of her compact body enticed him a little more.

He hadn't joined her in bed last night as he had every other night they'd spent at the cabin. After the evening's heated embrace, he hadn't trusted himself to cuddle all night. He wanted her badly but wanted to respect her desire to keep it platonic. He would. Even if it killed him. And the way he felt right now, it damned well might.

"I'll have to do some grocery shopping soon too. We're running out of everything."

"How far is the closest grocery?"

"I can pick up necessities at the truck stop and gas station on the main highway. It's less than ten miles. It's a good half-hour to a supermarket."

"How far is the ravine?"

"It's about a half mile down this road and then another half mile up the opposite road. The fork is narrow, and it's easy to make a wrong turn, especially when the foliage is overgrown at the intersection. I've done it myself a couple times when I wasn't paying close enough attention."

"So no one questioned the fact that your mom took the wrong road?"

"No. The road to this cabin is more of an offshoot of the main one. Nearly everyone has overshot it at some point."

Nick heard the tension in her voice and knew how hard it must be to face the scene of the crime. Her mood had been subdued this morning, and he wanted to ease the strain.

"I'll go with you. I need some exercise anyway. One more day of confinement, and I'll be climbing the walls."

Their gazes met, and she stared at him for a long time. "You can't risk being seen."

"I'll stay out of sight or just hide if we hear a vehicle approaching."

"What if we run into Russ and his warriors?"

He hadn't thought about the militia men. "Think they'll be patrolling their perimeters?"

She shrugged. "Who knows? They didn't look like hunters or fisherman. What else would they do day after day, night after night, holed up on this mountain?"

Good question. Another one he wanted answered as soon as possible. Deciding to drop the subject, he watched her get ready to leave. She pulled on a light jacket. The action stretched her breasts taut against her shirt, reminding him of having the firm fullness pressed against his bare chest. He closed his fist, remembering the satiny feel of her skin with its diamond-hard nipple. His pulse hitched and blood heated. Every move she made had him wanting her more.

Keri shot him a strange look. "I won't be long."

"Okay."

As soon as the front door closed, he grabbed his jeans from the back porch where she'd hung them to dry. He tugged off the sweat pants, struggled into the stiff denim, and shoved his feet into tight leather loafers. His high-dollar shoes hadn't faired too well in mud and water. The hooded sweatshirt went on easier. Then he collected her dad's gun from the first-aid kit and tucked it into the waistband at the small of his back.

When he finally moved to the front room window, he saw Keri disappearing behind a cluster of trees at the end of the clearing. She carried a large stick and prodded the ground ahead of her. Probably watching out for snakes, he thought. He hoped she scared them away because he sure as hell didn't want to encounter any of 'em. He had a gun but strictly for emergency. Using it would bring the whole militia down from their mountain lair.

He followed her quickly, relieved she never looked back. The foliage grew so thick along the road he didn't have trouble staying hidden. She didn't move nearly as fast as she had when she'd gone to collect apples. He wondered how badly she dreaded going back to the ravine.

The accident haunted her. That much he knew. He'd heard rumors of the weeks she'd spent in the hospital and months of physical therapy after the wreck. It took courage to face that kind of nightmare head-on.

It made him proud to know her. And that made him frown. He had no right to feel proud of her, yet he did. He felt a whole lot more than he should for his *infermiera d'angelo.* Complications. He'd always avoided emotional complications in his work. Now duty and desire had gotten all tangled.

In addition to being seriously hot for her body, he enjoyed every minute they spent together. He liked her independent spirit and her sharp mind. She challenged him with the mental sparring, and he never got tired of listening to her soft, sexy drawl.

She'd advised him against following her, so he kept his distance. Vegetation encroached over most of the road, but Keri had trampled a path. When he reached the fork, he caught sight of her again. She reversed directions and headed north. He waited, listening carefully for traffic, and then made the turn himself.

Despite the mud and gravel on the new fork, Nick soon felt the change in pavement under his feet. This section had an extra layer of blacktop, more recently poured. To support heavy-duty trucks? Could Keri and her mom have happened on a work crew the night of the wreck? Or maybe even an arms shipment?

They'd gone a few hundred feet when her pace slowed even more. He stayed hidden on the left side of the road and watched her approach the guard rail on the right side. The ravine couldn't be seen from his vantage point, only the repaired and reinforced railing.

As he watched, hoping he hadn't buried himself in a cluster of some kind of poison, she stiffened her spine and walked to the center of the guardrail. It came to her waist, and she grasped it with both hands. Her head slowly moved back and forth as she surveyed the overgrown, boulder-lined ravine.

He saw her shudder and ached to hold her, to offer support while she faced her demons. It had crushed him earlier in the week when she'd shared her pain over her mom's death. He didn't like to see her hurting and didn't want her dealing with the trauma alone. He started to go to her when he heard the rumble of an oncoming vehicle.

Pressing himself deeper into the bushes, Nick watched as a black, jacked-up pickup approached from the direction of the camp. It skidded to a stop, and he reached for the gun at his waist. Keri swiped her hands over her cheeks before turning to greet the newcomer.

Russ Carson jumped from the truck and joined her at the guardrail. Nick couldn't hear the conversation, but an alien emotion squeezed his chest as the militia leader slipped an arm around her shoulders. When Keri dropped her head to his shoulder, all the air whooshed from his lungs.

The sting of jealousy hit him hard. A direct jab at his heart and his ego. He didn't want any other man touching her, comforting her. He'd never been the possessive type, but Keri stirred a whole wealth of unfamiliar emotions in him. So did Carson—all negative.

He watched in frustration as the two of them quietly talked. Carson pointed to an area of the ravine, and Nick supposed he knew exactly where her car had crashed. He hoped Keri didn't share any of her recollections with soldier boy. The man couldn't be trusted. Of that, he felt certain.

After a few minutes of quiet conversation, Carson dropped his arm and turned toward his truck. Nick heard him offer her a ride back to the cabin. She shook her head but thanked him. Soldier boy climbed in his truck, revved the engine and roared past him in a cloud of diesel fumes.

Once the truck moved out of his line of vision, Nick started backtracking to the cabin. He'd made it to the edge of the clearing when Keri hailed him in a loud, hissing whisper.

"Lamanto!"

He turned and gave her a grin, disguising his emotional upheaval with the playboy façade. Jealousy still roiling inside him, he kept a smile locked in place while waiting for her to catch up with him.

"I thought I told you it wasn't safe to follow me."

He ignored the intended reprimand, choosing not to discuss the subject at all. "You could call me Nick, you know."

The change of subject gave her pause, then she said, "Russ happened by. What if he'd seen you?"

"It's my given name. It's a nice name." He kept his tone matter-of-fact while carrying on a totally separate conversation. "Nick is short for Nicholas, you know."

"You took a big risk!"

"I think once you've shared a bed with someone it's okay to be on a first-name basis," he continued the teasing vein.

"You're impossible!"

He laughed at her indignation and shot her a wink then bumped shoulders with her as they climbed the steps to the porch. She put a hand behind his back and patted the gun.

"Did you really think you might have to rescue me with gun blazing?"

"Nah, I just took it as a precaution against bears."

"Well I hate to burst your macho bubble, but that pistol would only madden a bear."

Nick pushed open the cabin door and waved her ahead of him. "Nice day for a walk, wasn't it?" he said, studying her face for some clue to what she'd felt at the ravine.

"Nice day," she agreed, turning her head while she tugged off her jacket. "I guess we both needed some fresh air, but I hope you didn't do any damage to your shoulder."

"You said I needed to use it more. It didn't hurt to walk."

"Maybe not, but getting into those jeans must have been a challenge." The fleeting glance she shot at his lower body shouldn't have affected him, but it heated his blood.

"They are rough and stiff. I'm ready to get out of them again. Wanna help?"

"You got into them, you can get yourself out," she chided.

"Spoilsport."

"I can still see some of the blood stain down the left side. I'll wash them again this afternoon. The sun should dry them pretty quickly."

"Good, because I'll need 'em again tomorrow."

She finally looked him in the eyes. "Why?"

"Because it's time for me to take an up-close look at the militia camp."

That had her propping her hands on her hips. "Are you totally insane? At best, someone will sic the dogs on you. At worst, someone will shoot you again."

"I've stayed here long enough. It's time for me to get back to work. I need to see what's happening at the camp before I report back to my lieutenant."

Her tone turned chilly. "You're impatient to leave?"

He didn't care for the closed expression on her face and hoped she wouldn't shut him out completely. Belatedly, he realized she might be thinking he wanted to leave because she'd ruled out sex.

Reaching out, he cupped her face in his hands, forcing her to look him in the eyes. The soft warmth of her skin encouraged him to gently caress her cheeks. As their gazes locked, an unsettling realization hit him. He could easily lose himself in this tiny, sexy woman and say the hell with everything else.

"Nothing personal, *la mia infermiera d'angelo* but the longer I stay here, the more you're at risk."

"Nobody's gunning for me."

"Yet."

"Why would they be?"

"What did you tell Carson? Did you mention your returning memory and suspicions?"

"You think whatever Mom and I encountered that night

might make me a target?"

"If they killed your mother to silence her, they won't hesitate to do the same to you. If anyone believes your memory is returning or you're questioning the details of the accident, you become a liability to the cause."

Her sigh tugged at his heart again.

"I told Russ it's all still a total blank."

"That's my girl," he said, relieved and pleased to know she hadn't trusted anyone but him with her secret.

The feel of her pleased him too, so he sank his fingers deep into her hair and pulled her close for a kiss. Just a little kiss, he promised himself until their lips met and hers parted in sweet invitation. An invitation he accepted with enthusiasm, dipping his tongue into the sweetness of her mouth. The need to lay claim on her, however minimal, urged him to deepen the kiss.

Keri shifted closer and lifted her hands to his chest. Her touch was light, but it seared him like a brand. She smelled of sunshine and mountain air. The scent and feel intoxicated him. Too quickly his pulse accelerated, and the blood surged through him in a heated rush.

They kissed until they grew breathless, and then kissed again as passion slowly escalated. He used his tongue to explore the sweetness of her mouth and shuddered when she did the same to him.

"You go to my head," he whispered against her lips. He loosened his hold and met her sultry gaze. She dropped her lashes to conceal her eyes, but he'd already felt their heat.

"Maybe it is time for you to move on, city boy, before we make the mistake of succumbing to this insane attraction."

"Would that really be so bad?"

Her lashes flew up, and she stared into his eyes. "I don't know. I'm still considering all the options."

Her quick smile eased the tension a little. He fought to regain control of his desire and return the smile.

"Not the impulsive type?"

She slowly shook her head.

Stepping away from her, he said, "Let me know when you've reached a decision."

"Will do, Lamanto."

"Nick," he corrected.

Instead of repeating it after him, she laughed. "I'll have to think about that too."

Chapter Nine

Just after midnight the following night, Lamanto looked at her and asked, “Do you have any ski masks around here?”

Keri threw him a questioning glance. They’d both dressed in dark pants and dark, hooded sweatshirts for their late-night excursion. He’d planned to leave her behind, but she’d convinced him he needed her knowledge of the woods and surrounding properties.

“We don’t do much skiing on this mountain,” she taunted. Just thinking of the covert trip had her adrenaline pumping.

“Smartass. I mean something that covers most of our faces.”

She went to a storage bin on the back porch and pulled out a couple of stretchy toboggan caps with holes for eyes, noses and mouths. “Like these?” She tossed one to him.

“Exactly like these,” he said, pulling one over his head.

“Less skin showing means a less conspicuous target.” Before covering his whole face, he drew her close and gave her a swift, hard kiss. “Be careful and don’t take any unnecessary chances.”

He’d warned her to abandon him if the situation turned dangerous. When she’d caught her breath again, she said, “Stop worrying about me. You’re the one they’ll shoot on sight.”

With that, she pulled the cap over her face, and they quietly left the cabin. Outside, they took time to trace circles around the yard, trees, fire pit and propane tank, spreading their scent over a wide area. If dogs tried to track them, they’d get tangled in a crazy circular pattern and hopefully discourage their handlers.

They’d discussed the best plan for checking out the camp.

Keri would lead the way, but they'd depend on hand gestures to communicate and take a long, circuitous route through the woods. The trip back would be a straight shot. Should anyone follow them, she'd return to the cabin while he went to the safe room.

A full moon lit the clearing directly behind the cabin, but inky darkness descended once they plunged into the woods.

Lamanto drew her close and whispered in her ear.

"We'd better stick to a straight shot there and back."

She nodded in agreement, having forgotten how pitch-black the woods could get. The penlight she'd found to illuminate their path wouldn't be much help in the darkly shadowed gloom. Depending on instinct and a thread of light, she followed the path she'd used to get to the orchard. They scared a few small animals from their nests. Keri shuddered when bats swooped close, but they didn't run into any unexpected problems.

They left her dad's property just beyond the orchard and crossed onto her uncle's land. The closer they got to the compound, the better they could see. High-powered pole lights shone over the entire camp, illuminating impenetrable security fencing.

Lamanto pulled her close again and whispered, "Electrified fence, motion sensors and cameras. Stay at least twenty feet back."

Keri followed his instructions and kept a safe distance from the fence. As they circled behind the new metal buildings, they took stock of what they could see without taking needless risks. Although no expert, she realized everything in sight went beyond what she'd imagined in Russ's operation.

The high radio tower stood in the center of the camp with a red warning light flashing atop it. Two big, military-style jeeps were parked between long, narrow buildings. Three fuel tanks stood in the center of the camp. Keri knew the collective cost had to be more than Russ would earn in a lifetime.

What looked like a firing range ran the length of one

building. At the far end of the property, a smaller building appeared where the old shack used to stand. Lights blazed from the small windows, despite the late hour. A heavily armed man stood guard outside the door. Several pickups had parked in front of it, but she couldn't get a clear enough look to identify any except Russ's.

While they watched, the door opened and several men exited the building. Keri tried to move closer to see if she recognized them, but Lamanto grabbed her by the arm and tugged her backward. She started to argue when three large Doberman dogs came charging out of the house.

"Night patrol," he hissed near her ear, pulling her deeper into the natural cover. They backtracked to the orchard before they heard the frenzied barking of the dogs and the sudden wail of a siren.

"Run."

She didn't need his terse command to shift into a faster gear. The threatening sounds coming from the camp scared her spitless. The adrenaline she'd experienced earlier was nothing compared to the panicked rush she felt now. Using a forearm to protect her face from low-hanging branches, she raced toward the cabin. Ducking and dodging as best she could, she tried to lead Lamanto back without leading him into harm's way. The sound of him following closely kept her momentum pumped.

It felt like an eternity before the cabin clearing came into sight. Her lungs burned. The raggedness of her breathing roared in her ears, so loud she could no longer hear Lamanto breathing. When they hit the edge of the clearing, they separated. He ran toward the propane tank, and she raced to the cabin, slamming and locking the door behind her.

Propping her hands on her knees, she bent double, chest heaving as she pulled in gulps of air. Her side ached from running so hard, making it even harder to catch her breath. Damn, she hadn't realized how out of shape she'd gotten these past couple years.

No time, no time, she told herself, jerking off the cap and her jacket to stuff them into the trunk. Her shoes followed, and then she headed to the bathroom and switched on a light. The image in the mirror staggered her breathing even more.

Sweat matted her hair flat to her head. Her cheeks had a deep blush of exertion. She needed to find a way to disguise both. If Russ showed up at the door, she had to look totally innocent. Stripping down to her underwear, she tossed her sweaty clothes into the shower and searched for something concealing to wear.

Her mother's old, full-length terry bathrobe still hung on the back of the bathroom door. Keri shook the dust off it, pulled it on and cinched the belt at her waist. She wrapped a towel around her head turban style. Body shaking with nerves and still struggling for breath, she searched the bathroom cupboard. After finding a jar of pasty white cleansing cream, she slathered it on her overheated cheeks.

Now she looked as though she'd just climbed from the shower except she smelled of sweat and fear. The dogs would tear her apart if the militia men didn't shoot first and ask questions later. Another quick search unearthed some old talcum powder. Partially caked, she thumped the container against the sink and then powdered herself liberally.

The suffocating cloud of sweet-smelling dust gagged her and threw her into a coughing fit. She'd just caught her breath again when the banging started at the front door. Someone yelled her name. Russ. He'd sure made good time.

"Coming!" The walk to the door helped her steady her nerves and breathing. Switching on the living room light, she approached the front door with one last deep breath.

"Who's there?"

"Keri, it's Russ. Open up!"

Her hand shook as she grabbed the door knob, and she willed herself to settle down. Opening it just a crack, she saw Russ and three other men in full combat gear. The dogs went wild at the sight of her. Teeth bared, they leapt in the air, straining against their leashes. She quickly slammed the door again.

"Get rid of them!"

He gave an order. When the sounds of their barking diminished, she cracked the door again.

"Russ, it's late. What in the world are you doing here?" Then inspiration struck, and she allowed some of her panic to show.

"Dad? Has something happened to Dad?"

"No, no." He shook his head and stepped closer.

"Jack?"

"No, nothing's wrong with either one."

"Then why in the world are you here with those vicious animals?" she asked, hoping she sounded more indignant than scared. "They sure aren't coon hounds!"

"We had intruders at the compound. The dogs followed the scent back here."

"Well, that's no big surprise. My scent is probably the only human one in the woods."

"You haven't seen or heard anything tonight?"

"How could I hear anything with all that racket?"

She could still hear the dogs, but their handler had moved them out of sight. She nudged the door open a little farther, not wanting him or his hostile buddies to think she had anything to hide.

"Maybe the rotten thieves who stole my gas were trying to steal something from your camp."

"Thieves?" he snapped, his expression going grimmer. "What thieves? You never mentioned 'em to me."

"I filled my car at the station when I came up, but someone emptied my tank that same night."

"Did you call your dad or report it to anyone?"

She nodded, almost dislodging her towel. Holding it steady, she replied. "Dwayne stopped the next morning and gave me enough to get back down the mountain. If the thief or thieves are hiding out in the woods, I hope you track 'em down and feed 'em to the dogs."

"If they're still out here, we'll find 'em," he promised in his tough-guy tone. "I'll leave a sentry here tonight to keep watch over you."

"Forget the sentry," she snapped, glancing at the cold, expressionless faces of his pals. They weren't even breathing hard. She gave them each a warning glare. "If I see any strange men lurking around the cabin, I'll shoot them myself and ask questions later."

"Okay, okay, don't get all fired up. We probably scared off the intruders. Just lock your doors and be watchful."

Keri managed a smile for him. "Thanks, Russ. I appreciate you looking out for me, but I'm not stupid or careless. I've had caution drilled into me since my toddler years."

He bobbed his head. "I reckon you have."

"Now I really want to finish getting ready for bed."

"Sure, you have a good night," he said, taking a step back from the door.

"Good night."

She closed the door, threw the deadbolt into place and switched off the lights. Taking a step toward the bedroom, she nudged aside the curtain and watched out the window until they'd all moved from sight.

"Damn, you're good." The whispered praise reached her ears seconds before a strong arm nudged her back against the wall. Lamanto pressed his body close to hers. The heat radiating from their bodies fused them together. One of his hands slipped beneath the opening of the robe and clasped her waist. His hot touch sent fire coursing through her.

Keri lifted her hands to his chest and felt the mad pounding of his heart. Her heart beat a matching rhythm as she tipped her head back to look into his eyes. Relief made her giddy. Her response came out low and husky.

"You don't know the half of it, Detective."

He dipped his head low until his mouth just brushed hers.

"Ever consider a career in undercover?"

"Undercover as in police work or undercover as in bed?"

Her sexual innuendo drew a pained sound from him. His guttural moan deepened her smile. He pressed himself closer and started to spread kisses over her face. The cleansing cream had him spitting and backing off.

"What the hell?"

Keri giggled. She'd never been the giddy type, but once she started giggling, she couldn't stop. The sounds kept slipping past her throat, one after another after another. He made a low sound of warning, but it just tickled her more. She slapped a hand over her mouth to muffle the sound, but the feel of the stinky cream on her face stirred another round of the giggles. Using the sleeves of the bathrobe, she swiped at her cheeks as tears ran down her face.

He locked his good arm around her waist and practically dragged her to the bed. Her body shook with laughter verging on hysteria. He shoved her down on the mattress and followed. She continued to laugh until he draped his body across hers and squished the breath out of her.

When she gazed into his eyes and saw the concern on his face, it made her giggle again.

When his frown deepened, she asked, "What's wrong, Copper? Didn't they teach you how to deal with hysterical women in cop school?"

In response, he dropped his mouth onto hers, kissing her hard and deep. His tongue invaded and swiftly conquered. Within seconds all her emotional tension found a new release in his kisses. Keri welcomed the hot, passionate invasion with fervor.

She put her arms around his waist and gripped him tightly, sliding her hands under his clothes to reach warm, damp flesh. The feel of him reassured, comforted and inflamed her. So many conflicting emotions whirled through her, with the joy of being safe in his arms superseding the others.

They finally broke off the kiss and stared at each other in

the dim light. Lamanto supported most of his weight with his good arm, with his injured one resting on the bed. Keri knew the position had to be uncomfortable for him. She rolled sideways, easing him with her. When they lay face-to-face, they continued to search each other's features.

"At the risk of another giggle fest, I have to tell you that you really stink, lady. What's all that sour-smelling stuff on your face and the sickening-sweet stuff on the rest of you?"

She grinned. "Menthol cleanser on the face. Talcum powder on the rest of me. I had to do something to disguise the BO."

"You succeeded. No wonder the dogs went berserk."

She shuddered. "They did track my scent. I wonder how crazy they acted in the woods."

"I heard 'em racing around the propane tank shortly after I locked myself in. I figured they'd start digging at the trap door, but they moved on."

"No trouble in the tunnel?"

"Pitch-black, but it's tight enough to find your way."

"How badly is your arm aching?"

"Like a sonofabitch."

Keri reached over and touched his shoulder. She couldn't tell if the dampness stemmed from sweat or if he'd pulled his stitches. "I'll have to check it as soon as we've cleaned up. By the way, you do not smell like roses yourself."

"It was worth some sweat and pain to get a look at that compound. I would've liked to get inside the fence, but an outside look confirmed my suspicions."

"Not your typical backwoods militia camp," she said on a sad sigh.

"No."

"What's happening over there?"

"A terrorist camp with a dangerous agenda."

"What's your connection to all this? Your coming to Thornsbury can't be a coincidence."

She stiffened when he hesitated too long. After all they'd

been through in the past few days, she deserved more respect and his trust. When she started to turn her back on him, he halted her with a touch and quiet explanation.

"A few months ago, we heard rumor of an illegal gun-running operation. It originated in Dade County, but we had no idea how the guns were being transported or their destination. My superiors contacted the Department of Alcohol, Tobacco and Firearms with what little information we had. They launched an investigation that went nowhere until someone in Thornsbury contacted them directly."

"Don Monroe?"

"If it was, they didn't share the information with me."

"I thought you and Don were old buddies?

Lamanto shook his head. "He worked in Miami after graduating from the academy and we met before he took the position here."

"So, he's just part of your cover? Why send a Miami detective to investigate? Why not an ATF agent?"

She saw a glint of speculation in his eyes, and knew he didn't want to tell her more. "My dad always says it's safer to tell the truth than get tangled in your own lies."

His voice went low and soft. "Your dad never worked undercover. It's all about lies."

"And you're an expert at lying?" she asked just as softly.

After a long, thoughtful minute, he said, "Truth is, my last undercover op made me unpopular with some thugs in Miami. Not the first time, but the lieutenant thought I should leave town until the dust settled. ATF is short-staffed, like every other federal agency, and they signed off on the plan. Now I need to report back to them before these guys get any closer to their targeted date of execution."

"When do you plan to head out?"

He quickly corrected her. "We're heading out first thing tomorrow."

Keri shook her head. "I'll be fine here."

"Too risky. Men with militia mentality are notoriously unstable. Your friend Russ might have a change of heart and decide you're a threat. He could take you hostage or worse."

She gave that some thought. "I can't just disappear or the cavalry will be searching country-wide for me."

"You can stick a note on the door or radio the rangers. If you get word to your dad, it should buy some time."

"I did tell Dad I might do some shopping in Knoxville."

"He'll figure you're restless after a week of alone time."

"If he only knew," she mumbled, her gaze locking with his. They'd had time to cool off and relax, but the haze of desire lingered. His expression gradually changed and her heart began to pound.

"One of these days, when we're in bed together, I'm going to make love to you and totally rock your world."

Keri caught her breath at the conviction in his tone. She felt hot color returning to her face and her pulse accelerated.

"You're sure, huh?"

"Sure I want to destroy your inhibitions and satisfy every fantasy you've ever imagined. Yeah."

Throat tight, she whispered, "Pretty big order."

"I'm a quick study."

She didn't doubt it. He probably had oodles of experience in pleasing women. Her body craved his touch with increasing urgency. Desire pulsed between them and they weren't even touching. What would it be like to lie with him, naked and as close as they could get?

The question brought another to mind. What about the scars? Her abdomen featured a road map of ugly scarring after being crushed in the wreck. Her thighs bore scars from skin grafts. Would it repulse him? Was he the type of man who could ignore the scars, or had he gained all his experience with physically faultless, beautiful women?

She thought of Miami and beaches and an abundance of perfect bodies in miniscule bikinis. No doubt his life had been filled with them. The sting of jealousy she felt at the thought caught her by surprise.

"What's going through that active little mind of yours?" he wanted to know. "I don't like the furrow between your eyes."

She wished she had the courage to tell him, but why bother when the need might never arise. Time to change the subject and lighten the mood.

"Little mind? I resent that. Didn't I lead you to the camp and back safely tonight? Am I not an undercover genius?"

He didn't respond for a long minute, and she held her breath, hoping he wouldn't press her for more personal answers.

"Okay, *la mia infermiera d'angelo.* We'll play it your way. You're a genius."

Keri gave him a grin and rolled off the side of the bed. "I'm also sweaty, stinky and exhausted. I'm headed to the shower."

Lamanto rolled onto his back. She felt his gaze on her as she moved around the room collecting clean clothes.

"By the way, that robe is very becoming."

"Thank you. My mom called it her vacation robe. I think it's at least as old as I am. It's stiff with dirt."

His chuckle followed her to the bathroom. She closed the door, smiling. Lamanto had a healing effect on her, she realized. A week ago she couldn't have joked about her mom or even thought of her without hurting. Sharing memories with him had helped her to heal.

He made her happy, she realized with a jolt. Happier than any man had ever done. Happiness didn't come easy for her, but she enjoyed his company and matching wits with him. She liked the way he challenged her, yet wasn't too arrogant to concede when she bested him. It would be way too easy to get addicted to his charm.

As water poured over her body, she remembered his promise they'd be lovers. Her body quivered at the thought, nipples pouting. Heaven only knew how she'd be able to make love with him and then say goodbye.

Their parting was as inevitable as day following night. They belonged in two different worlds. Her community and lifelong friends depended on her as well as her family. She couldn't imagine leaving Tennessee, and she couldn't imagine Lamanto leaving his career and life in the city.

Nick. She grinned, remembering his teasing request to be called by his first name. Lamanto she could keep at arm's length, but Nick might bury himself in her heart too deeply to ever remove.

Chapter Ten

"I'm guessing you have a GPS tracking system on your SUV," said Lamanto as they exited the cabin just after dawn the next morning.

Keri hadn't slept well and she doubted he had, either. She blamed it on pent-up sexual tension. They'd carefully avoided touching or kissing again last night. Neither wanted to cross the invisible line they'd drawn between them.

"Of course it has a GPS, my dad helped me buy it," she said while tacking a note on the door. Turning, she gave him a grin. "But I also know how to disable it."

"A woman of many talents," he teased.

They shared a smile and headed toward her vehicle. Though chilly, the cloudless sky indicated another sunny day. The temps could climb into the seventies before noon. She'd dressed in layers but left most of her things in the cabin. They planned to drive straight through to his home in Miami and purchase whatever she needed there. Anybody checking on her would find all her belongings at the cabin.

He took a minute to smear the dirt on her license tags, adding a little more and making it difficult to read the numbers. She hadn't thought to do that but she liked the idea of being harder to track.

"You should hide in the back until we clear the state line. On the off-chance that someone recognizes me, it wouldn't be a good idea to be seen with a strange man."

She pressed the release button of her remote and heard the familiar *thunk*. He'd already filled the tank with the gas Dwayne had left her.

Lamanto groaned. "I already have intimate knowledge of

the discomfort of your backseat."

"At least this time you're not feverish and bleeding."

"There is that."

She tossed her satchel-sized purse into the front seat and set about removing the fuse for the GPS while he tried to make himself comfortable. He gave her a thumbs-up when she came around the car to close his door. Grabbing an afghan she carried for emergencies, she tucked it under his legs.

"Just be ready to pull it over your head, if we get approached by anyone wearing a uniform."

"Will do, not that it'll help if anyone takes a close look back here."

"It'll help if you stay out of sight until we hit the Georgia line. Then nobody is likely to care if I have a passenger."

"Maybe if you sing for me, *mia l'angelo*, I can take a long nap."

Keri's heart tripped at the endearment. It rolled off his tongue with such velvety sweetness it warmed her from head to toe. She'd promised herself not to let his charm penetrate her defenses, but he melted them more each day.

"You're a menace, Lamanto," she charged, slamming his door and moving around to the driver's side.

"Nick," he corrected, chuckling.

"Don't mock me," she warned as she started the engine and shifted gears. "It's a long, rough ride down this mountain, and I can make you seriously miserable."

"Didn't you take some kind of Hippocratic oath that forbids you to deliberately do harm?"

"I can't remember," she tossed over her shoulder. "I'm on vacation. I don't have to think about professional responsibilities."

The banter continued while she drove to the gas station. Lamanto went quiet when she jumped from the SUV to fill her tank, buy a few supplies and a throw-away cell phone he'd requested. He tinkered with it while she headed south to

Interstate 75 and cranked up the radio.

In another hour, they'd passed into Georgia and stopped long enough for him to climb into the front seat. Once they'd driven through Atlanta, they shared a quick lunch, and he used a pay phone to activate his temporary cell.

Keri continued to drive while he checked in with his lieutenant and his family. She could tell by his end of the conversations they'd all been worried about him.

When they stopped briefly to eat in the late afternoon, she stripped to a T-shirt and gym shorts. The temperatures had slowly risen through their drive and reached well into the eighties by midway through Florida.

Lamanto took over the driving when they neared the outskirts of Miami. Keri happily relinquished the wheel. She had no desire to navigate through the insane traffic and unfamiliar streets. He whipped from intersection to intersection with no problem, but she knew she'd be lost in a heartbeat.

As evening approached, the heat and humidity had steam rising from the pavement. Instead of using the air conditioner, Lamanto rolled down his window and sucked in the heavy air.

"Ah, the smell of home!"

Keri wrinkled her nose. "You live in an exhaust pipe?"

He shook his head and gave her a reproving glance. "Can't you smell the water? We're almost there."

She sniffed again but didn't smell water for another fifteen minutes when they neared one of the many harbors framing the city. She caught her breath at the sight of sunset sparkling on the water with kaleidoscope brilliance. The harbor pulsed with activity and an amazing spectrum of color.

From dull-gray, slow-moving tugboats to rainbow-painted, racy speedboats, the entire area hummed with rich color and continuous activity.

"Miamarina?" she said, reading the name of the huge complex they'd entered.

"Miamarina at Bayside," he said with a laugh and a shrug.

"Where else would a good Italian settle?" They circled the parking lot and pulled into an empty end row spot overlooking the water. A concrete dock spanned out below them, just a few feet lower than the parking lot.

"So, what do you think?"

She couldn't drag her gaze from the beauty of the water, wanting to absorb as much detail as possible. People zipped around on Jet Skis and she saw boats of every imaginable size and color.

"About what?"

"About my home."

His words finally drew her attention, and she spared him a quick glance. "You live here?" Glancing around, she looked for residential buildings.

He unsnapped his seat belt and reached over to do the same with hers. Cupping her face in his hand, he turned her head to the left.

"See that pretty little cabin cruiser about middle way down the pier. Between the red and yellow sailboats?"

Keri slowly searched the row of slips. "The white one with the turquoise trim?"

"Yep," he said with pride. "That's my baby."

Her eyes widened. "It's your child, your girlfriend or your home? Be a little more specific, please."

"I guess it's a combination of all three," he said on a chuckle. Then his voice went low and sexy. "At least it used to be my best girl. Lately, there's a mouthy ER nurse nudging it aside in my affections."

Keri's heart stuttered and her breathing stilled, but she didn't want to admit how deeply his casual teasing touched her. She covered the emotional reaction with a smile and light sarcasm. "I'm impressed. I don't think I've ever vied with a boat for someone's affection."

"Only coon hounds and jacked-up trucks?"

He surprised a laugh from her and she smacked his arm.

"You're bad."

Lamanto swooped in for a quick, hard kiss, and then reached for his door handle. "Grab some stuff, and I'll take you to meet my girl. I don't know about you, but I'm more than ready to stretch my legs."

Once her feet touched pavement, Keri groaned and stretched, trying to work the kinks from her muscles. It felt good to be out of the vehicle. She drew in a deep breath, trying to absorb all the unfamiliar scents in the heavy air. The strong smell of fish mingled with floral sweetness and some oily scent she attributed to keeping all the watercraft in running condition.

Lamanto rounded the vehicle and opened the back door. After handing her the giant handbag she always carried, he grabbed a couple bags of groceries and clicked the door lock.

"A little different from the sights, sounds and smells of Thornsbury?" he asked.

"Majorly different."

"Unpleasantly so?"

She shook her head as he took her arm to steer her in the right direction. "Not unpleasant, just unfamiliar. The only time I ever visited Florida was for spring break at Lauderdale."

He dismissed that with a grunt. "Kid stuff. Tonight you're in for a pleasure beyond your wildest dreams."

The certainty in his tone made her lift her brows and give him a wary glance. "I'm almost afraid to ask."

"We'll be sleeping on the *Adrianna*."

"Adrianna's your girlfriend's name?"

"*Adrianna* is my cabin cruiser. She's named after my paternal grandmamma. Nonna Lamanto passed a few years ago, but left me enough money to buy the *Adrianna*. It's been my home ever since."

"You actually live on it? Fulltime?"

"Sure. Nothin' like being rocked to sleep every night. No problem with neighbors. Most of these boats are docked year round but only used on the occasional weekend. It's a perfect place to live."

She knew nothing about boats or living on the water, so she couldn't help being skeptical. "What about electricity and heat and bathroom facilities?"

"Got all that," he said as they stepped down from the parking area to the pier and started toward his slip. "It's compact, of course, like an efficiency apartment. And it has a nice little galley."

"Galley's the kitchen, right? I do read and watch some TV. I just don't have any practical experience."

They passed a couple boat loads of people docking for the evening. They looked relaxed, though sun baked and windblown. Lamanto shared casual greetings with them but didn't stop to talk. He kept moving at a quick pace, and Keri could almost feel his pleasure when they reached his slip. Up close, the cruiser was larger than it had appeared from the parking lot.

"It's a pretty big home," she said, giving it a once-over. Mostly white, it had a wide turquoise stripe down the side and the name *Adrianna* scripted in the same color. "You'll have to tell me more."

"She's a twin-engine, thirty footer, about average length for a cruiser. The top is hard. The fiberglass hull is V-shaped with a sundeck." He pointed to the front of the boat with a chrome railing and built-in deck chairs on either side of a small table.

"A little dirty from lack of attention, but she's a real beaut when she's clean, and she really flies across the open water. Nonna would have loved her. My nonna was a bit of a speed demon. She lost her driver's license at the age of eighty because she had too many points for speeding."

That brought a smile to her face. "I think I'd have liked the original Adrianna," she said. It sounded as though he'd been very fond of his nonna too.

"She'd have liked you," he replied with certainty.

He jumped from the dock on to the back of the boat and

helped Keri do the same, then steadied her until she'd adjusted to the gentle undulating of the deck beneath her feet.

"Welcome aboard," he said with a grin, taking her arm and leading her to a cushioned, built-in bench.

"Sit tight until you get used to the motion, and I'll do a quick check down under."

"Something objectionable in your floating bachelor pad you don't want me to see?"

He grinned and winked. "Just a little precaution since I've been gone so long," he said, turning. He gathered the grocery bags, found what she assumed to be a spare key and unlocked the cabin door. Then he disappeared down the stairs.

She glanced around while waiting. The slips on either side of his held tethered sailboats. Each had their sails tucked out of sight and heavy canvas covers over the cabins, a red one on the left and a bright yellow on the right. They didn't look as though anyone used them on a regular basis.

The slips beyond the sailboats held sleek speedboats and a variety of other watercraft. Farther in the distance, the area teemed with nightlife and a myriad of neon signs. This end of the pier had quieted. The well-placed security lights created a shadowy darkness as dusk descended. One or two of the crafts were well lit and had people aboard. She'd have to ask Lamanto how well he knew his neighbors.

He returned after just a few minutes, but the sight of him knocked all thoughts from her mind. His stunning good looks still caught her off-guard sometimes. With his hair tousled, his mysterious dark eyes and a five o'clock shadow, he looked beautifully dangerous.

After catching her breath, Keri tried to disguise her reaction with more teasing. "All's well? No dead bodies?"

"No dead anything," he said with another wink and a crook of his finger. "Come into my parlor."

She laughed at the wicked gleam in his eyes and headed in his direction. "Said the spider..."

Excitement coursed through her as their gazes locked and their hands touched again. His grip felt warm and sure, giving her pulse a jolt as she followed him down the steps. When her feet touched the floor, he dropped her hand and slipped his arm around her waist. More heat flooded her as she absorbed the feel of having him hip-to-hip close. Unused to casual intimacy, Keri decided she could get used to it pretty quickly.

"This is called the saloon. It's Italian in design, of course, in honor of her namesake."

"Of course," she repeated breathily. As her eyes adjusted to the change in light, she took in the compact beauty of the boat's interior. Most everything, including the globed lights, was secured to the walls. "The paneling is gorgeous."

"All natural teak," he explained with pride. "It smells a little dank in here right now, common in this climate, but we can air it out better tomorrow. I can't wait to take you out for a ride. There's nothing sweeter."

Keri made sounds of agreement as he slowly twirled her around to see the other features.

"The bed's up here," he said, pointing to a platform with heavy drapes. He pulled them back to show her a queen-sized, rumpled bed. The sight of disheveled sheets made her heart thump a little harder. The tight confines of the cabin enveloped her with romantic intimacy.

"The true head is at the foot of the bed and galley to the right," he continued. "Nothing ready to eat, but I can remedy that pretty quick if you want first shot at the shower."

"A shower sounds nice, but I don't have any clean clothes."

Lamanto pulled her fully into his arms. Hunger tightened his expression and she expected a kiss. Instead, he brushed his nose back and forth across hers in a gentle caress.

"Do you trust me? Really trust me?" he asked softly.

"Trust you how?" she replied just as softly. "Trust that you're honest? Trust that you wouldn't hurt me?"

"Trust me with your body, even your life?"

Keri looked into his eyes and tossed the question around in her mind. The answer came quickly. Of course she trusted him. If not, she'd have turned him over to her dad days ago. He'd had plenty of time to do her harm or take advantage of her at the cabin.

On the other hand, he'd needed her up to this point, as a nurse and a means of transportation out of Tennessee. He'd needed her to get them from her home turf to his. Would their easy rapport and budding relationship end now that he'd returned to his normal life? She'd never really asked if he had a significant other waiting for his return.

Lamanto's good arm tightened at her waist, crushing her breasts against his chest. She felt the strength of his arousal when their lower bodies bumped.

"You're taking a damned long time to answer."

Keri rose on tiptoe and brushed a kiss over his tight lips. "If I didn't trust you, I would have let Russ sic his dogs on you days ago."

"But? There has to be more. I can see the wheels of your brain spinning."

"Well, I'd be a fool not to realize everything changed when we came south. Now that you're home safe and sound, you really don't need me, do you?"

"Maybe not, but I sure as hell want you." He rolled his hips, rubbing his erection against her belly. "Does that count for anything?"

"It's pretty important to me."

She felt as well as heard his sigh of relief. The gentle movement of his chest teased her nipples to tightness. Need spiraled through her.

"In that case, you're welcome to wear one of my shirts after your shower. I'll buy you new clothes tomorrow."

She nibbled on his chin, enjoying the sexual teasing. "I have clean underwear in my tote. I always carry the basic necessities in case I get held over at work."

"Remember, you're on vacation," he reminded quickly. "There's no need to break out emergency gear tonight."

"Just commando under the shirt?"

Lamanto groaned and set her aside. Keri laughed softly, feeling deliciously naughty and desirable for the first time in years. She let her fingers slide down his chest to the waistband of his jeans.

He quickly grasped her hand to waylay it. "You're a wicked tease. I promised myself I wouldn't jump your bones the minute I brought you into my home. No matter how much I've fantasized about it. Take a shower while I fix us some food. Then we can sip wine out of each other's navels."

Her pleasure dimmed at the image, but she tried not to let it show. For just a little while, she'd felt normal and sexy. She'd forgotten her disfiguration. No way would she let him get a close look at her scars. If they made love, it would be in the dark.

"Aye, aye, Captain. Where might I find a shirt?"

Lamanto pulled a soft green T-shirt from a drawer built into the bedframe. He showed her how everything worked in the miniature bathroom and explained the importance of securing things in cabinets.

"Otherwise, the rocking of the boat would toss your belongings all over the place?" she asked.

"Right you are, mate."

Keri shook her head, and then slid the door closed, effectively cutting off his teasing.

"Make it quick. I'm starving," he called to her.

Ten minutes later, she reentered the saloon and confronted him with her hands on her hips. "You neglected to mention the lack of hot water. I didn't even manage lukewarm."

Her stance pulled the thin fabric of his shirt tight across her otherwise bare breasts. He stared into her eyes for a long, pregnant minute then lifted his hands to cup the firm mounds and thumb her rigid nipples.

"Guilty," he whispered hoarsely. "It takes awhile for the hot water tank to warm the water. But I can't say I'm sorry since the result is so damned pleasing."

Keri gasped at the sensual assault. She couldn't find the will or words to stop him as he fondled her sensitive breasts, molding and caressing until her knees grew weak. His hot hands quickly dispelled the chill of her shower.

"See how well my arm is healing? I can use it without breaking a sweat," he said, using his left as effectively as his right.

"Physical therapy is important," she managed through a tight throat.

"I'm looking forward to a lot more," he swore softly.

Heat continued to course through her until he abruptly dropped his hands. "I need a shower too, and I promised you dinner. I won't take long."

She nodded, will and words abandoning her as she tried to tamp down the desire raging through her body. He'd barely touched her, through clothing, and she'd nearly fainted at his feet. It didn't bode well for maintaining control of the situation, she thought, crossing her arms over her chest protectively.

Get a grip, Merritt! You're behaving like a sex-deprived wanton, she admonished herself while studying Lamanto's home. Soft, romantic music surrounded her, but she couldn't find the source. Everything from photos to personal possessions had been secured for safety. Most of the surfaces were bare except for the supplies he'd put in the galley. She wondered if he kept the bulk of his belongings in drawers or if he didn't keep much beyond necessities. Tempted to snoop, Keri refrained.

When Lamanto emerged from the shower a few minutes later, his dark hair glistened with moisture. He wore tight, faded cutoff jeans and a light blue, short-sleeved cotton shirt. He hadn't buttoned the shirt. Dark, swirling hair on his chest sparkled with moisture too, and the sight of him had her breath hitching again.

How would she survive intimacy with a man so gorgeous

and so sexy he made her head spin without even touching her? How could she be expected to eat with him so close?

Lamanto showed her amazing possibilities. He pulled her onto a bench behind a table and started feeding her bites of meat and cheese and yeasty dinner rolls. He followed the first course with fresh sweet grapes and succulent strawberries. She licked the juice off his fingers, and he licked it from her lips. He stole a kiss and then another and another, each one longer and deeper than the one before.

The only thing he allowed her to do for herself was lift a glass of wine to her lips. She drank thirstily as he pressed kisses along her jaw to her neck and the sensitive spot behind her ear. He sucked deeply, and she shuddered.

Her breasts swelled with arousal, her nipples begged for attention. He didn't disappoint. Using both his hands, he clasped them tightly, rolling his palms hard against their turgid tips.

Keri moaned and he swallowed the sound with another deep, wet kiss that had their tongues dueling and dancing. She moaned again and the sound echoed from deep in his chest. She felt him shudder as she sucked his tongue deep into her mouth, adoring it with her lips and teeth and tongue.

When they came up for air, he stared into her eyes, his own glazed with passion. "Want anything else?"

"You, in me," she whispered roughly.

His responding groan was guttural as he pressed her back against the cushions and slipped his hands under her shirt. Keri barely had the forethought to wiggle out of his reach.

"Bed," she insisted, scrambling off the bench. Legs trembling, she headed for the shallow steps to the platform bed. "Lights out."

"No way," he insisted.

She turned to him. "Yes way!"

"Do you know how badly I want to see you naked?" came his hoarse reply.

Chapter Eleven

"You'll have to settle for feeling me this time."

Something in her tone convinced him not to argue anymore. He doused the light, leaving them bathed in shadows and the dim illumination from the port holes.

Relief washed through Keri as she climbed onto his bed and crawled forward to make room for him. Lamanto halted her progress by grasping her ankles. He flipped her onto her back. The low ceiling and limited overhead space didn't give them much maneuvering room. It didn't matter because she couldn't bear having too much space between them.

She breathed in the scent of him from the cool sheets. He started a new assault on her senses by kissing her ankles and massaging her feet. Nurses had a special kinship with foot massage.

She sighed with pleasure that quickly escalated to humming desire as he kissed his way up her calves to her thighs. Not wanting him to explore the scarred flesh too much, she slid downward until they were face-to-face.

With their gazes locked, she slowly lifted the T-shirt and tossed it aside. He did the same with his shirt. She reached for the button of his cutoffs, but he clasped her hand and pulled it to his lips.

"As bad as I want to feel your hands on me, this might not be the best time," he confessed gruffly.

"A little needy, are we?" she whispered, putting her hands to better use against his chest. She plucked at his nipples with her fingertips, and then dropping her head to gently lick and suck them.

"A lot needy," he said in a graveled voice. "Dangerously,

explosively needy."

Pulling her hands above her head, he pressed them against the sheets in a silent request that she keep them there. He caressed her arms with gentle fingers and then cupped her breasts again. For a long few minutes, the only sounds they heard were the gentle lapping of water against the boat and her strangled gasps of pleasure.

Lamanto adored her breasts with biting little kisses and tongue-lashing gentleness. He plucked at her nipples until they were engorged with blood. He played with one while sucking the other deeply into his mouth. His tongue lashed and laved, making Keri twist and squirm impatiently. She dropped her hands to clutch at his hair. He pressed himself against her body, damp naked flesh against damp naked flesh.

When she tugged fiercely on his hair, he lifted his head for her kiss. It seared them both with hunger and need. She got lost in the heat and excitement he aroused as mouths greedily sucked tongues.

Then she felt his good hand sliding down her hips, dragging the tiny panties off her legs.

"You promised commando."

She kicked the scrap of fabric aside, feeling totally wanton. "Suggested, not promised."

He grunted but brought his hand back to the juncture of her thighs, searching and finding super-sensitized flesh. She arched against probing fingers, moaning and twisting as he slowly stroked her desire. Then he pushed her harder and higher until she thrashed wildly against the sheets. Whimpering and pleading without words, she begged him to make them one.

"Nick, please!"

"Ah, now it's Nick," he taunted huskily. "I like the sound of you begging." He brushed a kiss across her mouth. "I like the sound of my name on your lips and all the other sounds of arousal. Tell me how much you want me."

Already sheathed and straining, he shifted fully over her. She parted her thighs in primitive welcome, but he waited for the words.

Panting, barely able to articulate her needs, Keri did as he asked. "I want you very, very much."

"More than you've ever wanted anybody in your life?" he demanded hoarsely.

She scolded him. "That's blackmail, Detective."

"I want you more than I've ever wanted any woman," he amazed her by confessing. "More than I want my next breath." With that, he slowly joined their bodies and they both gasped at the intimate pleasure.

Nick pressed his forehead to hers. "*Cristo, mia l'angelo,* you feel good. So wet and tight, I'm afraid to move."

Keri solved the problem by grinding herself against him with all her strength. She bucked her hips and kept bucking until satisfaction exploded through her body, drawing a low, keening scream from her throat. Nick slammed his mouth onto hers, absorbing the sound and then thrusting into her until they shared another shout of satisfaction.

For long minutes afterward, they lay panting and sweating. He shifted his weight off her and collapsed onto his back, his arms thrown over his head. She gulped in deep breaths of air, trying to regulate her breathing and slow her racing heart.

"Wow," he finally managed.

"Wow," she reiterated.

A few minutes later, he turned on his side, facing her. Resting his weight on his good arm, he draped his other one across her waist. The dim light allowed them to see each other's expressions. The turbulent emotion on his handsome features awed her.

"I wasn't lying earlier and I wasn't using any standard line on you," he swore softly. "I can't remember ever wanting a woman as desperately as I wanted—want—you."

She knew he wanted her to admit the same. She felt the same, but she couldn't formulate the words. A long-term relationship with him didn't stand a chance, and she couldn't bear to commit her heart at the risk of losing it.

"That's pretty scary territory," she whispered.

He searched her face for a long, tension-filled moment, and then shifted off the bed. "Tell me about it," he mumbled before excusing himself to hit the head.

Keri listened to him moving around the saloon but couldn't find the energy to move. She couldn't remember ever feeling so comfortable with her sexuality or so completely sated. She didn't even worry about covering her nudity.

Nick caught her attention when he started back up the steps to the bed platform. Totally naked, partially aroused and sheathed with a fresh condom, he carried two glasses of wine and literally stole her breath with his pagan beauty. Handing her a glass, he plumped some pillows at the head of the bed and patted them in invitation. She scooted up beside him.

He'd turned on a night light in the galley, so it wasn't quite as dark as she'd like. Grabbing the corner of a sheet, she tugged it across her waist.

"Scars?" he queried with unerring insight.

"Lots of ugly, puckered scars," she declared grimly. "The surgeons assured me they'd look less horrible in a few years, but I don't really believe it."

Nick downed his wine in one long gulp. "And you think I'm so shallow I can't be trusted to see them?"

Keri downed her wine thirstily too, setting her glass on the headboard. "I don't think you're shallow. It's not so much about you as it is my own self-consciousness."

He took a while to consider that angle. "So how do we get past the sensitivity?"

"We did just fine a few minutes ago," she said lightly. The wine and the man both went to her head. Turning to him, she put a hand on his chest and began tangling her fingers in the tight, silky curls.

"If we only make love in the dark, how am I ever going to see your breasts? I want to see their fullness and watch your nipples go all hard and tight," he told her, his tone dropping an octave.

She felt the heat of his hand as he cupped her breast, absently teasing the nipple with his thumb until she felt the pull deep in her womb.

"I have a solution," he declared gruffly. Before she realized what he intended, he'd slid down the bed and tugged the sheet off her stomach. He poured the remaining drops of his wine in her navel. She gasped a little at the sensation.

"Maybe you'd better explain your solution," she whispered.

"I'll just do a Braille study of your scars without looking at them. Once I'm familiar with every inch of your body, you should trust me to see it in the light."

She had no snappy comeback or arguments to wage. The feel of his tongue lapping her belly brought every nerve in her body to full attention. Her legs stiffened, toes and fingers curling as he slowly, thoroughly explored her midsection with his mouth. His hot lips made her flesh quiver. His kisses seared her flesh while healing wounds she hadn't even known existed. His tenderness brought tears to her eyes.

Working his way slowly down her abdomen, he clasped her thighs in his hands.

"Scars here too?" he asked, his fingers finding the tiny ridges at the back of her legs.

"Skin grafts," she explained.

No man had ever kissed her thighs. A shudder coursed through her when he pressed wet kisses over her skin. His tongue gently bathed the front with moisture while his fingers caressed the hidden scars. Tears overflowed her eyes.

She grasped his head with both hands and pulled him over her body. Looking at him through a shimmer of tears, she whispered, "I want you more than I've ever wanted any man in my whole life."

He moaned, low and long then made them one again.

They fell into a deep sleep, their bodies snuggled close

wearing nothing but a sheet.

Keri woke a few hours later and carefully searched the bed for her shirt. After slipping it over her head, she made her way to the bathroom. A glance at the digital clock showed two in the morning. Still sleepy, she crawled back into bed and drifted to sleep with the sound of Nick's breathing.

He woke her later when his hands began to caress her again. Lying on his right side, he pulled her close with her back to his chest, spoon fashion, and used the hand of his bad arm to knead her breast.

"More therapy?" she mumbled.

He rested his chin at the curve of her neck and teased her with his lips. "Amazing results."

"Amazing," she repeated drowsily.

"Why'd you go and put this shirt back on?" he grumbled.

She didn't bother to respond. The shirt had hitched up to her waist, leaving her mostly nude and exposed to his caresses. It didn't hamper him much at all.

His unselfish loving really was amazing, she thought a few minutes later when he expanded his therapeutic massage to the tender folds between her legs. He tickled and teased with his fingers, making her breathless with need. Then he filled her with hard, powerful demand. She moved against him with driving urgency until they'd both found complete, shuddering satisfaction.

Hot and sweaty again, they collapsed against the sheets and sucked in ragged breaths.

Nick finally spoke in a low, gruff voice. "That's some great therapy, *mia l'angelo.*"

"Exhausting but restorative," she agreed, and they shared soft laughter.

"It also requires a lot of energy," he said. "You goin' back to sleep?"

"Are you starving too?"

"Uh-huh."

"Do we have any food left?"

"Not much, but there's a café down the street that serves the best breakfast in the city."

"Doughnut shop?"

He growled and smacked her bare behind. Keri heard herself giggling. He had her giggling again.

"It's still the middle of the night," she argued.

"They open at five and it's after four now. Fishermen need an early start and a hearty breakfast."

"You get the first shower," she said. "I'll wait until the water heater has time to actually heat the water."

Nick chuckled and pressed a kiss to her lips before crawling from the bed. Despite the dim lighting, Keri enjoyed the sight of his tight, naked, incredibly sexy tush. The man really had a great set of buns, she thought. Another giggle bubbled up her throat.

She hadn't felt so happy and content for a very long time. Maybe never. Not knowing how long it might last, she decided not to worry, but just enjoy. After all, she was on vacation. What more could a woman want than a fabulous vacation fling with an incredibly gorgeous, sensitive lover? She also loved the gentle rocking motion of the boat.

Dragging herself from bed, she collected her pocketbook and was waiting when Nick exited the bathroom. *Head,* she mentally corrected. In nautical terms, the head meant the bathroom.

"Stupid name for a bathroom," she told him.

"What? The head? It's not stupid. There's no bathtub in there so why would you call it a bathroom?"

"I'll have to think about that for a while." Meanwhile, she soaked up the sight of him bare-chested with a towel draped around his waist. There was still so much of his body she wanted to explore.

"Water's warmer now. You want to borrow something else

to wear?"

"I have fresh underwear and yesterday's clothes aren't dirty, just a little wrinkled. They'll be fine."

"After breakfast, we can go shopping. Not that I mind having you naked, but we'll need to leave the *Adrianna* occasionally, and I don't really want anyone else seeing you that way."

"I'll have to go home shortly," she reminded.

He frowned and moved closer. Cupping the side of her face in his hand, he brushed his thumb across her lips and then kissed her lightly. His gaze held hers captive.

"One night with me and you're thinking about leaving? Why don't you just stab me in the gut?"

She didn't blink but held his steady gaze. "You know I can't stay very long."

His brows creased. "You're on vacation. Nobody expects you home for two more weeks."

They stared into each other's eyes for a long time. Despite the desire to be together, to shut out the rest of the world, they still had serious issues to deal with in Tennessee. Most importantly, whatever Russ and his militia were up to at home.

"Isn't your vacation officially over?" she asked softly. After another long few seconds, Nick sighed.

"Damn, sometimes it's real annoying to be one of the good guys."

"Obligations? Responsibilities? Annoying stuff like that?" she asked.

"We'll worry about that later. I should hear something from Lieutenant Alexander by afternoon. Until then, we're just a carefree couple enjoying vacation. Okay?"

She offered him a smile. "Okay,' she agreed, and then slipped out of his arms.

Keri took a shower and dried her hair, thankful her short style didn't require much attention. She dressed quickly and found Nick had dressed as well. He wore jeans and a dark blue

T-shirt. The well-worn fabrics hugged his hips and waist and muscled chest with loving familiarity. Even though he'd dressed casually, he looked good enough to eat.

"Ready?" he asked.

"My hair's damp, but that's no big deal."

He turned the key of a locked drawer, opened it and withdrew his wallet, badge and a small gun. He tucked the wallet and badge in his back pockets, and the gun into his waistband at the small of his back. To conceal it, he pulled on a lightweight sport coat, also blue.

"You need a weapon to get breakfast?"

"I'm still a cop, you know."

She'd deliberately put that out of her mind. Knowing men were always ready to do battle, she still found it hard to get her pacifistic mind around the concept.

As they made their way off the *Adrianna*, Keri glanced at the now-peaceful docks. The hustle of the city's nightlife had faded to dead-of-the-night quiet. A light fog drifted over the water. The air felt heavy and humid on her skin. Despite the warm temperature, it gave her goose bumps.

Nick put his arm around her shoulder and pulled her close. He chased away the chill and the eeriness she attributed to being in a totally foreign environment. As they moved across the parking lot to her SUV, she slipped an arm around his waist, but the bulge of his gun made her shiver again.

He clicked the remote to release the locks and opened the passenger door for her. Sensing her discomfort, he turned her in his arms and gave her a long, slow kiss.

"Stop thinking and worrying so much," he ordered. "Trust me for a while."

Keri relaxed and gave him a smile. "Aye, aye, Captain."

In the predawn hours of the morning, Walt and Jack Merritt moved around their home in compatible silence. They took turns in the shower and making coffee. Both dressed in standard gray uniforms, a style the Thornsbury sheriff's department had used for half a century.

Juice, toast and cereal sufficed for breakfast. Their morning routine didn't vary much without Keri in the house.

"You got home really late," Walt said as they sat down at the table.

"I stayed at the cabin until midnight and didn't want to wake you that late. Keri wasn't there."

"Not there?"

"A note on the door said she'd gone to Knoxville."

The sheriff frowned. "She said she might, but she didn't mention staying overnight. Did anything look out of place?"

"In my sister's typical fashion, she left the cabin super tidy and organized. Not a thing out of place."

"But?"

"But something didn't feel right. All my old spare clothes had been washed."

Walt brushed that off and took a big drink of coffee. "She's probably bored. The place has been empty for two years. I bet she gave it a thorough cleaning. Russ did say she'd baked pies. Hasn't made time for that in a long while."

Jack swallowed a mouthful of toast, and added, "She must have been really thorough because I could tell she'd cleaned the first-aid kit. The gun and handcuffs too."

Walt set his coffee cup on the table and stared at his son. "She never touches that gun. You know she hates it. What else?"

"I snooped around in the trash. She'd burned everything in the barrel, but I found a couple bits of gauze. Looked like blood stains on it."

The sheriff held his son's gaze. "She could have cut herself. Maybe just a finger prick and nothing serious."

"Well, since I had time to poke around, I also checked out the safety hatch in the bedroom closet. It's been used recently too. Lots of disturbed cobwebs and dust through the whole passageway and the trap door's been opened."

"I wouldn't put it past her to clean down there."

Jack shook his head. "I couldn't make out all the footprints, but there were definitely two sets of prints, one male and one female."

"Damn!" Walt whispered softly.

"Yeah, I'm thinkin' Lamanto never really made it out of the county."

"Why do you think Lamanto?"

"The footprints in the bomb shelter looked more like fancy Italian loafers than sneakers or boots. Maybe his lieutenant didn't lie to us when he said he hadn't heard from him. My guess is he's been holed up at the cabin with Keri."

"Double damn," swore Walt. "You think she deliberately sneaked him out of town?"

Jack frowned and took a sip of his coffee. "That's what I can't figure. She didn't seem too taken with the guy, and she's always gotten along well with Don. I don't know why she'd have helped Lamanto."

Walt's voice went grim. "Maybe he forced her."

"She passed me at a check point outside of town. I ran a quick flashlight through the SUV but didn't notice anything out of place."

"He could have highjacked her somewhere along the way. Then again, we did find a blood trail, and she's always been a sucker for a wounded animal of any sorts."

"He could have flagged her down later or just stood in the road and dared her not to stop."

"Whatever happened, she took him into the bomb shelter."

Both men understood the implication. "So she trusts him."

"At least we know she's not his hostage."

"They've been up there for almost a week. How the hell did they pull it off right under Russ's nose?" wondered Jack.

"Just outsmarted him. Keri's been doing that since kindergarten."

"Well hell," added Jack as he rose from the table and cleared their small amount of dishes. "It's bad enough having her near the compound, but if Lamanto's in any condition to snoop, he might stir up a whole hornet's nest of trouble."

"We sure don't need any more trouble."

Gathering their guns and jackets, they shut off lights and headed out the door. Both went quiet as they left the house and climbed into the sheriff's SUV.

"Want me to go back up today? Or send Dwayne to check on her? Maybe she took Lamanto to the nearest bus station and went back to the cabin."

"I'll try to track her first with the GPS on her phone and car. No matter where she is, she may not be willing to cut her vacation short and come home. You know she hates being told what she should or shouldn't do."

"I'll tell her Don is asking to see her since he regained consciousness."

"Is he?"

"He asked if she was working. He denies it, but I think he's pretty hung up on her."

"Good idea. I don't like not knowing exactly where she is. I want her safe at home."

"You think it's time for combat?"

"It won't be long now."

Nick and Keri shared a leisurely breakfast at a hole-in-the-wall café with surprisingly good food. Next they hit a twenty-four-hour superstore for a few items of clothing she needed. She argued about him paying, but he reminded her that a personal credit or debit card purchase could be traced.

"Do you want your family and the entire Thornsbury sheriff's department homing in on our location?"

"A rhetorical question," she replied tersely.

He paid for their purchases and they returned to her car, arms loaded with plastic bags. Once they'd stashed them in the back seat, Keri promised to repay him.

"Do you ever let anyone do anything for you? Just because?" he asked, drawing her slowly into his arms.

She lifted her hands to his chest and gazed into his eyes. "Because why? Because I'm a woman? Because I'm single? Because they want something in return?"

"Stubborn woman," he argued, dropping a kiss on her lips. "Just because I enjoy doing things for and with you? Is that so hard to accept, *mia l'angelo*? Do you always have to be the one doing the giving?"

Keri smiled slowly and arched her hips closer to his. She enjoyed the swift reaction of his body and nudged him harder. "If you really want to do something for me, why don't you take me back to your floating bachelor pad and seduce me in your big, comfortable bed?"

Nick made a rough sound in his throat and stole a long, deep kiss. Keri tightened her hold on him and wiggled closer, loving the feel of his hard, demanding body. They shared kiss after kiss, trying to satisfy an overpowering need to be closer.

Minutes later, the loud slam of a nearby car door dragged them from the passion-induced embrace.

He cursed softly and eased his grip on her. "I can't believe we're making out in the parking lot of a discount store," he said in self-disgust, turning to open the passenger door for her. "You're a constant temptation."

She laughed, "So it's all my fault, huh?" Taking her seat, she fastened her seatbelt while he circled the car and climbed into the driver's seat. One he'd settled, she reached over and rested her hand on his thigh. The muscle jerked in satisfying reaction. "Just get me back to your boat, ASAP, and I'll show you temptation."

Nick grasped her hand and slid it to the bulge between his legs, drawing a delighted sigh from her. Her fingers curled around the hardening evidence of his desire. Keri felt the flush of arousal creeping over her chest and neck.

"So sexy," she whispered. "So very, very sexy."

"And so very distracting," he replied gruffly, nudging her hand gently aside. "Now, behave for a while or I can't be responsible for my actions. I'd hate to wreck this pretty little SUV of yours."

Keri clasped her hands in her lap and tried to be patient when what she really wanted was him naked. She wanted them cocooned in his cozy, rocking bed with the sheets kicked aside and nothing between them but hot, steamy passion. Then she wanted to explore his body as thoroughly as he'd explored hers during the night.

The thought and accompanying mental image startled her in a deeply private way. She'd never been the aggressive sort in any relationship. A bit sassy and provocative, maybe, but never bold and uninhibited. An innate modesty and sheltered upbringing kept her from exploring the depths of her own passion, yet Lamanto blew reticence right out of the water.

The pre-dawn traffic grew heavier as they returned to the Bayside area, yet not nearly as heavy as when they'd arrived last night. She realized it was Saturday and assumed that accounted for fewer cars on the streets.

"You went awfully quiet," said Nick a few minutes later as they reached the entrance to the marina's parking lot.

"You told me to behave," she said, flashing him a grin.

"You can't talk and behave at the same time?"

"I'm doing some serious thinking."

"About what?"

Her smile deepened. "About stripping you naked and having my way with you."

A low rumble of complaint accompanied the tight smile he flashed her. "You're gonna pay for that."

He parked them near the railing overlooking the dock, shut off the engine and jumped from the SUV while she slowly unsnapped her seat belt. The sun had just risen above the water, casting a brilliant billowing glow across the bay area. She glanced toward the *Adrianna*, but the dock and slips still lay in shadowy morning fog.

Excitement bubbled inside Keri as Nick swung the door open and pulled her into his arms. She locked her hands on his neck and pressed herself close to his solid frame. He kissed her greedily and she returned his open-mouth kisses with equal fervor. Hunger swelled into a life of its own

Wrapped in their own private world, they had no forewarning of the explosion that rocked the pier and knocked them right off their feet.

Chapter Twelve

The force of the blast slammed Nick and Keri to the concrete. He landed on his back with her sprawled across his chest. Unhurt but winded, it took a few seconds to regain his senses. A plume of acrid smelling smoke followed the explosion and debris rained down on them. He ducked his head and crossed his arms over hers to protect them until the worst had passed.

“Are you okay?” he asked once the air cleared a little. An instant of panic followed as she gazed at him with a dazed expression.

“I’m fine, just a little stunned. What in the hell happened?” she asked, slowly rolling off his chest. They both sat up, brushing at their hair and clothes.

“I don’t know, but keep your head down,” he warned, cop instincts kicking into gear. He rose high enough to open the back door of the SUV. After fishing around in their shopping bags, he pulled out two hats. He’d made her buy a sun hat for boating, so she’d picked out a baseball cap for him. He tore the tags off both and handed her one.

“Put that on and keep your face hidden as much as possible,” he said, jamming the hat on his head.

Drawing his gun from his waistband, he hid it under his jacket, and pulled her up to his side. “Stay close and don’t make any unexpected moves until we find out what’s going on.”

She shook her head, brushed more dirt from her hair and donned the hat. “You think this has something to do with us?”

“Better to be cautious.”

Sirens began to wail and people shouted from all directions. More people raced across the parking lot and dockside to see what had happened. Flames shot into the sky, nearly two stories high, keeping onlookers at a distance. They felt the heat of the blaze as it sucked all the fog and dampness from the air.

With a firm grip around her waist, he moved from the partial protection of the vehicle to the iron guard rail overlooking the docks. A sickening sense of dread filled him as he looked toward the source of the raging fire. He knew before he actually saw it that the *Adrianna* had gone up in flames. His jaw locked in anger.

"Oh, Nick!" He heard her hoarse, sympathetic whisper. She hugged him tighter, but her attention stayed riveted on the burning boat.

He didn't have time to grieve or watch the rescue efforts. A crowd had collected at the railing, and he didn't want to get pinned in a mass of bodies. Tightening his hold on Keri, he slowly began to edge her backward. Someone had blown up his home in an attempt to kill him or at least send a deadly message. If they hadn't left the cruiser under the cover of darkness, they'd both be dead.

The attack and the destruction of the *Adrianna* made him seethe with fury, but the thought of something happening to Keri sent a horrified shudder over him. He briefly wrapped her in his arms. She returned his hug, holding him close. He allowed himself a minute of relief mixed with pleasure, but didn't want to stand in the open too long.

As more people rushed to the dockside, he led her back to the relative safety of the SUV. Shards of wood and fiberglass had riddled the front end of her vehicle as well as the door they'd stood behind. The windshield had cracked but not broken. He opened the passenger door for Keri, helped her in and then rounded the back to the driver's side. A quick survey of the parking lot didn't net any possible suspects. Too many thrill-seekers had begun to fill up the area.

They sat quietly for a minute, trying to catch their breath while listening to the roar of sirens and watching people run madly along the pier.

Nick adjusted the rearview and side mirrors. “Whoever did this is probably close by or patrolling the area to make sure the job got done. Keep a watch in the mirrors. Look for a dark SUV, a panel van or anything suspicious.”

“Nick, someone tried to kill you!” she declared gruffly. She stopped picking debris from her clothes and stared directly into his eyes. Her expression held a mixture of horror and outrage.

“They must have known you came home last night,” she echoed his thoughts. “What if they see you here? Will they try again?”

Reaching out a hand, he cupped her face and gently brushed a thumb across her lips. He desperately wanted more time with her, lots more time alone. But circumstances had a way of raging out of control. Right now, protecting her had to be his first priority.

“Probably not in broad daylight with so many witnesses. We’re safe for now. Since this isn’t my vehicle, nobody will be on the lookout for it. We just have to sit tight a few minutes until I can get a good look at all the people coming and going.”

His phone rang and he dropped his hand to pull it from his pocket. Glancing at the caller ID, he flipped it open.”

“Lieutenant.”

“Nick, you okay? A call just came through about an explosion at Miamarina. Are you there now? Tell me it’s just a freak coincidence.”

Cars and trucks swarmed into the parking lot, trying to get closer to the source of excitement. Nick tried to split his attention on his boss, his worried lover and the trolling sightseers.

“I’m fine, but some sonofabitch blew up the *Adrianna*.”

“With you on it?” Alexander yelled loud enough to make him hold the phone from his ear.

“No, no. I spent the night aboard but left early this morning.”

With a relieved sigh and a calmer tone, Lieutenant Alexander drilled him with questions. "Did you see anything suspicious? Notice anything unusual? Someone follow you from Tennessee or do you think someone local had your placed staked?"

"Negative on the tail. I'm sure of that. I greeted a few people on the docks last night but didn't see or hear anything out of the ordinary."

Not that he'd have noticed, he thought in self-disgust. He'd been totally captivated by Keri and having her aboard his beloved cruiser. A situation that had nearly gotten them both killed. He shifted his gaze from the circling traffic to her. She sat stiff and still beside him, staring at the rear-view mirror. Her clothes still held a layer of dust and ash. He realized in that instant, he'd do anything and everything in his power to protect her from any more traumas.

"My guess is the McDowell family made good on their threats."

Alexander uttered a few choice words Nick hoped she couldn't hear. Her gaze swung and locked with his. He could tell the news of a death threat didn't sit well with her.

His boss regained his attention. "You suppose they knew you weren't aboard and just wanted to scare you? Or do they think they've killed you?"

"Hard to tell."

"I'll see if I can hold off an official report and hint at a body being found in the wreckage. That should buy you a little breathing space."

"Sounds like a plan," said Nick.

"What about you? Do you wanna go into protective custody?"

He had a better option in mind that included Keri. Nobody knew about her being with him and he sure as hell wouldn't mention it over the phone.

"I'll lay low for a while longer."

The lieutenant wisely didn't ask for details. "Good. Don't contact anyone in the department but me. I'll send someone down to the marina to do damage control and see what kind of device they used. You want me to contact you on this phone?"

"I'll swap it for a new one and call you later," Nick told him, disconnecting the call.

Alexander's warning about contacting other detectives meant his boss suspected someone under his command of being dirty. He hated to think one of his police buddies would orchestrate his murder, but big money or extortion sometimes brought down the best of men.

"Someone wants you dead?" She leveled a stare at him.

"It's part of the job description," he told her, holding her gaze. "You should know that."

"Wanting someone dead and acting on it are two different things," she replied. "Who or what is the McDowell family?"

He hesitated, not wanting to involve her more, but needing her cooperation. When his lack of response had her eyes narrowing and lips thinning, he caved a little.

"They're a dysfunctional family of gangbangers who got chased from their own neighborhood. They tried to save face by escalating their criminal activities with extortion and smuggling. Their ambition is to bring notoriety to the family, and they boast they'll do anything for a price."

"Including murder?"

His response was terse. "Anything."

"Are they part of the reason you came to Thornsbury? The undercover operation you mentioned?"

"Partly. I was the front man for a sting that netted Reggie, the oldest brother and leader of the pack, along with a low-level cousin. The cousin bragged about the gang's newest scheme making McDowell a household name in this country."

The informant also offered warnings about the Thornsbury connection in a plea deal. He didn't mention that to her because he still wasn't sure where her family stood in the scheme of things.

"So is the top dog still in jail?"

"Yeah. We have evidence to send him to prison for a long time, but he's still controlling the family business."

"And they want you dead."

"They threatened me and several other guys on the force. That's the normal reaction to being caught red-handed, but most don't want to risk going down for killing a cop."

"So why risk it?"

"Incarceration is a perfect alibi. Even if we know he's giving orders from jail, it's hard to prove."

"So what now? I vote on going back to Thornsbury."

"No."

"Just no?" she snapped. "No discussion? No 'what do you think'?"

"You said you trusted me."

"And I do," she replied, "but I don't trust whoever is trying to kill you, and I don't trust that it's safe here."

"I swear we'll be protected. Give me an hour or so and I promise I'll have us in one of the safest locations in the country."

Since joining the police force he'd avoided mixing his work with his family and private life, but her safety had to come first now.

Nick's breathing stalled while Keri mulled over his promise. She held his gaze without flinching and then finally nodded her head in agreement. The simple nod squeezed his heart with emotion. He needed her to have faith in him, wanted her complete trust even in the face of disaster.

"So you have a plan?" she asked.

He scanned the parking lot again but didn't see anything or anyone suspicious. "They won't be watching for a couple, only a lone man. We need to get the shopping bags and head down the dock like tourists returning to their boat. And we need to do it before the police can cordon off the area around the *Adrianna*."

"But we don't have a boat to return to," she reminded.

"My family has one docked farther down the pier."

She shifted her gaze from the rearview mirror and stared at him, one brow cocked. "Your family lives on a boat too?"

Her tone made him grin. "No, but they own one, and I swear nobody will get close enough to blow it up." A full-time security team guarded that big ole water vessel.

He saw indecision in her eyes and didn't want to give her time to change her mind. With one last, sweeping glance behind them, he jumped out his door and rounded the SUV. After gathering the shopping bags from the backseat, he opened her door and she joined him on the pavement. Handing her a few bags, he hung a couple on his bad arm and slipped it around her waist, leaving his gun hand free.

They made their way slowly through the sea of people and headed down the steps to the docks. A marina guard tried to stop them, but Nick told him they needed to get to the opposite end of the pier. He knew the guards had instructions not to offend other owners, so he allowed them to pass.

They skirted the confusion near the *Adrianna* and slowly walked by it like any of the other curious bystanders. Anger curled in his stomach as he gazed at the darkened, smoldering carcass of his cruiser, but he didn't stop to watch as they pumped water onto her charred decks.

When they cleared the main congestion, he exchanged nods with a short, stocky man standing just beyond the wreckage.

Nick touched the bill of his hat to Gus Puppuna, one of his family's security team. The other man's expression didn't show a spark of recognition but relief flashed briefly in his dark eyes as he returned the nod. Gus had worked for the family so long he'd become a trusted member.

He and the others would be alarmed by the annihilation of the *Adrianna*. Nick hated that they worried so much about his job and lifestyle. Just a few hours ago, he'd assured them all he was safely home. The destruction of his cruiser would cause his parents more worry and stress. He wasn't too damned pleased about it, either.

The farther they walked the fewer people they passed. Nobody followed them as they moved from the center of activity. Gus had his back, and nobody could slide past the long-time bodyguard unnoticed, so Nick allowed himself to relax a little.

"Do you actually have a destination in mind?" Keri interrupted his thoughts with a complaint. "Or are we just going to walk off the end of the pier?"

"Almost there," he assured her.

The slips for smaller crafts gave way to extra wide slips for bigger crafts. They passed two empty ones and then approached the *Gianovelli.* The beautiful white yacht gleamed in the sunlight. The words *Gianovelli Chocolates* graced the side in bold red lettering. His steps slowed as he neared it.

Then Keri came to an abrupt halt. Nick wondered if she'd explode or gush. He should have known she'd be less predictable.

"Gianovelli?" she asked in a soft, inquisitive tone that worried him a little. "That's your family name?"

"My mother's family. I carry my dad's family name."

"Your mother sells candy?" she said in a little louder tone. Her irritation grew with each indrawn breath. "You told me your mother sold candy. That's like saying the Pope says prayer. This is how you describe the matriarch of one of the world's finest names in chocolate?"

"The finest," he corrected, but the distraction didn't ease the tension he felt in her body. Nor his own as he registered her level of annoyance.

She pulled from his grasp and glared at him. "You expect me to meet your family looking like something the cat dragged in? My hair's a wild mess, I'm filthy and more than a little battered. I cannot go aboard a yacht like that," she pointed to emphasize her words, "looking like this!"

"None of the family is aboard the *Velli,"* he assured her.

"You have a nickname for the family yacht?"

"It's really not much bigger than the *Adrianna*. Technically, it belongs to the company and it's just part of doing business in a port city."

"Except your family owns the company?"

The sudden appearance of another big, broad-shouldered man saved him from having to respond to her question.

"Brice," said Nick, stepping forward and offering a hand to his mother's head of security. Brice Carlisle's Italian heritage had a blend of Scotch Irish to make a tall, striking man with dark eyes and auburn hair. He grabbed Nick's hand and then slapped another on his arm, shaking firmly.

"Good to see you, man. We've been worried."

Nick gave him a smile and nod of understanding before turning to Keri. She watched them with a wary, calculating expression. Never quite sure how she'd react in any given situation, he introduced the two.

"Brice, this is Keri Merritt. Her dad is the sheriff in Thornsbury where I spent the last couple weeks."

"Ma'am." He nodded to her and they briefly shook hands. "You just got back?"

"Last night."

"You spent the night aboard the *Adrianna*?" Although the other man's voice didn't alter much, it held a rare touch of alarm.

"Left early for breakfast."

Brice gave them a quick once-over and his jaw tightened. "You came back to an explosion?"

"That's about the size of it," said Nick. "We need a shower and change."

"Sure thing. When Gus gets back we'll pull up anchor. You're goin' out to the house, right?"

"Right. When I talked to Mom yesterday she said they planned to leave for Italy."

To Keri, he explained. "We have extended family over there. My folks go a couple times a year and combine business with an extended visit."

"Your mama refused to leave until you called yesterday and assured her you're okay," said Brice. "But they flew out last night."

"We need to disappear for a few days too," Nick told him.

"Good idea. Anyone know you've got company?"

He shook his head and slipped an arm around Keri's waist, pulling her close to his side. He shot Brice a look that made words unnecessary. He'd wanted her under the umbrella protection extended to any member of the Lamanto family.

Brice gave him a slow nod of understanding and gave Keri a more thorough scrutiny.

"If you two are done exchanging macho, irritatingly silent messages, I'd really like a shower," she declared tersely.

"Now, honey," Nick placated, bracing for the elbow he knew she'd slam into his ribs. She did, and he grunted. Then her sexy country accent deepened as it always did when she was pissed.

"Don't 'now honey' me, Lamanto. My mood is rapidly deteriorating."

That surprised a bark of laughter from Brice. "Looks like you have your hands full, pal."

"You might say that."

"I'm standing right here, wiseasses!"

Brice reached out a hand for the shopping bags. "Let me take those. You two go ahead and board while I wait for Gus. I'll see if he learned anything. There are plenty of supplies."

"We'll shower first, but Keri needs some clean clothes."

"In the bags?"

"Yeah."

"I'll have Gus wash 'em up when he gets here. He'll bring 'em down when they're laundered."

Nick handed him the keys to her car. "Dark green SUV in the parking lot with Tennessee tags. It got hit pretty hard with debris. Can you arrange to have it repaired?"

"Sure thing."

"I have insurance," injected Keri. "I don't know the policy on bomb damage, but I'll take care of it myself."

He didn't want his problems costing her more time or money, and he wasn't ready to have her tracked down by the Thornsbury sheriff's department.

"We need to get it off the lot now before someone notices the out-of-state tags. You'll be under suspicion for the bombing and they'll run a background check."

After a few heartbeats, she nodded understanding and stopped protesting. He took her elbow and guided her onto the yacht. The interior saloon looked similar to the *Adrianna's* but more spacious and elegant. It featured genuine leather seating, chandelier lighting, a stocked bar and state-of-the-art entertainment options.

"There are four staterooms, the master one my parents use, a VIP one and two smaller guest rooms. The master and VIP both have their own showers, so we can use them to get cleaned up. There should be spare robes and toiletries in each room. Gus'll bring fresh clothes soon."

"There's a laundry room aboard?"

"Yeah, all the modern conveniences."

"Pretty impressive."

He didn't want her judging him by his family's lifestyle. In the past, women had both loved and hated him due to the Gianovelli wealth. He'd stopped sharing this side of his life years ago. "Don't be too impressed, it doesn't belong to me."

Keri didn't respond but stared at him and lifted a brow at his prickly tone. He signed and ran a hand through his hair.

"Sorry. I'm a little testy this morning."

Her expression softened a little. "Why? Just because someone destroyed your home in an effort to kill you?"

Her mild teasing made him smile. He reached out and pulled her into his arms, loving the way she molded her body to his. The fit was perfect. They shared a long, slow kiss. He eased his tongue into her mouth and shuddered as she slowly sucked it deeper. His whole body reacted to the caress. He wanted to lose himself in her again and block out the rest of the world. He wanted days and weeks and maybe more to explore the extraordinary chemistry between them.

The sound of the anchor being retracted snapped him back to reality. He withdrew from her seductive kisses and eased some distance between them.

"We'd better get a shower. It won't take long for us to clear the dock, and I want to show you around the bay when we leave the port."

"Point me in the right direction," she said.

Nick showed her to the VIP stateroom and told her where to find the necessities. Then he took a long, hot shower in his parents' room. His left arm still smarted when he moved it in certain directions, but the stitches had healed nicely and the bruising had faded to a dull green. It no longer throbbed and it felt stronger each day.

The bureaus in the master stateroom always held a variety of spare clothes for the family, so he donned a pair of black swim shorts and a gray T-shirt.

Less than half an hour after leaving her, Nick crossed the hall and entered the VIP room. Keri exited the shower wrapped in a white terry robe and drying her hair with a towel. The robe stopped at midthigh, giving him a glimpse of bare, shapely legs. The sight kicked his libido into overdrive, forcing him to stifle the urge to disrobe her.

"You're quick. Ready to go up top?"

She finger-combed her hair and tossed the towel onto the back of a chair. "I can't go on deck in a robe."

"Sure you can. That's more than some guests wear. Not much different than a beach cover."

She looked unconvinced, but then conceded and crossed the room toward him. "If you say so."

"I say so."

As he took her hand to lead her through the saloon, he felt

the tremble of the powerful engines. By the time they reached the deck, the yacht had begun to ease from the slip. After a few minutes of maneuvering, their horn sounded and they started to glide through the heavy traffic toward the inlet of the bay.

"The color and clarity of the water is amazing," commented Keri as she gazed around them at the white sand beneath the deep blue.

"Bayside is beautiful," he agreed. "A lot more congested than I'd like, but definitely special."

They settled on a wide, cushioned deck chair. "Who's our captain?"

Nick looked up toward the highest level of the yacht. "Brice is in the cockpit. He and Tony, who probably went with the folks, can handle the *Velli* with ease. Gus, not so much."

"Gus is the short, stout-looking man we passed near the *Adrianna*?"

He gave her a long look. "You noticed Gus?"

"Law enforcement officers aren't the only people with honed observation skills. I noticed the flicker of relief in his eyes when you tipped your hat to him."

"Gus is a treasure. There's not much he can't do except pilot this thing. He's worked for the family for as long as I can remember."

"Doing what, exactly?"

"Lots of stuff. Chauffeuring, shopping, cleaning, even a little gardening when he's in the mood."

"And bodyguarding?"

"That too."

"Does your family have a big need for bodyguards?"

"Maybe not full time, but a certain level of wealth necessitates state-of-the-art security."

"Because that level of wealth also entices a high level of criminal mentality?"

"Yeah, unfortunately."

Nick didn't want to talk about wealth or bodyguards or

anything else right now. He slid his good arm around her shoulders and drew her closer. Then he placed his other hand on her knee, slowly edging his fingers under the hem of her robe.

Her quickly indrawn breath pleased him immensely.

Chapter Thirteen

"I owe you a little payback for some earlier teasing," said Nick, caressing the warm, supple flesh of her thigh. "Do you have anything on under this robe?"

"A bright purple thong," she said, shifting out of his reach and modestly tugging the sides of the robe together.

"You're puttin' me on. You're not the thong type."

"That's how much you know," she shot back at him. "When I pack spare undies in my pocket book, I have to keep them as tiny as possible. You should see the itty-bitty matching lace bra."

His breathing shattered and his imagination went wild. Just a tiny little strip of fabric tucked between smooth, rounded cheeks. Only a scrap of lace covering those beautiful breasts. Her nipples probably peaked through the lace. He uttered a low groan of regret because the chance of him getting her alone anytime soon was slim to none.

"I think you might have a sadistic streak," he charged.

"I think you should concentrate on showing me the sights."

He sighed deeply. "Okay, I'll play tour guide. If you look to the port side," he pointed to show her, "we'll soon be approaching Millionaire Row."

"And what is Millionaire Row?"

"It's a barrier island with shops, restaurants and homes only millionaires can afford."

Although he'd seen it hundreds of times, he tried to imagine seeing it for the first time. Private pools and miniature, manicured lawns dotted the landscape. Luxury condos and elegant mansions stretched from end to end, gleaming like flamboyant jewels.

"And is that where your family lives?"

"Nope." Despite his own background or maybe because of it, he'd never liked the ostentatious display of wealth.

"So where is the family home? We're not cruising to the Bahamas, I hope."

When he didn't immediately respond, she flashed a questioning look at him.

"Well? It's not in the Bahamas, is it?"

"No, but it is an island."

"What island?"

"The Gianovelli Island."

Her expression went from quizzical to amazed. "Your family owns its own island?"

"A small one. I've heard my great-grandpapa bought it for a song."

Keri rolled her eyes and then her expression went blank. Nick wasn't sure how to interpret the reaction. She didn't comment on the island again, but he knew her mind must be reeling with all the information he'd thrown at her in the last twenty-four hours. Besides complicating their relationship with sex, he'd offered her plenty of reason to ditch him as soon as possible. He didn't like it when she went into her quiet, withdrawn mode.

She did ask general questions about the area, and he enjoyed sharing facts with her. The sun rose higher and warmed them, even though the speed of the yacht kept a stiff breeze blowing across their skin. A small awning protected them from the direct sunshine as well as prying eyes. He slipped his arm around her and drew her close again, relieved when she snuggled into his embrace.

They'd passed Millionaire Row and headed out of the bay when Gus came topside to let them know he'd put Keri's clothes in the VIP room. Nick made introductions and the two greeted each other with reserved politeness.

"Want I should fix you something to eat?" asked Gus.

"We had breakfast, thanks," Nick told him. "We can wait and have lunch at the house."

"I'm sure Teresa will like that. She's always in a better mood when you're at home. I'll just go to the cockpit to harass Brice. Yell if you need anything."

"Will do."

"Teresa?" asked Keri when they were alone again.

"She's a distant cousin of my dad's. She lives and works at the villa."

"Villa?"

He didn't know how to describe his family home without sounding like a braggart. "My great-grandpapa bought the island from one of his old-country friends. It came complete with an Italian-style villa."

"So," said Keri. She turned her gaze from the waterway and stared at him. "Have you been waited on all your life? Is that how you grew up? With servants and chauffeurs and someone always catering to your needs?"

Her total lack of expression worried him, but he didn't take offense at her curiosity. He gave her an honest answer.

"I guess I had a sheltered adolescence. Not that I realized it at the time. The typical angst-ridden teen years. Mom and Pop tried to instill good values. I had chores, responsibilities and summer jobs. I had to use my allowance wisely and work for what I wanted. My sisters thought I got special treatment because I'm the only son, but I never bought into that."

"Just your typical family dynamics?"

"Yeah. Privileged for sure, but my parents worked hard to keep our family life as normal as possible."

"So why in the world did you pick law enforcement for a career?"

He frowned and shrugged his sore shoulder. "I've been asking myself the same question lately. A cop can't just do his job anymore. Everything gets bogged down with paperwork and politics. It drives me crazy."

"Your parents must have wanted you to join the family business."

He gave her a long, hard look, wondering if she thought the same. She wouldn't be the first woman who'd preferred to date a high-salaried executive.

"I wanted something more challenging and unpredictable. I'm not cut out for the corporate world, the boardrooms and nonstop meetings," he argued.

Keri shook her head, her tone sardonic. "You'd rather have people shooting at you and blowing up your home?"

"Extreme situations," he argued. "I'm a detective. I have the mindset for it. I like the problem solving and probing for the truth. I believe in the justice system and our responsibility to uphold the law."

"Me too, but I could do without the violence involved," she said, settling back into his embrace.

He held her tighter. "Ah, but what would a trauma nurse do without violence?"

"There are other forms of trauma."

"I'm dealing with a little problem that needs your attention now," he said, sliding his arm around her waist and tugging her on top of him. What better way to change the subject?

"Nick!"

"Nobody can see us." He swore softly, brushing his lips across her mouth. Slipping both hands under her robe, he palmed her bare flesh. A rush of air burst from his chest. His body hardened. "You really are wearing a thong."

"Told ya so." She nibbled on his chin, and he shuddered.

He squeezed her firm, baby-soft skin and pulled her tighter against his erection. She squirmed, and need slammed through him. He wanted to forget everything and everybody but the woman in his arms. They had so much more loving to do.

"Done sightseeing?" he whispered gruffly.

The slumberous look in her eyes answered his question.

She slowly detangled herself from his grasp and offered him a hand. He clasped it tightly and led her back down to the VIP stateroom. As soon as he closed the door behind them, he simultaneously kicked off shoes and tugged off his shirt. In another instant he'd shoved shorts down his legs and stood fully naked while she watched with hungry eyes.

"Damn, condom." He didn't have one.

Keri gave him a slow smile and reached into the pocket of her robe. "Found this in my bag too."

She pulled out a condom, lifted it to her mouth and used her teeth to open the package. Nick didn't think he could get any hotter or harder. Then she touched him, using both hands to slowly sheathe his straining flesh. His knees went weak.

"Let me see that bra and thong," he whispered roughly.

She hesitated and he remembered her sensitivity about the scarring. He held his breath until she slowly shrugged out of the robe and let it drop to the floor. By revealing her body to him in broad daylight, scars and all, she afforded him the trust he badly wanted. He silently vowed to reward her once his pulse stopped pounding in his ears and pooling in his groin.

"I'd like to take my time with you, but I'm really needy right now," he warned her. Reaching out both hands, he cupped her breasts, rubbing his thumbs over the lace-covered nipples until they grew hard and tight.

In response, Keri shoved him backward across the bed and climbed on top of him. Nick thought the breath-staggering anticipation might kill him. But what a way to go.

She didn't bother to remove the thong but nudged it aside and eased herself down onto his shaft. He uttered a deep moan of pleasure as their bodies locked. Pulling her close, he licked her nipples through the lacy fabric. She moaned too, grinding herself against him with greedy feminine demand.

As she writhed against him, he tried to hold back the spasms stealing down his spine. Lifting his hands, he pulled the straps of the tiny purple bra off her shoulders, freeing her breasts. Then he scooped the soft mounds into his hands and squeezed them tightly, plucking at her nipples until she quivered and groaned. Seconds later, when she cried out in satisfaction, he exploded with mind-blowing pleasure.

Dressed in new khaki walking shorts and a turquoise knit top, Keri joined Nick on the deck of the *Gianovelli.* The yacht had slowed speed as they approached his home. He handed her a small pair of binoculars so she could get a better view of the island.

She supposed it would be considered a tiny island. The stretch of emerald green couldn't be much more than a couple miles in circumference. Right in the center, atop a slight hill, sat a pale pink stone building with more windows than she'd ever seen on one house. Correction, a villa. She'd never seen an actual villa, but it sure matched her imaginings and images in history books.

The villa stood three stories high with what looked like marble pillars and a huge archway over the entrance. A wide porch circled the entire ground floor. Most of the collection of windows had balconies with wrought iron railings.

Besides the main building, she could see what looked like a three- or four-car garage as large as her home in Thornsbury. She saw a boathouse and another smaller, matching structure between the villa and the dock. Palm trees and a kaleidoscope of colorful flowers framed the property, making it look like a gleaming gem in a sea of blue.

"Wow." The hushed admiration in her voice had Nick pulling the glasses from her face.

"Wow, what? Tell me what's going on in that active little mind of yours." He turned her so they faced each other again.

"Little? I resent that," she teased lightly, pressing a hand flat to his chest. She loved the warmth and solid feel of him. Loved the new intimacy they shared. Loved the way he loved her with no thought of her scars and emotional baggage.

"So what do you think? Too ostentatious? Too regal for twenty-first-century America?"

"Is that what you think?" she shot back at him.

He gave her a grin. "I guess, but it's still home. My childhood playground. Know what I mean?"

"Home means a lot of different things to people."

"It's where your heart, your history and your future all get tangled," he said.

The engines of the yacht began to gear down and they turned their attention back to the island. The closer they got, the more astounding its beauty. Keri tried to take it all in but she'd never even stayed in a hotel so elegant. Never one to feel awed by wealth, she thought her attitude might be undergoing some adjustment.

"Doesn't your family worry about hurricanes? It looks like the whole island could be swallowed or blown out to sea."

"That's a huge risk of living out here, but the place has stood strong for over two hundred years. The shores are reinforced every year. There's a twenty-foot stone wall on the south side of the island to protect against the worst Atlantic storms. And the family always heeds hurricane warnings to evacuate. We're in season now, but you don't have to worry."

"Hurricanes are the least of my worries."

He tugged her closer and dropped a kiss on her lips. Keri returned it with enthusiasm. She'd never liked demonstrative men, yet she found herself blossoming under Nick's attention. He liked touching, kissing and being close. She liked it too, but the little intimacies kept her hungry for more of him. That growing need surprised and concerned her. It wouldn't be smart to become too dependent on Detective Lamanto, she reminded herself frequently.

The yacht gradually came to a halt under the stone archways of the boathouse. Gus extended a ladder then Nick helped him tie down the mooring ropes while Brice killed the engines. The men offered her a hand while she disembarked. Gus assured them he'd bring all their belongings to the house, so they headed up a cobbled stone path to the main building.

Flowers lined the walkway along with flowering bushes,

palm trees and a flowing fountain. Despite temperatures in the eighties, Keri didn't feel the oppressive heat of the city.

"All eco-friendly," Nick assured her, taking her left hand into his right. "Pop's a stickler for keeping the place green and safe for future generations of Lamantos."

"It's all so gorgeous," she said. "Does your dad take care of the landscaping too?"

"He helps, depending on how busy he is with other stuff. We have extended family that helps too."

"Who all lives here on the island? Your parents and sisters? Brice and Gus? It looks big enough to house an army."

"The Gianovelli and Lamanto clan probably equates to a small army, but living here isn't practical for everyday work schedules," he explained. "My two older sisters and their families have suites in the villa, but they live, work and go to school in Miami. The twins just started back to college. They live in dorms during the school year but at home during the summer."

As they talked, they approached the front of the villa. Keri noted the marble pillars, grand archway and imposing bronze door flanked by bronze statues. Her breath caught at the elegance and beauty, but Nick didn't appear affected at all.

"The house has three floors," he continued to explain. "The ground floor has a formal sitting and dining room for entertaining on the west side. The east side has the kitchen, breakfast nook and family room. The first floor has six small suites with bedrooms, baths and sitting rooms. There's also a library, fitness center and music room on that level. The second floor has more suites for guests and our security team."

"Brice and Gus live on the second floor? But it's really the third level?"

"Yeah, and Tony when he's not traveling with the folks."

He pulled open the door and ushered her inside. Once her eyes adjusted to the more dim interior lighting, they widened in amazement. The entry hall opened into a double curving staircase that lead her gaze straight up to lavishly painted ceilings. She'd never seen anything so grand outside a museum or history book.

"Wow!"

"Yeah, a little overpowering at first," he said.

Before she could respond, they heard a shout from the back of the house. "Is that my Nico?"

Following the heavily accented question, Keri saw a short, round woman hurrying toward them from the right side of the staircase. Dressed in a simple green skirt and flowered blouse, the fifty-something, dark-haired woman threw herself into Nick's arms and hugged him tightly. Her dark eyes gleamed with genuine warmth and affection.

"Hey there, Teresa. How's the world been treatin' ya?" Nick asked as he returned the woman's hug.

"I'm so happy to see you!" She shook her finger at him. "It's been way too long."

"It's good to be here," he returned warmly. "I brought a friend." Turning he introduced Keri. "She's special so we have to be extra good to her."

The other woman took Keri's proffered hand and shook it firmly.

"Welcome, welcome," she said. "Nico doesn't bring many friends to us. He hardly comes to visit at all. I'm glad he's making time now, although his mama and papa will be sorry to miss him."

She turned back to Nick. "You want me to make up a guest room for your friend?"

"Nah, she can use Maria's old room."

"Please don't go to any trouble on my account," added Keri. She didn't know where his sister Maria's old room might be, but she figured it was close to his.

"No trouble. I'll freshen both rooms, but first come to the kitchen and get some lunch. I know Brice and Gus will be hungry." With that, she turned and hurried back the way she'd come.

"Teresa's a regular whirlwind," said Nick. "She always moves in high gear."

"She lives here too?"

"She and her husband, Tiko, live in a cottage on the property. He helps Pop with whatever projects he's into at any given time. The security guys help with maintenance around the place too. There's always something that needs work."

"Just one big happy family?"

"For the most part." He turned her in his arms and gave her another long, deep kiss. When they needed air, he rubbed his nose against hers and spoke softly. "Don't be intimidated or enamored of all the wealth and opulence. It's not who I am."

She replied just as softly but with genuine curiosity, "You can take the man out of the mansion, but can you really take the mansion out of the man?"

"I'm proof of it, but not this minute. As much as I'd like to spend the day introducing you to my private suite, we'd better go see what Teresa whipped up for lunch."

"I am getting a little hungry."

"I'm starving."

"You're always starving," she chided as they headed down the hallway toward the kitchen.

"Only because you worked off all my morning calories."

"Reminder, Nico, you initiated that workout."

He laughed. "Nico is just my family nickname. And reminder, Miss Merritt, your purple thong was the catalyst."

Keri shook her head and followed him across ceramic tiles and plush carpeting to a kitchen with a view that stole her breath.

Reggie McDowell paced the small, windowless jail cell, impatiently waiting for a visit from his lawyer. A few weeks in the Dade County detention center had dampened his plans for becoming a big-time crime lord. He'd settle for being free right now.

The clothes he had to wear were rags compared to his own bangin' threads. The food looked and tasted like barf from the alleys of his youth. The dank, rotting smell of the jail reminded him of those same seedy streets. He hadn't risen above all that just to be socked in the slammer for the rest of his natural life.

He had to get the hell outta this place. His lawyer said the DA had enough evidence to send him to death row. The judge nixed his bail option, so he was screwed unless his stupid kid brother, Knifer, could get rid of the evidence and the cops who'd put him here. But Knifer never did anything right without minute-by-minute instructions. Mostly, not even then.

His loser of a brother had gotten him into this mess in the first place. Knifer had wanted one more score against the Paulson family before they broke with the old crowd for good. He'd trusted that cop Lamanto and the whole deal had gone from bad to worse. Too many people had seen him gun down Rafe Paulson. A self-defense plea wouldn't fly, and he wasn't pleain' to some mental incompetence crap.

He had a plan, though, he always had a plan. That's how he'd pulled the family from the gutters and caught the attention of the Cooper guy. Cooper was a high roller with really ballin' plans, but he couldn't risk drawing too much attention from the cops.

A guard interrupted his angry thoughts and led him to the visitation lockdown. Ronald Mansune, another loser, greeted him nervously. He had plenty of reason to be nervous. The main one being his meth habit the McDowell family fed or starved, depending on the family's needs. Right now, the Ivy League loser looked to be in a bad way.

"What's the haps?" he asked, knowing how much his lawyer hated him and the street slang.

"I got a message you needed to see me," said Mansune.

"I wanna know what you're doin' to get me outta this stinkin' rat's nest."

Mansune cleared his throat. His right eye twitched, and he played with the catch on his briefcase. "I'm doing everything possible. Since the judge refused bail, the only option is a speedy trial. A preliminary date's been set, but I need time to prepare your defense."

"Cop-shop rumor is a certain detective's boat got wasted with him onboard. Any truth to that?"

The lawyer's head bobbed like one of those toys on the dash of a car.

"I heard it on the news. Apparently a male body was found, but no positive ID has been made. The police department is being very secretive about it."

"I wanna know positive," said Reggie. He glared at the little puke for a long, tense minute and then added, "Find out and report to Knifer. He'll have a little reward for you."

"Even without Detective Lamanto's eye-witness account, there's a lot of solid evidence against you."

Reggie'd had plenty of time to weigh the odds. With Lamanto dead and the other cop in Cooper's pocket, his odds improved. Last resort would be double-crossing Cooper. If he sold him out to the feds, he'd have the best odds for a plea deal. But that carried other risks, life-threatening risks and the need for relocation.

Death row compared to targeting himself as a snitch.

At least a snitch had a chance to run, hide or disappear. The clang of jail cells had him grinding his teeth and running another option by his lawyer.

Chapter Fourteen

In the afternoon, Keri and Nick lounged by the crystal blue water of the Olympic-size pool behind the villa. They soaked up sun and enjoyed the serene beauty of the landscaping. She didn't think he should swim until his stitches came out, so they cooled off by dangling their feet in the water. Playing footsie with bare, wet feet led to some heated foreplay and a sensual siesta in his king-sized bed.

They surfaced again near dinner time, neither bothering with many clothes. He wore old cutoff jeans. She dressed in gym shorts and a white tank top. Teresa had left the house for the day, so they raided the refrigerator. Nick whipped up a feast of leftover manicotti, garden-fresh veggies and home-baked bread. For dessert, he found vanilla ice cream and topped it with caramel syrup.

"Way better fare than I provided at the cabin," she said as she licked the last drop of sweetness from her spoon.

"Except for the apple pie," he reminded with a warm, flirty smile.

She returned his smile with a nod. Despite the short amount of time they'd known each other, she felt a deeper connection with him than any man she'd ever known. He'd shifted her world on its axis. His smile made her heart pound and her insides tremble with pleasure. She felt alive and happy and whole with him.

Even if they couldn't sustain a long-term relationship, she'd treasure every memory they made together. The thought sent her into an emotional tailspin. Her pulse skittered in panic, so she covered her reaction with mindless chatter.

"My mom tried hauling ice cream to the cabin years ago,"

she said, breaking eye contact and focusing on the spoon in her hand. "We celebrated Jack's birthday up there, and she wanted him to have cake and ice cream. She bought dry ice to keep it frozen for the trip up but the freezer at the cabin didn't keep it cold enough. We had really sloppy ice cream."

"Jack's birthday in the summer?"

She nodded again, but didn't look directly at him. "July. We used to go to the cabin for two weeks every summer. Jack and I loved it until we got into our teen years. Then we whined a lot about leaving our friends and being bored."

Feeling a sudden urge to burn off nervous energy, Keri gathered their dirty dishes and carried them to the sink. She needed a minute to gather her wits and deal with the emotional jolt she'd given herself.

"The lack of phones, television and computers?" asked Nick. "Sounds like a familiar teenage complaint when you take 'em out of their comfort zones."

She made a sound of agreement and they both got lost in thought. As she cleaned the dishes, he dried them and they slowly returned the kitchen to its earlier pristine condition. Still not looking directly at him, she drained the dish water and asked more questions.

"How does your family bring in groceries? With the year-round hot weather, I'd think hauling by boat would get tricky."

"They use the chopper."

That had her raising a brow and staring at him. He tossed his towel aside and gave her a shrug.

"Brice is a helicopter pilot too. The family uses it for quick trips to the city."

Why should that surprise her? Keri wondered as she dried her hands. For all she knew the family could afford a whole fleet of aircraft. In an emergency situation, having air transportation from an island could mean the difference between life and death.

"And Millionaire's Row is closer by boat," he said,

"Sometimes Teresa shops there."

"I didn't see a helicopter anywhere. Do your folks leave it in the city?"

"No. It's on the roof. You can't see it from the ground because it's hidden behind all that fancy architecture on the top of the house. When someone wants to come or go, they just call Brice."

Nick took her hand and led her outside as evening approached. She twined her fingers with his and felt the thrill of the physical connection as his warmth permeated to her.

They strolled around the beautiful property. He showed her his favorite spots and told her he used to compare his family's compound to Alcatraz, the old island prison. As a hormonal teenager, he'd hated the isolation and yearned for a more normal lifestyle.

"So when did you escape?"

"We have a home in the city and spent most of the school year there. Summers and holidays we were stuck here."

"I'll bet that really cut into the social life of a studly young Romeo."

He grinned and wrapped his arm around her waist. "Until I escaped to college," he teased as they strolled up the hill to the villa.

"What college?"

"Miami U, of course."

"East Tennessee for me," she told him.

"You always wanted to be a nurse?"

She nodded. "Once I got past the ballerina, horse-trainer and firefighter stage in grade school. I suppose you studied law enforcement."

"Criminal justice. I considered going to law school but didn't have the patience or ambition for it."

For most of the day, they'd ignored the more pressing problems of bombs and militias and terrorist threats. As they settled into a comfortable glider on the back terrace, Keri broached the subject.

"What next, Detective? Lovely as your family home is, we can't stay holed up here very long. I need to head back to Tennessee or at least touch base with Dad."

"You're on vacation, remember?" He ignored her questions and pressed warm kisses along her neck.

She felt his teeth on her ear lobe and shivered. A couple minutes in his arms, and she wanted him again. The hunger increased each time they made love, the need escalating rather than diminishing. His uninhibited desire had given her fragile self-confidence a badly needed boost.

"What better place to spend it than an island paradise with a guy who's crazy for your bod," he added.

"Just a vacation fling with a hottie?" she replied as his mouth sent goose bumps down her spine.

"You think I'm a hottie?"

"Of course, or I wouldn't have bothered to take you to my bed," she parried, tilting her head to give him better access.

"I think you're a hottie too." His mouth found its way to her lips and he nibbled, coaxing for deeper penetration. "I want you again," he whispered.

She didn't think any man had ever wanted her more. Or maybe she hadn't ever wanted one so much. Call it fate or kismet or destiny, they were perfectly in tune with each other.

"You're insatiable."

"Only for you," he swore. "Wanna call it a night?"

"The sun's just setting, and I'm not sleepy."

"Guess we'll have to find something else to do in bed. We're damned good at that, aren't we?"

"Just a couple of hotties," she agreed, running a finger down the five o'clock shadow on his cheek. "But as inventive and distracting as you can be, I still need to call my dad."

"Give me another day to stir up information."

"We already wasted this day."

His seductive tone turned to indignation. He pulled her

across his lap and leveled a frown at her. "Wasted? That's how you describe a day spent with me?"

Keri grinned and cupped her hands around his face. "Sorry if I bruised your ego, Detective. It's certainly been a fascinating day but wasted in the way of furthering our investigation."

"Our investigation?" he prompted.

"We need answers. I want to know what's going on in Thornsbury and if it has anything to do with what happened in Miami this morning." Her tone grew more serious. "The only thing I know for sure is you're the catalyst."

"Which makes it dangerous to be near me," he declared softly.

"So now you think you're going to stash me in paradise while you continue to make a target of yourself?"

He didn't immediately reply. She dropped her hands to the cushions on either side of his head and stared directly into his eyes. His facial expression didn't offer a clue to what he was thinking. Her eyes narrowed, brows furrowing.

"That is your plan, isn't it?"

He finally spoke in a low, steady tone. "It's not a bad plan. You call your dad on a disposable phone and tell him you're sight-seeing. It wouldn't be a lie, and he wouldn't worry about you not returning to the cabin. Meanwhile, you'll be protected and pampered here."

"Only one little tiny problem with the plan, Lamanto," she said as she shoved herself off his chest.

"And what would that be, Merritt?"

"I don't like it."

He sighed heavily as she shifted off his lap.

"Maybe you'd better tell me exactly what you've got planned," she said.

"Keri—" he started, but she swiftly interrupted.

"Don't Keri me in that tone. Where you go, I go. What you do, I do. It's that way or the highway, Detective, so you'd better give me some details."

Nick turned to face her. “It’s not like I have some secret plan. I want to take the speedboat back into the dock after dark and nose around a little. There’s no need for you to go with me.”

“Are you planning to take Brice and Gus?”

“Brice will go with me. Gus’ll stay with you.”

“How about I go with you and Brice while Gus stays here as our backup guy? I’ll keep an eye on the boat while you and Brice investigate whatever you want to investigate.”

Nick went quiet for a few long seconds, and then said, “The only way you go is if you go with a bodyguard besides me. We’ll both have backups, okay?”

“And do what? Make out in the boat so we won’t look suspicious?”

“You wanna make out with Gus?”

“I could make out with you while Brice and Gus investigate,” she argued. “We could even do that from your bedroom upstairs.”

“I’m not sending them to do my work,” he insisted stubbornly. His darkened gaze locked with hers.

She could be just as stubborn. “Then we all go.”

After heaving a frustrated sigh, Nick rose from the glider and offered her a hand. “We’ll do it your way, except for the making out with Gus bit.”

Keri took his hand and stood. “What time do we leave?”

“About the same time we left the *Adrianna* this morning. I want to see who’s snooping around the docks at that hour.”

She put her arms around his neck and pressed her body tightly against his. He slipped his hands around her waist and tugged her closer. Despite their difference of opinion, as soon as their bodies touched, the simmering passion re-ignited.

“I guess that gives us a few hours to kill,” she said, pressing her lips to his. That’s all it took to light a fire, their disagreement forgotten as desire flared. Nick held her while they watched an amazing sunset and then led her back to his bedroom.

Hours later, Keri watched him as he slept in his big, tousled bed. Despite some very strenuous sex, she couldn't sleep. Her mind wouldn't stop whirling and her emotions churned along with it. Moonlight filtered into the room through half-drawn drapes at the balcony doors. A cool breeze fluttered the sheers at the windows. One small lamp illuminated the wall opposite the bed.

As she looked around his childhood bedroom, she saw the signs of a happy, healthy teen growing into manhood. The bookshelves held popular teenage titles as well as true crime and college text books. Sports trophies mingled with photos of his family and friends.

Wearing only a tank top and panties, she slipped quietly out of bed and crossed the room. A picture of Nick's family sat on the bureau. He wore a cap and gown while his parents beamed with pride. His mother looked slim, attractive and very sophisticated. His dad had a full head of thick white hair, a thickening waist and a twinkle in his eyes.

Sonia and Sophie had been in their tween years and looked alike, but she didn't know which was which. Though she hadn't actually slept in Maria's bed, she recognized his oldest sister from photos in her room. Liz was shorter and more full-figured. All Nick's siblings had inherited dark hair, eyes and complexions.

She knew from a casual conversation he wanted a big family too. Lots of little additions to the Lamanto brood, he'd said with a laugh. He just hadn't found the right woman to be their mother. Keri thought he'd make a good father if he'd give up the police work. Getting shot at by thugs didn't factor into the raising of children, in her opinion.

One thing she knew for certain, she had no chance of being that woman. The car wreck two years ago had crushed her abdomen and destroyed her reproductive system. She wouldn't be conceiving, carrying or bringing anyone's children into the world. Everyone back in Thornsbury knew about it, of course.

The news had created a ten-day gossip fest back then, but she hadn't seen a need to mention it to Nick.

Setting the photo back on the bureau, Keri wondered what his family would think of her and if she'd like them. They looked friendly and good-natured, but most people did when they posed for pictures. She wondered about his brothers-in-law, nieces and nephews. Did they all share the Italian heritage? Not that it really mattered. She wouldn't be around long enough to meet them. They were strangers indulging in a brief affair. That's all she and Nick meant to each other. She'd thought their differences, country girl versus city boy, would be too much of a hurdle for any relationship to survive.

Now that she knew more of his background and his family's incredible wealth, she knew they had no chance for a future. Their lifestyle differences had shifted from diverse to poles apart. When he did marry, it would probably be to a woman from his own social set. One with a perfect, unscarred, child-bearing Italian body.

She'd always wanted children, but she'd come to terms with the fact she'd never have any of her own. Still, it hurt. It made her sad to think of leaving him too, but she needed to make the break before she fell more deeply in love. Each time he smiled at her, teased her or made love to her, he stole a little more of her soul.

After turning off the small lamp, she moved back to the bed and snuggled up to his warm body. He immediately reached out and drew her close. Keri laid her head on his chest and listened to the steady beat of his heart, wondering if it was already too late to salvage her own.

Dressed in jeans and dark hooded sweatshirts, Nick and Keri met the bodyguards at the boathouse just after three a.m. They untied and boarded the family's speedboat. She'd thought it might be crowded with all four of them, but the streamlined craft had plenty of room.

Brice drove with Gus as navigator while Nick tucked her

beside him on a narrow bench. They traveled slowly through the water to avoid a strong wake or spray. The big engine hummed softly as they made their way inland.

"The air must be really clear tonight because the stars look extra bright," said Nick.

"The moon and stars really are beautiful. I hate to think about evil goons with guns and explosives. Why is it that men aren't satisfied unless they're waging some kind of war?"

Nick's reply came swiftly. "Brice can take you back to the villa."

"No," she responded just as swiftly and succinctly.

"Okay then."

The wealth of resignation in his tone made her smile. She knew he wanted to protect her and keep her safe. She'd dealt with the sentiment all her life. Mostly she appreciated the caring and concern, but sometimes she thought any more would surely suffocate her. Just another reason she needed to guard her heart.

When she'd made her vacation plans, she'd never imagined how much it would complicate her life. She couldn't regret meeting Nick and spending time with him, or getting a glimpse of the luxurious Gianovelli world. The hard part now would be figuring when and how to go home.

Home brought thoughts of the cabin, the militia and her family. Something bad had to be brewing in the mountains. Did Russ and his cohorts plan to keep their activities local or did they hope to expand? Worse yet, did they plan to attack someone or something on a grand scale? Could they really want to kill or injure masses of innocent people? What cause could possibly warrant that sort of terrorism?

"I need to get another disposable phone so I can check in with the lieutenant and you can call your dad," said Nick as the lights of the harbor gradually changed from fairy-dust size to a sparkling crown of jewels.

"I have to decide what I'm telling my dad. He knows I'm not big on shopping, so that story won't fly any longer."

"Visiting old college roommates?" Nick suggested.

"Too easy to verify."

"Didn't you say you visited Lauderdale on spring break once? You could tell him you wanted some beach time and headed to the coast."

"He'll want specifics. Where are you? Who's with you? How long will you be gone? It's the story of my life."

"He loves you."

"Yeah.

"You can pretend to have really bad phone reception. Lots of static and interference."

She'd thought of leaving a message on the home answering machine during their work shift, but they rotated weekends. Hard to tell who'd be hanging around the house on a Saturday.

"If I wait much longer, Dad'll have an APB out for me."

"You're sure he knows you didn't return to the cabin?"

"No doubt in my mind." Between Russ and her extended family, someone would be reporting to her dad.

"Maybe just hearing from you will pacify him right now."

Keri nodded. When he started demanding details, she'd give him her *I'm a big girl, don't baby me* attitude. That should reassure him.

As they neared the bay, she felt Nick withdrawing both physically and mentally. He reached to the back of his waist and checked his gun, refocusing on his investigation. Yet another trait she'd lived with her whole life—the ability to concentrate on the job in exclusion of all else.

She'd once asked her mother how she could stand it. The family would attend a school or community function and her dad would zone out on them. Her mother had smiled and said his dedication made her proud, and the benefits of loving such a man outweighed minor annoyances.

Now Keri understood a little better. She appreciated Nick's commitment to get to the truth. This case had impacted him personally and professionally. He'd taken a bullet and lost a home. Not small sacrifices.

Despite the early morning hour, lights sparkled on the water and illuminated the bay. Keri watched as Brice expertly maneuvered the boat through the inlet to reach Miamarina. A thick haze rose from the water, shrouding the row of slips along the dock. She felt Nick tense as they approached the burned out shell of the *Adrianna.*

When they eased closer, he handed her a pair of binoculars. Lifting them to her face, she got her first experience with night-vision. The glasses cut through the fog and darkness to bring the *Adrianna* into clear focus.

Not that she could see much. Yellow police tape draped the carcass, giving it a ghoulish appearance. Most everything above water had burned or melted. An empty hull gently bobbed on the waves of their wake.

They didn't linger near the destroyed cabin cruiser. No more than any other curiosity seeker might do. Keri shifted her gaze from the destruction to the parking lot above it. She quickly zoomed in on a vehicle that looked just like hers, only undamaged.

"Is that my SUV?"

Nick swung his glasses in the same direction. "Yeah, Gus arranged for it to be repaired, repainted and brought back to the lot. We took the liberty of giving it Florida tags so your out-of-state ones wouldn't draw attention. The Tennessee tags are under the backseat."

"How in the world did he get all that accomplished in one day? On a weekend, no less."

He didn't immediately respond, but the answer came to Keri as soon as she'd posed the question. "I guess the Gianovelli name gets results where others wouldn't have a hope."

"That's about the size of it."

He didn't sound too happy about it. She wondered why. Maybe for the same reason she'd always used her family's name and reputation with reluctance. She didn't approve of nepotism. She'd always wanted to make her own way, but circumstances sometimes warranted extra influence.

"Thanks."

Nick shot a quick glance at her as if he didn't trust his hearing. His voice softened in his reply. "You're welcome. I'm sorry it got messed up in the first place."

"I know," she said. "Whose Florida tags are on it? They can't be traced to your family, can they?"

His tone hardened. "The tags are from a rental agency the police department uses on occasion. I've never involved my family in any traceable fashion. They're not even listed as next of kin on my personnel files."

Until now and for her. He didn't say the words but they hung between them. She couldn't bear to think he'd endangered his family by trying to protect her. They'd all be safer when she went home.

Brice slowly guided the speedboat past a dozen or so slips and then eased them into the Gianovelli family spot they'd vacated yesterday. Nick jumped to the dock to secure the ropes as the engine rumbled to a halt.

Keri grasped the edge of her seat to steady herself and rose to her feet. She kept the binoculars trained on the parking lot and dock. Two men with fishing poles and tackle boxes walked toward a boat close to the marina. Farther down the dock, at a fueling station, an employee appeared to be opening the door of the business.

"See anything suspicious?" Nick asked as he rejoined her, lifting his glasses to his face.

She'd agreed to stay with Gus, but they'd have his back from a distance. A lot of good that would do if someone decided to shoot at him again.

"Just the same things I saw yesterday morning."

"Brice and I are going to look around the *Adrianna* first. Then we'll try to find the night watchman who patrols this time of day. Maybe he saw something after we left yesterday. We won't be long. I want to head back to the island before it gets too busy here."

"Okay," she said, lowering the glasses long enough to accept the kiss he aimed at her mouth.

The boat rocked as they disembarked. Keri steadied herself and Gus came to stand near her. He put a hand under her arm for support but quickly dropped it once she'd found her legs. Then he picked up Nick's binoculars and they both watched the dock.

She got briefly distracted when her gaze drifted to Nick's retreating form. The man had gorgeous written all over him from the front, side and the rear. In his tight, well-worn jeans, he oozed sex appeal. It wouldn't be easy to walk away when the time came.

In a matter of minutes, the two men had walked halfway to the marina. When they grew too small in her magnified vision, she secured the binoculars around her neck and jumped from the boat to the dock.

"Miss!" Gus hissed and quickly followed.

She tightened the hood around her head and offered him reassurance. "I'm not going to follow them to the *Adrianna*, but I want to keep them in sight. Otherwise, we're not much of a backup team, are we?"

She couldn't see his features in the dim light, but she didn't care if he disapproved. Short of physically restraining her, he didn't have any option but to follow her lead. He fell into step beside her, and she lifted the binoculars back to her face. He did the same.

They slowed their steps as Nick and Brice neared the *Adrianna*. Keri had a good view of them as they split up and approached the boat from opposite sides. The next instant, they heard shouting and Gus dragged her behind his broad body. It took a minute to regain her footing and then an exchange of gunfire shattered the early morning stillness.

Gus shoved her into the hull of a nearby sailboat and shielded her with his body. When she'd righted herself again, all she could see was a lone man racing toward the parking lot.

She raised her binoculars to her eyes and tried to focus on the moving target. A big black car appeared near her SUV, the man jumped in, and the car sped out of the lot, tires squealing.

In the next instant, Keri shoved her way past Gus and started running, covering the fifty or so yards in record time and flying straight into Nick's arms.

"I'm fine," he assured her as he wrapped her in a tight embrace and rocked her gently. Then the softness in his tone hardened with annoyance and he set her away from him. "Why the hell didn't you stay on the boat like we agreed? Gus?" he glared at the other man.

"Don't yell at Gus. I may be small but I'm way faster than most men. And I do have a mind of my own."

Nick shook his head, and gave her his hard-ass detective stare. She stared right back with her most intimidating trauma nurse glare.

"What happened?" she finally asked, breaking the tense silence and shifting out of his arms.

"We flushed out a rat," he said.

"Did you recognize him?"

"Yeah, he's the other cop who saw Reggie McDowell commit murder. He has to be on the take. I need to tell Alexander, but I wish to hell I knew who's paying him."

"I might be able to help there," she said, garnering the full attention of all three men. "I saw a logo on the door of the car."

"I didn't see anything but black," said Brice. "Not even an interior light when the door opened."

Gus shook his head.

"I had binoculars and there's a small logo on the passenger door. It's Cooper Caskets. I've seen the logo on their vans when they deliver caskets to the Moville mortuary in Thornsbury."

"Damn," Nick swore softly. He grabbed her again and hugged her tightly. "A casket company. That's how they transported the stuff for so long without drawing attention."

"That's the connection," they said in unison.

Chapter Fifteen

Across town, in a well-lit gated community, Harold Cooper made the final lap in his five-mile jog. Lungs and legs burning from exertion, he took a seat on the marble bench in his carefully manicured lawn. Inhaling deeply, he drew heavy, moisture-laden air into his body and exhaled toxins.

He hated jogging. Always had, but he applied willpower over excuses and weakness. He believed a man should stay fit and active. By jogging before the start of his business day, he could get his exercise, avoid other sweaty people and quickly shower off the disgusting body odor. Besides, he didn't tolerate sun on his skin. He prided himself on being a white man and had no desire to change the color of his skin.

He exercised because a man needed strength and fortitude to deal with life's stresses. His father had frequently told him a businessman had to deal with a lot of unpleasantness to be a success. Well, there was no doubting his success. Besides the multi-million-dollar home where he lived, he also owned hundreds of acres of prime Florida ranchland and one of the finest casket companies in the country.

A frown creased his brow as he thought of his father and all the changes he'd seen since his death. They'd shared so many traits and secrets. His father had introduced him into the society of White Supremists at an early age. They'd shared the passion and pride in their heritage.

In the family business, they'd had to allow for change. Society forced them to accept all religions and nationalities. More change came every year as more and more immigrants filtered into the country, changing the complexion of people at work, in their schools and even the churches.

It made him sick to his stomach. Mabel, his wife of thirty years, had understood the pressure of success. She'd commiserated with him when he had to smile and shake hands with people he despised. She'd kept him sane in an increasingly insane world.

He'd lost Mabel shortly after terrorists attacked the twin towers on 9-11. He held all Muslims responsible for the heart attack his wife suffered that same day. He knew she'd died because she didn't want to live in a desegregated society any longer. The America they loved and life as they knew it had irrevocably changed that day.

Sometimes, he wished he'd gone with her. He'd grown tired of it all too. The only thing that had kept him alive was his plan to avenge her death. It had taken a lot of time, patience and money, but he'd know satisfaction soon. Someone had to pay for the loss of his wife and the purity of their existence.

As he started to rise from the bench, the cell phone in his pocket vibrated. The only person who had the number was Raymond McDowell. Harold refused to call him by the ridiculous nickname of Knifer. Mongrel would be a better description of the mixed-heritage thug. Just another of the disgusting people he had to deal with to obtain his goal.

"Cooper here," he said into the phone.

"This is Knifer. We got a prob."

Harold closed his eyes in exasperation. The man sounded like gangster, and he never called unless they had a problem. Too many lately.

"What this time?"

"Me and Detective Jenson just left the marina where that other cop was supposed to have fried. Didn't happen."

"What didn't happen?"

"Lamanto didn't burn to death. He jumped Jenson when we was there checkin' out the boat we blowed up yesterday."

Harold closed his eyes and sighed. It hurt his head just to listen to McDowell talk. Every report from the man gave him stress-induced indigestion.

"Lamanto saw Jenson?"

"Yeah. It was dark but we figure he still got a good enough look to ID him."

After a brief hesitation, Harold said, "Then it's time to cut all connections with the police department." He hoped he didn't have to spell out his instructions, especially over a cell phone.

"Jenson went into the convenience store for coffee. Want I should put him on the phone when he gets back?"

"No. I have nothing to say to the detective. He's no longer of any importance to our mission. Just listen carefully and do exactly as I say." Harold spoke slowly and concisely, so there'd be no confusion. "I want you to eliminate Jenson permanently and make sure his body is never found."

A pulse throbbed in his temper, the beginning of a headache as he waited for McDowell's response. He wished them both dead, but he still needed a driver stupid enough to haul volatile explosives over rough country roads.

McDowell's voice went low, his words no-doubt mumbled through a mouthful of smokeless tobacco. "That's an expensive order, ya know."

"I know the price, and you know I'm good for it. Once it's done, your payment will be waiting in cash."

"We could sure use the extra dough. Reggie's got legal bills."

Harold locked his jaw. He couldn't begin to describe his frustration at Reggie McDowell's arrest for murder. The older brother's stupidity at such a delicate stage in his plans had enraged him. He'd thought Reggie the dependable one, but he refrained from commenting.

After a short pause, Raymond asked, "Killin' a cop will cost ya extra."

"You didn't kill the other one."

Harold assumed the next long pause was due to the fact that Raymond couldn't think very fast.

"I reckon you're right, but we did blow up his boat. Here comes Jenson now. You'll leave the payment at the usual drop spot? It'll be there when I get back from the mission?"

"Yes. I expected you to be on your way to Tennessee by now."

"I was all set to leave when Jenson called this morning. He wanted me to take him past the marina in case somebody recognized his car."

"So you drove my van to the marina?" Harold felt the blood pounding in his ears.

McDowell was slow to answer. "It was pitch-dark out there. I reckon it don't matter now anyways. I'll do Jenson and make sure the body don't get found, then I'll get the van out of town, pronto."

"When you dispose of the body, dispose of the phone too. Don't just toss it in the trash somewhere. Make sure it's totally destroyed. This will be our final communication. You need to get to Thornsbury today, get the van loaded and get your final orders from my partners there."

"Sure thing. It's been a pleasure takin' your money," he said with a chuckle.

Harold didn't see the humor. He snapped the phone shut, hoping he never had to speak to the mongrel again.

The gunshots at the marina had brought people running from every direction, so Gus hustled Keri back to the yacht. She didn't argue, not wanting to be recognized or questioned, but she waited impatiently for the excitement to settle.

The sun had risen high over the water by the time Nick and Brice rejoined them. Brice jumped aboard and went straight to the driver's seat. Nick cast off the ropes and hopped on to the boat as the engines flared to life.

"Nick! What the hell?" she asked, trying to maintain her balance as they pulled from the dock. "Why are we leaving now and where are we going?"

"Back to the island," he said, gathering the mooring ropes and securing them in the bottom of the boat.

"I need to call my dad."

"We need to regroup before we make any calls."

"Regroup how?" she demanded.

He took hold of her arm and guided her to the bench. She sat beside him but didn't stop questioning him.

"What else did you find out? Did you call your lieutenant?"

"I talked to the night watchman. He said he noticed you and me leaving in the early hours yesterday. Then he saw a man return to the boat. He was about my height and size so he thought I'd taken a date home and returned. He heard the explosion a short time later."

Keri wondered if the watchman saw a lot of women coming and going from Nick's boat, but she put the question on the back burner while she bombarded him with others.

"And you recognized the cop who shot at you? He's the dirty cop in your department? With your height and build? Did you get a new phone to call your boss?"

"Yes to all that. I called Alexander and told him about Jenson. I doubt he'll show his face at the precinct. He'll be lucky if he doesn't end up in the bottom of the bay. He sold his soul to the devil, and then screwed up, so his life isn't worth shit."

"If something happens to him, you'll be the only witness against the McDowell guy?"

"Yeah."

"So you're planning to stay at the villa for a while?"

Nick went quiet and a weird shiver ran down Keri's spine. "You're not planning to stay hidden, are you?" she asked, suspicion coloring her tone. "What exactly is the new plan?"

"Alexander is getting in touch with McDowell's lawyer. Now that we know Cooper is involved, we're betting he's the money man as well as the mastermind. The lieutenant said he owns several big farms, so it wouldn't be hard for him to stockpile extra fertilizer like they use for bombs. McDowell is probably responsible for buying the illegal firearms."

"Has he confessed to any of it?"

"Not yet, but McDowell doesn't have the finances or the smarts for a big operation. We're hoping he'll give up more details to save his own ass."

"And what then?"

"Then we shut down the whole damned operation."

"Including the militia camp in Thornsbury?"

"Sure, if we get proof of the connection."

"And your Lieutenant Alexander will be coordinating this with my dad's department?"

Nick just returned her steady gaze without responding. She narrowed her eyes and her tone got grim. "You have no intention of coordinating with Dad, do you?"

His frustrated sigh annoyed her as much as his next words. "I'm sorry, Keri, but we're not sure he can be trusted."

"I *know* he can be trusted."

"Think about it from my viewpoint, sweetheart. That compound is on Merritt land. Your family either has to be involved or turning a blind eye. Either way we risk the whole operation if we include them in our plans."

She let his words sink in a moment, trying to be impartial, but she knew her dad and brother too well to accept his reasoning.

"Believe what you want, but I want Brice to turn this boat around and take me back to the marina. And I want my car keys. Now."

Nick returned her unflinching stare with one of his own. "It's not gonna happen, babe."

A host of emotions hit Keri—hurt and betrayal, but mostly pure, unadulterated anger.

"So you're kidnapping me, which is a federal offense, I remind you. Now who's operating outside the law? You plan to keep me imprisoned at the villa while you and your team attack my family and home. All in the name of justice? Because you're not sure the Merritts are trustworthy?"

"Forget the kidnapping crap," he said, standing to put distance between them. Then he turned back to her. "You came with us willingly and nobody in their right mind would consider spending time at the villa an imprisonment."

"I'm in my right mind," she challenged, tone and body stiff with tension. "I just don't believe the results are more important than the method."

Nick ran a hand through his hair in frustration. "Be reasonable, sweetheart. You're not trained in law enforcement. We can't take you with us and we can't let you go home. You won't have to stay at the villa long. Just trust me on this."

Keri waited several heartbeats before responding. "Trust is a two-way street."

He moved close again and reached for her, but she shifted out of his reach. His expression went grim. "You know I trust you. With my life. But I won't risk your life, and I can't risk you alerting anyone in Thornsbury. They have too formidable an arsenal at the camp. They could destroy most of the county or just destroy the evidence and start up somewhere new."

She stared at him a moment longer and stopped arguing. During her lifetime, she'd wasted far too much time and energy trying to reason with overprotective, all-knowing males. She pulled her legs up to her chest and wrapped her arms around them, turning her attention to the passing scenery.

They passed Millionaire Row, yet she barely noticed the glitz and glamour. Paradise had lost its appeal. The wild beauty of the bay had dimmed. Whatever Nick had planned from here on out didn't include her and that worked both ways. She'd wondered how she could make a break from him, but she needn't have worried. He'd solved the problem for her. He'd made it easy for her to declare her independence—emotionally, at least, if not physically.

Keri didn't speak to any of them as they disembarked at the island. She ignored the hand Nick offered her and jumped to the dock. The men started discussing lunch since it was past noon already. She headed straight for the villa and straight upstairs to Maria's room.

Once there, she stripped and took a long, hot shower. When she'd finished and towel-dried her hair, she pulled on clean panties and the tank top she'd worn earlier. Then she climbed into bed and pulled the sheet over her head.

Nick came to the room a short while later, asking if she wanted something to eat. She pretended to be sleeping, telling herself to start cutting him out of her life. After another hour or so, physical exhaustion finally won over temper, and she slept. She dreamed troubled dreams, reliving the night of the wreck as she had many times over the years.

She remembered waking at her mother's scream, the car rocking on the guard rail and a man approaching the car. A man her mother recognized and trusted, who'd done nothing to stop the car from careening into the ravine. As always, the identity of the mysterious man eluded her.

The sound of the door opening and Nick speaking her name roused her hours later. Keri pulled back the sheet and blinked at the late-afternoon sunlight pouring into the room. She glanced at the bedside clock, realizing she'd slept most of the day. She'd obviously needed sleep.

"You okay?" asked Nick.

She didn't respond but sat up, tugged at the twisted tank top and squinted at him.

"Sorry to wake you. I thought you'd be getting hungry. We ate already, but there's plenty in the kitchen."

Keri ran her hands through her hair and ignored him. Nick closed the door and moved farther into the room.

"Look, I know you're pissed and you don't want me protecting you. I get it, but there's a lot more at stake than your personal loyalties."

Keri refused to even honor that statement with a response. What meaning did life hold without loyalties? If faith in your family held no importance, what would? They really did live in different worlds.

He didn't get too close but tossed a cell phone on the bed. "Call your dad. Tell him you're okay. Just don't tell him anything else."

She reached over and picked up the phone, a new wave of fury rushing through her body. First he held her against her will, and now he wanted to manipulate her a little more. Apparently he didn't even respect her intelligence.

Drawing back her arm, she hurled the phone at him with all her strength. She'd never had a very good aim, but she managed to graze the corner of his forehead. His expression went from shocked to furious and that tempered her temper.

Nick started toward her and then checked himself.

She taunted. "A little angry, are you? Seething and wishing you could slap some sense into me? Well now you know exactly how I feel!"

He picked up the phone, walked out the door and slammed it hard. She threw herself back against the pillows. Tears welled in her eyes but she swiped at them impatiently. Her stomach growled. She ignored it too. Rested and with renewed energy, she needed to formulate her own plan of action.

Deciding to keep busy until dark, Keri hopped out of bed and started cleaning. She returned the bath and bedroom to immaculate condition. The ultrafeminine décor and pastel colors of Maria's suite didn't suit her personal tastes, but it couldn't be faulted for good taste and cleanliness.

Next she sorted through the clothes she'd brought to the island until she found the only outfit that belonged to her. Some super-efficient soul had laundered her ER nurse T-shirt and favorite jeans. Probably didn't want bomb residue dirtying the place, she thought spitefully.

After dressing in her own things, she made a neat pile of the clothes Nick had bought. He could give them to the next woman he held hostage. Her pocket book was the only thing she planned to take when she left the island. Her stomach growled again, and she searched the bag for food. She always carried energy bars and chocolate in case of emergencies. He should have confiscated her big tote.

Mistake number one, Detective.

A search for her cell phone came up empty, so she dumped the bag on the floor, sorted through the contents twice and then swore profusely. No phone meant Nick had confiscated it while she slept. The dog. The villa didn't have a landline, so she couldn't sneak a call. That ruled out contacting anyone by computer too.

Her wallet still held a little cash, a debit card and her driver's license. She tucked them in her back pocket along with the spare key to her SUV. She didn't know how to get off the island, but once she did, she'd need money and identification.

Next Keri decided to do a little recon. She knew someone would be guarding the boathouse, so she'd just have to outwit the men. They might have physical strength on their side, but she'd spent her lifetime mentally sparring with smart men.

Another thought popped into her mind. Had Nick locked her in the room? She quickly checked and just as quickly slipped into the hallway. He probably hadn't bothered to lock the door because he didn't think she had anywhere to go.

Mistake number two, Detective.

One thing for certain, even if she didn't leave the island, they'd have a hell of a time finding her again. In a house this size, there had to be hundreds of great hiding places. She just had to stay one step ahead of them.

Feeling something of a voyeur, Keri moved from bedroom suite to bedroom suite, familiarizing herself with the layout of the house. This floor also had a small chapel, a library and a huge recreation room. In it, she found fitness equipment, a billiard table and media center.

A wall of glass faced the sea and offered a gorgeous view of sky and water. She took a minute to enjoy the sheer beauty of it as the orange of the setting sun glistened on the deep blue of the ocean. Then she quietly opened the French doors to step onto the balcony. The sound of voices drew her closer to the railing until she stood directly over the patio.

She strained to hear their conversation but could only catch the occasional word. Brice mentioned *hungry* and Nick replied something about *temper*. Their shared laughter had her gritting her teeth.

Her brother loved to say, "Don't get mad, get even."

The ring of a telephone had her holding her breath and listening intently. Nick answered, excused himself and moved closer to her. She heard him addressing Lieutenant Alexander. Now she could hear better but only one side of the conversation.

"Did you talk to McDowell's lawyer?"

Damn, she wished she could hear Alexander's reply. Next Nick mentioned someone named Paulson and then the dirty cop, Jenson. He made a few grunts in response to whatever the lieutenant said, and she heard him ask about the ATF.

ATF? The Department of Alcohol, Tobacco and Firearms? What did they have to do with anything? *Oh, the gun trafficking,* she thought. Then she heard him mention Homeland Security. What in the world did they think the Thornsbury militia had planned? They intended to organize a multi-organizational attack without contacting her dad. She understood, to a point, but still resented the fact that Nick totally disregarded her judgment.

Her dad despised bigotry of any kind. Her mom had worked in the Peace Corps and taught them to respect all nationalities of people. They'd preached the right to religious freedom and beliefs even if you couldn't understand them. Her parents and brother loathed anti-Semitism sentiments and terrorist actions against innocent people.

Keri knew with every fiber of her being they couldn't be involved with whatever the militia had planned. They wouldn't turn a blind eye to illegal activities if they had knowledge and proof. Maybe they didn't know how dangerous the militia had gotten. They'd avoided the mountains since her mom's death. Which, she supposed, gave Russ and his military fanatics the perfect opportunity to thrive.

Nick's voice started to recede again, and she only caught a couple more words—*later* and *chopper.*

Aha! They'd be leaving by helicopter, not boat. She had to find the helicopter pad on the roof. She needed to get to it before the men. Hopefully she wouldn't run into any of them on the top floor.

It took awhile, but she wound around the halls to the central staircase, passing through the second story without encountering anyone. The villa didn't have an attic, just a small top floor with doors opening on to the rooftop.

Expecting a small, two-seat chopper, it surprised her to find a really large one. Perfect for big families or hauling supplies, she supposed. The shiny red whirlybird had to be the top of the line in the 'copter world. It had the name Gianovelli emblazoned on the side.

Keri hurried toward it to check the doors, happy to find them unlocked. She jumped into the cockpit and studied the control panel. During her teenage years, she'd begged her dad for flying lessons and learned a little about piloting a plane before her interest waned.

No way would she try to fly this bird, but a quick look behind the passenger compartment showed plenty of storage space. Turnabout's fair play, she told herself. Nick had used her to get out of Thornsbury.

A more thorough search unearthed a tarp. She could easily hide under it. With Brice and Nick up front and nobody in the second row of seats, they'd never realize they had a stowaway.

"Another mistake, Detective," she whispered. "That's three strikes."

Chapter Sixteen

An hour later, Brice expertly landed the helicopter near a row of police choppers and shut down the engine. While the noise and vibration slowly settled, Nick pulled the earphones off his head and turned to his friend. He yelled above the fading noise of the blades.

"Thanks, Brice. I know hauling me around isn't part of your job description, but I appreciate the help."

"No problem," said the other man. "Breaks up the boredom while your folks are gone."

"Want to come in for coffee before you fly back to the island?'

"I've had enough coffee for the night, but I'd better make a pit stop before I take off again."

They jumped from the chopper and locked the doors as the propellers came to a slow halt. Nick didn't see anyone as they started walking toward the back entrance of the police station. Most of the day shift had gone. Due to budget cuts, the night shift had a lot fewer people on staff.

He did notice a few ATF vehicles parked in the lot.

When they entered the building, he pointed Brice in the direction of the bathroom. Moving farther into the reception area, he spoke to several fellow officers. They exchanged handshakes and small talk as he studied the unfamiliar faces mingling with familiar ones. After a few minutes, he saw Alexander, a tall, heavy man with a receding hairline and weather-worn features.

The older man separated himself from a group and came to meet him. "Good to have you back in one piece, Lamanto." His tone and expression held genuine warmth.

They shook hands, and Alexander gave him a welcoming slap on his shoulder.

"Good to be here in one piece, Lieutenant."

"How's the shoulder? I didn't just pound on it, did I?" he asked, dropping his hands and frowning.

"No," Nick reassured. "It's my left, and it's better now."

"You're gonna give this old man a heart attack if we don't get the McDowell mess cleared up soon."

"I hear ya," said Nick. "What's happenin'? Did you learn anything more from McDowell?"

"The feds made a deal with him. He couldn't give them the name of the head man in Tennessee, but he spilled on the plan in hopes of getting immunity from terrorism charges. He tried to get out of the murder wrap too, but since we already knew about Cooper and Jenson, he lost some of his bargaining power."

"What about Jenson? Is he on the same payroll? Any word from him since he shot at me on the dock yesterday morning? He has to know he's been made."

Renewed anger surged through Nick as he remembered how close he and Keri had come to being victims. He had no doubt that Jenson's greed had cost him the *Adrianna*.

"Nobody's seen or heard from Jenson since your shootout yesterday. We don't even have a valid address in his files. Since his divorce a couple years ago, he's spent a lot of time drinking and gambling. He fell behind in child support and got evicted from his last known address."

"Stressors, to be sure. Any proof he's on the take?"

"We dug into his personal finances and found a mountain of debts he recently paid. I hate to think he's on the take, but it's pretty obvious he's getting money from someone. If and when we track him down, he's got a lot to answer for. You never want to believe one of your team could stoop to murdering cops and domestic terrorism."

"So when and where is the attack planned?"

"It's scheduled to go down on 9-11."

Nick whistled softly. "Damn, that's Tuesday, we're cuttin' it really short. What's the target?"

"The target's a mosque in western Virginia. They'll have to start moving off the mountain soon. Best guess is they'll be using one of the casket vans filled with bomb material. Rig it to drive directly into the building. McDowell says the militia will follow at a distance, but launch a second attack on survivors and rescue teams."

"Pretty damned bold move. They must all be suicidal."

"You got that right. These aren't backwoods terrorists. They're dedicated fanatics."

"What's our plan?"

"We don't have one. It's out of our hands now. The ATF is in charge of the operation in conjunction with Homeland Security. The FBI could be involved too, before it's done. They've agreed to let you ride along if you want because you know the lay of the land."

Before Nick could reply, a stranger approached them. Alexander introduced him as ATF commander, John Samuels. He shook hands with the big, brawny man as they briefly searched each other's expressions.

"A pleasure, Lamanto," said Samuels. "We've been trying to pin down the Miami-Tennessee connection for months. Your identification of Cooper pulled it all together just in time."

"I can't take all the credit for that," he said, thinking of Keri's invaluable help. "What I can't figure is why we were able to ID one of Cooper's vehicles in the first place. Why would he send one to the marina?"

Samuels shook his head, "Doesn't make sense. He's been planning for months, maybe years, and this is the first time we can trace a mistake back to him."

"I might have the answer to that," said Alexander. "Reggie McDowell said his brother Raymond, nicknamed Knifer, is doing a lot of Cooper's driving. I guess that's about the only thing he does right. Cooper probably didn't know he made that early morning run."

"Are you planning to pick Cooper up for questioning?" asked Nick.

"We can't risk having him pull the plug at this point. We need to put a permanent stop to it and get these people behind bars," said Samuels. "We'll keep round-the-clock watch on him until we have the others in custody."

Nick nodded in understanding. "I'll be happy to see it resolved on our end."

"They will be on the Thornsbury end too," Samuels surprised him by saying. "Our man there is fightin' mad and ready to kick some ass."

"You have someone undercover in Thornsbury?" News to him. "Don Monroe?" Why wouldn't Don have told him about the ATF connection? It didn't make sense. "You know he's in critical condition, don't you?"

Samuels shook his head. "I'm not at liberty to share our man's identity, but I did hear Monroe's doing okay. His injuries weren't as bad as they first thought. The bullet didn't hit any vital organs. A blow to the head required a drug-induced coma, but he's doing okay. The hospital released him a couple days ago."

"Glad to hear it," said Nick, wondering if Don had made any attempt to find out who had shot at them. Even more, if he'd had any luck.

His thoughts drifted to the trauma team who had helped Don, and especially Keri. An image of her popped into his mind, but not as a nurse. He visualized her sleepy-eyed, tousled and dressed in a tank top that outlined her breasts and tight, sensitive nipples. He got hard just thinking about it yet he couldn't get the picture out of his mind.

"Lamanto?"

Nick felt heat crawl up his neck as Alexander demanded his attention. Damn Keri, her beautiful body and his inability to get her out of his head. He'd never let another woman interfere with his work. There'd never been one who affected him so intimately. He wasn't pleased that one little spitfire could shatter his attention and divide his loyalties. He had to forget her until all risks to her home had been eliminated.

For the next few minutes, Samuels introduced him to his officers and a couple of men from Homeland Security. They decided to move to the conference room for more privacy. Alexander led the way.

"Hey, Nick, a minute please."

He turned to see Brice motioning from the doorway then excused himself for a minute.

"What's up? You headed back to the island?"

"I just got a call from Gus. Thought you'd want to know, he can't find Keri."

"What?" Annoyed, but not really worried, his expression tightened. "She's messin' with him. She has to be hiding somewhere on the island."

The security man shook his head. "I don't think so. He said Teresa and Tiko helped him search ever since we left. They even brought out Luther. He followed her scent all around the villa and dragged them clear up to the roof."

"The roof?" said Nick. Tiko's hound dog Luther could track anything, anywhere, anytime. He didn't make mistakes, so what the hell?

Then it hit him.

Brushing past Brice, he raced out of the station, across the parking lot and to the helicopter. He found the passenger door unlocked.

"You unlock this?" he turned and asked as Brice caught up with him.

"No."

"I know I locked it when we went inside."

A quick search unearthed a tarp and the faint smell of Keri. "Well I'll be damned—smartass-outsmarted, double-damned. She came with us." He shoved himself out the door, stood on the side-step and did a sweeping, visual search of the parking lot. Dark except for a few scattered pole-lights, he couldn't see anything moving. The streets were mostly deserted too. No sign of her.

"She has to be long gone," said Brice. "My bet she took off as soon as we went into the building. She wouldn't stay close, would she?"

Nick's reply held a grim note. "I doubt it." She was royally pissed at him and wouldn't ask for his help under the best of conditions.

Keri, alone at night, on the streets of a strange city without a cell phone or transportation. His chest tightened. He should never have assumed she'd accept his orders without a fight. How could he have been so damned careless?

"Did she leave her big pocketbook at the villa?" It held a collection of survival tools.

"Gus said it's there, but her driver's license is missing. There's no cash, phone or credit card, either."

Nick shook his head, amazed and furious yet reluctantly proud of her resourcefulness. He damned well wouldn't underestimate her again. When that woman got mad, she might pout and throw a temper tantrum, but she didn't concede defeat. He should have known. He touched the tender spot on his head, evidence of her fiery temper. The vision of her in his bed popped up again, but he shoved it out of his mind.

His Keri was a fighter, and he fell deeper in love every moment he knew her. Love. The concept tightened his throat. He loved her even if he found her annoying as hell sometimes. The depth of the love sharpened his concern. He had her cell in his pocket. He'd notify her dad and track her down eventually, but he hated not knowing. If anything happened to her, he'd never forgive himself.

"Can you do some checking for me?"

"Sure, anything."

"I want to know if she goes after her SUV. She probably has a second set of keys, but it could be compromised. I don't like the idea of her in the marina parking lot—someone might be watching the vehicle. It'd help if you got hold of the watchman we talked to this morning."

"Sure thing. I'll make some calls. Want me to have Gus come to the city too?"

"Not yet. I'll get back inside and check cab companies, see if a driver picked up a pretty woman near the police station. My guess is she'll head straight to the airport."

Keri had a little time to kill before the last flight out to Knoxville. She'd gotten lucky, the reservation clerk told her. They normally didn't schedule this late on Sunday. A series of delayed flights had made it possible for her to get a standby seat. There would be a short layover in Georgia, but she wouldn't have to change planes.

She poked around the airport shopping center, bought a romance novel, a disposable cell phone and a travel bag with a few basic necessities. She felt naked without her pocketbook, and didn't want to draw attention by not having any bags. The airline clerk had frowned when she said she wanted a one-way ticket and wouldn't be checking luggage.

Food came next on her agenda. The energy bar had long been digested and her stomach grumbled. A cheeseburger, French fries and strawberry milkshake settled that problem. A sleazy-looking guy with mustard on his chin tried to chat her up, but she brushed him off. She'd had it with men, whether sleazy or gorgeous ones, she didn't plan to trust another one any time soon.

After hitting the bathroom and washing up a little, she began to feel more human. A damp comb through her hair settled it back into its natural style. Her T-shirt had wrinkles and smelled faintly musty from the tarp she'd found in the helicopter. Some spray-on deodorant from the travel kit masked it a little. Now she smelled like musty baby powder.

Next she needed to call her dad and ask if he or Jack could pick her up at the airport. They'd be getting ready for bed, but one of them would have to leave home early to drive to Knoxville. It made no sense for her to rent a car. She already had one vehicle she'd have to retrieve.

The disposable phone didn't get very good reception, so she moved closer to a bank of windows. After a couple rings, her dad answered.

"Merritts." The deep, familiar sound of his voice made her feel weepy. *Silly woman*, she chided herself. *Get a grip.*

"Hey, Dad, it's Keri."

"Hey yourself, baby girl. Where are you? Jack said you left a note about shopping, but that was three days ago."

"Long story, Dad. I'm at the Miami International Airport, scheduled on a flight to Knoxville in a few minutes. I'm supposed to get there between six and seven in the morning. Can someone pick me up?"

"I'll be there. Everything okay? Lamanto with you?"

"I'm fine and alone." She shouldn't be surprised he knew about Nick. Her dad knew everything.

"We need to talk."

"Lots to tell you," she agreed. "I have to go now. Love you."

"Love you."

Keri closed the phone and smiled. Annoyed as she might get with his overprotectiveness, he never failed her. Nick would make the same kind of father, she thought—protective and dependable and loving. Providing he didn't get himself killed, she added in an afterthought, and then ordered the errant train of thought from her mind.

The boarding call went out for her flight. In less than a half-hour, they took off for Atlanta. Most of the passengers tried to sleep, but she'd slept all afternoon. Determined not to dwell on Nick or her current situation, she pulled a book out of the travel bag and got lost in the story.

The stopover in Atlanta was brief. Keri went to the toilet and stretched her legs, but settled quickly back into her seat. She continued to read as people boarded, the doors closed and they went airborne. When the cabin got dark and quiet for a second time, she dozed off to sleep.

The dream came to her again. The familiar, haunting dream of the wreck. Her memory conjured the sound of her mom's scream, her valiant efforts to free them, and the relieved greeting to a mystery man. This time, Keri heard her mother's voice more clearly.

When she saw her dad at the airport the next morning, she went straight into his arms. He hugged her and rocked her back and forth like he'd been doing all her life. When she'd cleared the tears from her throat, she tipped her head and caught his gaze.

"I know who's responsible for mom's death," she whispered softly.

He stared into her eyes for a minute and said, "So do I, baby girl, so do I. But I can't prove it."

"I can," she told him.

Nick boarded a military cargo plane early Monday morning along with a twelve-man team comprised of ATF and Homeland Security agents. They planned to meet up with a Tennessee branch of the FBI once they arrived in Knoxville.

The joint force had spent the remaining hours of Sunday going over plans to intercept the militia movements. Not wanting a standoff at a heavily fortified compound, they'd decided to spread their forces along the most barren stretch of highway between the mountain road and Thornsbury.

They'd have to synchronize the assault so nobody in the convoy could alert the rest of the entourage before they left the camp. Without knowing the militia's exact timetable, they'd need to spread out and cover miles of road.

An FBI chemist had warned them the van could be carrying enough explosives to wipe out half of Thornsbury should it detonate close to the town. Any vehicle in the direct path could be destroyed, as well. The timing of the joint assaults on the van and the follow-up vehicles was crucial.

Nick tried to catch some shuteye during the flight but couldn't get his mind off Keri. Had she flown straight home and told her dad everything? If she had, would it help with their operation or hinder it? If the Merritt's were involved with the militia, they'd have a head start on dispersing and relocating. He hoped her faith in them was well-founded. She'd complained about their overprotectiveness.

He'd tried calling her house several times from her cell phone but hadn't gotten an answer. He'd left a message for her dad. Now he wondered if she'd avoided his calls or if something had happened to her between Miami and Knoxville. Could her family be trusted to ensure her safety, regardless of the situation? He sure as hell hoped so.

As soon as they touched down at the airport, he planned to check with authorities there. He'd learned she'd booked a flight out of Miami. What he didn't know was if she'd gotten home safely.

He loved her. The shocking realization had come to him the instant he'd realized she'd stowed away in the 'copter. No other woman had ever intrigued him the way she did. None had challenged him so thoroughly or loved him so unselfishly.

Her love and loyalty to her family, though it annoyed him, had also endeared her to him more. He wanted the same level of unquestioning faith. He wanted her complete trust. He wanted her unfaltering love.

It had felt so right sharing his life with her, so natural, both on the *Adrianna* and at the villa. Whether in her home territory or his, they'd made a great team. And the sex. Wow. Just wow. The sex was phenomenal. She had a mouth made for kissing and a body that kept on giving. A lifetime wouldn't be long enough to indulge himself in her sweet-tartness.

Shifting restlessly in the tight seat, he knew he had to stop thinking about her and concentrate on the mission. But when he banished the image of her in the tight white tank top, another took its place. He saw her exposing herself to him in those tiny purple undies. So open and honest, so vulnerable yet so damned sexy. The memories kept him restless and needy. His body didn't appreciate the sudden forced celibacy.

"Lamanto?"

He turned at the sound of Samuels' voice. The older man looked at him in concern.

"You okay? Alexander said you're recovering from a gunshot wound. Are you sure you're up to this? You look like hell."

Nick grimaced. He couldn't help how he looked or the lack of sleep, but he wouldn't back down from the mission.

"I'm fine, just tired, and I'll be even better when it's all over."

"Remember, you're supposed to stay out of the line of fire. Alexander doesn't want you getting shot at again."

He'd given them all the information he could at this point. He'd warned them to keep a low profile. Any group of outsiders would create a stir if they approached Thornsbury. They'd have to move in slowly and with unmarked vehicles. He talked them into hauling Keri's SUV from Miami, so he'd be leading the pack in her car.

"Understood."

Samuels gave him another long, considering look. "Why doesn't that reassure me?"

Nick chuckled. "You have my word," he said, meaning it. He didn't plan to take any unnecessary risks.

For the first time in his career, he wanted to avoid the main action. Ensuring Keri's safety, and possibly the safety of her family, ranked higher on his priorities right now. He'd lead the team in the right direction, but then he planned to find Keri as soon as possible.

Chapter Seventeen

Feeling the urgency to move quickly, the team didn't waste time at FBI headquarters. Their Thornsbury connection had informed them the militia would move off the mountain in intervals. One jeep would take the lead, the Cooper van filled with explosives would follow, and a second jeep would bring up the rear. The militia would have to be on the road today in order to get to Virginia and get in position to implement their plans tomorrow.

They all had their orders and rolled out of Knoxville in several unmarked cars. When they neared Thornsbury, they planned to pass through the area in fifteen-minute intervals to avoid drawing unwanted attention.

Nick rode in Keri's SUV with a young FBI agent named Patty Edwards. She had a similar height and build to Keri. Her hair and eyes were darker, but she had her hair tied back and wore large sun glasses to shield her face. Behind the wheel, Edwards could easily be mistaken for the car's owner.

Even so, they took a ten-mile detour across back roads to avoid driving directly through town. Too many of Thornsbury's citizens would recognize her car and that could stir unwanted interest in their movements.

"We're less than an hour from the base of the mountain now," Nick told Edwards as he settled more deeply into the bucket seat. "If we're right about the terrorist timetable, we should see one or more of their vehicles soon."

She nodded and her hands tightened on the wheel. He'd tried making small talk to help the young agent relax, but it hadn't helped much. He didn't know if it was the mission or being paired with him that made her more nervous, but he didn't care. She handled the car with skill, and he'd never again underestimate the ability of a determined female.

That thought made him frown. All he really wanted to do was find Keri. Their mission was crucial, yet concern for her had his concentration splintered. An official at the airport had confirmed her arrival in Knoxville, but that didn't reassure him much. He hoped to hell she hadn't headed back to the cabin.

Lost in thought, he didn't see the jeep until Edwards drew his attention to it.

"Military vehicle approaching," she said tersely.

Nick slid low in his seat and watched the oncoming vehicle through his own dark glasses. He pulled the bill of a baseball cap low on his forehead and tipped his head back as if sleeping.

"Keep looking straight ahead. Don't glance their way when we pass and don't show any interest."

While Edwards kept her gaze forward, he took the opportunity to stare into the passing jeep. It held two unfamiliar men in camouflage uniforms. Nick flipped out his phone and called Samuels.

"Just passed the first vehicle. A closed, olive drab, heavily fortified jeep."

"That'll be the point men," said Samuels. "We'll stay out of sight and let 'em pass until we've dealt with the bigger threat."

"Right," said Nick, breaking the connection. He relayed the information to Edwards and they grew quiet for the next fifteen minutes. The road narrowed a little as they passed through a few miles of heavily wooded countryside. Tree branches overhung the road on either side, the canopy of leaves blocking most of the midday sun.

A teenage boy driving a compact car sped by them just before they cleared the dark green tunnel. Nick hoped the kid got wherever he needed to go quickly. A few miles later, Edwards alerted him to another oncoming vehicle.

"Black van approaching," she said.

He'd already noticed it. Hard to tell if it was the same van he'd seen at the marina, but definitely similar. Cooper had a fleet of them. He unfastened his seat belt and slid farther down in the seat. Edwards kept her eyes on the road while he watched out her window. The two men in the van didn't even glance their way.

Once they'd passed, he called Samuels again.

"The casket van just passed us twenty-seven minutes outside of Thornton. Knifer McDowell at the wheel but an unknown with him. They're driving at a moderate speed and didn't pay any attention to us."

"Good to hear. We'll set up road blocks ten miles out of town where the road splits and try the tire spikes first. Part of our team is ten minutes behind you. They'll stay hidden until the van passes. Then they'll be in place to block the rest of the militia. Let's hope they're on the road before we intercept the van, so they can't get back to the mountain. We sure as hell can't afford to lose any of them or take the fight to their stronghold."

"Damn straight. They're heavily armed and willing to fight to the death."

"Once we have 'em pinned with a road block, we'll bring in the choppers. Have you passed many other vehicles?"

"Nothing since the van."

"We don't want any civilian casualties, but I can't risk pulling cars off the road, either, or detaining them without reason. Once you're sure you're clear of the militia, watch out for family vehicles."

"Will do," said Nick. He broke off the connection and told Edwards the plan.

"Will you recognize all of them?" she asked.

"I got a look at the compound last week. Two jeeps and several pickups, plus the militia leader's personal truck. Hard to know how many will take part in the attack. I figure they'll use untraceable jeeps and mercenaries or fanatics, but the big men in charge won't be anywhere near."

"The militia leader isn't one of the masterminds?"

"Not the brains or the money man, just a puppet. A very dangerous, fanatic puppet."

"You've met him?"

"Yeah, he knows this car, its owner and me too. I haven't seen him yet. If we see another jeep or a black pickup, I'll duck out of sight. If he tries to get your attention, ignore him."

Edwards nodded in understanding.

The second jeep approached within a few minutes. Nick slid as far down in the seat as he could fit then ducked his head out of sight.

"Passing them now," Edwards told him quietly. "The driver threw up a hand to me, but I didn't look close enough to ID him. Two men in the jeep, dressed like the other ones."

Nick waited until she gave him the all clear, straightened into his seat again and phoned Samuels with the latest information. A few more miles down the road, they approached the filling station at the base of the mountain. The same station he and Keri had stopped for gas last week. One rusty pickup was parked near the back. A car sat out front, but he didn't see anyone milling around outdoors.

"Is this where we're supposed to wait for word from Samuels?" asked Edwards as she slowed to turn into the lot. At his nod, she continued. "How much farther to the militia compound?"

Nick started to explain but got cutoff by the sound of a distant explosion. A few seconds later, the shock waves rocked the SUV and had him swearing.

"The damned van must have exploded. That'll alert the final jeep. They'll be heading back this way, and we can't let 'em get to the mountain road. Turn around and go back the way we came," he demanded sharply.

"We have orders to stay here."

"You can stay if you want, but I'm gonna make sure Russ Carson doesn't go into hiding."

Instead of arguing, Edwards whipped the SUV through the filling station and reversed directions. Nick tossed the ball cap to the floor and drew his weapon.

Within a few minutes, they'd reentered the narrow, heavily wooded stretch of road. The sunlight filtered through the leaves, making crazy geometric patterns on the blacktop.

"Slow up. This is the best place to cut them off. They'll have to pass through here with your team members in hot pursuit," said Nick. "Block the road, and I'll see if we're carrying any flares."

She did as he said, parking the SUV lengthwise across both lanes of the road. Nick sent a silent apology to Keri for involving her SUV in another possibly destructive situation. The government might end up owing her a new ride.

They hopped out of the car and started to move to the rear when they heard the roar of an approaching vehicle.

"That's the jeep!" shouted Nick. It came hurling toward them at an excessive speed, traveling way too fast to avoid a collision with the SUV. "Get to cover!"

He grabbed Edwards arm and they raced to the side of the road. From the shelter of a massive tree, they steadied their weapons and prepared for a fight. Instead, they watched a horrendous wreck unfold.

The jeep's driver hit the brakes hard, burning rubber for half a mile before turning the wheel sharply to avoid the SUV. It spun on two tires and hit a tree on the right side of the road. Next it bounced across the road and hit a second tree on the opposite embankment. Sparks flew and smoke started rolling from the engine. Then it took another bounce and kept rolling like a giant, crumpling ball on a pinball machine.

Edwards whistled softly at the carnage.

The FBI's chase vehicles slammed to a stop farther down the road, agents piling out of the cars as the jeep shuddered to halt. Upside down, crushed and with tires spinning, it landed in a smoldering heap.

Nick and his temporary partner started moving toward the

wreckage.

Walt Merritt holstered his gun and picked up his hat. "Promise me you won't leave the house for any reason."

"Cross my heart," Keri told him, standing on tiptoe to press a kiss on his cheek. "I have no desire to see or talk to anyone right now. I plan to be the quintessential hermit."

"That's a damned big word for such a little person," chimed Jack as he joined his dad by the door. He grinned and pointed to his cheek. "But you can plant one on me too."

She swatted him with the flat of her hand. "I swear I'm not leaving this house. I'm not getting involved in any manhunts or undercover operations or militia plots. I'm still on vacation!"

"We'll be back or call you as soon as this thing is resolved. Lock the door behind us and don't let anyone trick you into leaving the house. Let the machine screen phone calls. Until you have an all clear from me, stay put."

"Yes, sir," she replied, nodding as she always did when he lectured her on safety.

Her dad shoved his hat on his head and then, in an uncharacteristic display of emotion, he pulled her into his arms and hugged her tightly.

"Love you, baby girl."

Keri hugged him back, tears clogging her throat. "I love you too, but now you're scaring me," she added, shifting out of his arms and staring into his eyes. She knew how badly he wanted to avenge his wife's murder, and now he had the ammunition he needed for a confrontation.

"Promise me you'll be careful and you won't take any unnecessary risks," she pleaded.

"I'm gonna do the same thing I've been doin' most my life," he said, opening the front door and stepping through it. "My job."

Jack followed his dad. Keri flashed her brother a look, begging him to be careful and watch out for their dad. He gave her a reassuring wink. "I'll have his back."

She closed the door behind them, locked it and slid the deadbolt into place. Not that she expected any visitors. Unless someone had caught sight of her returning home, nobody knew she'd cut her vacation short. She hadn't contacted anyone since returning. Didn't care to see or talk to anyone, either.

The Merritt home sat amidst three acres of woods just outside the corporation limits of Thornsbury. The decades-old, two-story frame house wasn't easily seen from the highway and most folks called ahead if they planned to visit. Her mother used to invite friends for coffee, card parties and various other social events, but the open-door policy and congeniality had died with her.

"I'm just not much of a socialite, Mom," Keri whispered to the photograph of her mother. "I'd rather curl up with a good book than entertain people," she said, glancing at the book she'd left on the end table.

For the next half-hour or so, she tried to lose herself in the story but couldn't concentrate. Nick filled her thoughts, shoving everything else from her mind. She missed him so much, and she hated missing him. Hated knowing he had such a stranglehold on her emotions. She'd never been the type to pine for a man. Hadn't even understood the old-fashioned term until she'd returned home alone.

Standing and stretching, she moved toward the answering machine and clicked the play button just to hear his voice. She hadn't erased any of them. His first call had informed her dad she'd left Miami. After that, he'd left several short, succinct messages in increasingly worried tones.

It served him right to be worried. He'd abandoned her in a strange place in the care of strangers. Maybe not strangers to him but definitely to her. And against her wishes. That was just wrong on so many levels, she reminded herself every time she thought about forgiving him.

He'd made his last call from Miami International Airport, just a few hours after she'd left Florida. He'd probably arrived in

Knoxville shortly after her too. Had they both been in the same building for a while? Had they missed each other by minutes?

Where was he now? Somewhere nearby with a posse of law enforcement officers? Neither her dad nor Jack had mentioned contact with out-of-town law enforcement authorities. They told her they'd received a reliable report regarding a militia movement today. After getting a good look at Russ's compound, it scared her to think everyone she loved might be in horrible danger.

Had Nick taken his team to the cabin? Had he shared his concerns about the Merritt's involvement in a possible terrorism camp? Had he listened to anything she'd said or trusted her at all? Did he really believe she could live with bigots and not know it? Hell, maybe he suspected her as well as the rest of her family.

It didn't matter what he thought. She had to put him out of her mind and out of her life even though her body craved his touch. Even though she missed him more than she could have imagined possible. Even though her heart wouldn't stop aching, she had to stop thinking and worrying about him.

With that thought, she went to the kitchen, poured herself a tall glass of sweet tea and carried it to the living room along with a bag of chocolates. Chocolate had a way of soothing her nerves, despite the overload of caffeine.

Making herself comfortable on the oversized blue-plaid sofa, she grabbed the remote and started surfing through televisions channels. The large, flat screen TV was the only change her dad had made in the house since her mom's death.

Otherwise, the Early American-style furniture in hues of green and blue remained the same. The only clash in an otherwise stylish décor was her dad's brown leather recliner. The plaid couch had a matching loveseat and easy chair. End tables flanked the couch with a long, oval-shaped coffee table directly in front of it. Her mom's hand-crocheted doilies covered the smooth walnut surfaces.

She propped her bare feet on the table and flipped the

buttons on the remote. Daytime TV left a lot to be desired, she decided a few minutes later when she'd run through all the channels twice. Talk shows and cooking shows didn't hold her attention for long. Maybe she'd try to read a while.

When Keri crossed the room to the bookcase, she heard what sounded like a tremendous sonic boom. It just kept rumbling and reverberating. The floor beneath her shuddered and the windows rattled.

What the hell? Her mind flashed back to the explosion at the marina and the devastation it had caused. Had the task force attacked the militia camp? Surely she wouldn't hear and feel an explosion that far away. So where and what had exploded? How close had they come to town? Judging by the direction of sound, it had originated south of them.

She moved to the window and looked out but couldn't see anything beyond the trees. The phone started to ring, but she ignored it. Anytime something the least bit curious happened near Thornsbury, the residents bombarded the sheriff with calls. This time would be no different.

Keri wished she knew what had happened too. How close had Nick been to the blast? How close had her dad and Jack been? Was anyone hurt? Would the emergency room at the hospital be prepared for an influx of injured? Was it her civil duty to help them in a crisis?

No, she'd promised her dad to stay put. If he told her to go to the hospital and help, she'd go. Otherwise, she'd just have to wait and worry. She picked up the book again and forced herself to pay better attention.

After a few chapters and a few too many chocolates, Keri set aside the book long enough to go to the bathroom. Next she made a trip to the kitchen for a refill of tea. She moved back into the living room and stuffed another chocolate in her mouth, following it with a long drink. Chocolate always made her thirsty. She'd probably be on a sugar high the rest of the day, but she didn't care.

A few minutes later, the ringing of the doorbell took her by surprise. Her first thought was of Nick, so she hurried out of the room to the foyer. Disappointment hit hard as she looked out the peep hole and saw Don Monroe. Swallowing her disappointment, she turned both locks and opened the door.

"Hi, Don. How are you? It's good to see you upright."

He laughed at that. "Good to see you too, Keri. I thought you planned to stay at the cabin for all three weeks of vacation."

She cringed at the reminder of how much attention her plans had garnered. No way would she discuss her messed-up vacation agenda.

"Slight blip in the plans, but that's the norm with any plans I make." Changing subjects, she added, "I didn't realize you'd been released from the hospital, but you look like you're doing great."

He gave her a warm, friendly smile. Keri knew several women in town were enamored of his blond, blue-eyed good looks. She found him attractive in an asexual sort of way. They'd dated awhile but never really clicked. At least she hadn't felt much beyond friendly affection for him.

"I'm told I had great care even though I wasn't conscious to appreciate it at the time."

"Your body took some serious hits, both by gunshot and the blow to your head. We worried about a fractured skull."

"My head's too hard to fracture," he teased. "But I don't ever want another concussion. It took longer to recover from than the gunshot. Who'd have thought?"

"Neither is very pleasant," she said. "I'm afraid Dad and Jack are both gone, if you wanted to catch them."

"Nothing that can't wait," he said. "I'm just bored with the whole rest and recuperation process. Mind if I stay and visit with you awhile?"

"Not at all. I'm totally bored myself." She motioned for him to come inside, and then closed the door. He waited for her to precede him down the short hall to the living room. When they passed through the arched doorway, she waved him into an easy chair and returned to her spot on the sofa.

"You must have heard the explosion," she said. "Do you have any idea what caused it? It sounded like sonic booms from a whole squadron of jets."

"I was hoping you could fill me in," he said, crossing one jeans-clad knee over the other. "Since I'm officially on sick leave, nobody tells me anything."

The phone rang again and Keri grimaced. "Everybody in town is asking the same thing. That's about the tenth call. They all want answers, and I don't have any." They listened as another tax-paying citizen demanded answers.

Don laughed. "Leave it to Hazel Smith to throw the tax issue at you. That's always her first line of defense. You'd think she's the only person who ever paid taxes."

Keri smiled and nodded. She'd known Don since his family moved to town during their high-school years. Some people still considered him a newcomer because he hadn't been born in the county, but he knew most of the residents by first name and all their quirks.

The thought reminded her of Nick and how little he knew of her way of life. He didn't like her community or anything about Thornsbury. He might as well be from another planet. It made her sad. To distract herself, she asked Don if he'd care for something to drink. When he said he'd like some tea, she went to the kitchen and poured him a glass.

"You like a little lemon in yours, don't you?" she called to him from the opposite side of the house.

"Just a little, please, if it's not too much trouble," he called back to her.

"No trouble," she assured him, adding a couple drops of lemon. She returned the pitcher and bottle of lemon juice to the refrigerator. "I didn't think to ask if you're hungry. Can I get you anything else?"

"No thanks, I'm fine," he replied as she reentered the living room and handed him the glass.

She moved to the sofa, picked up her glass and drank the rest of hers before it could get watered down by melting ice.

"Would you care for some chocolate? I've already had way too much."

"I'll pass, thanks. I don't have much of a sweet tooth, remember?"

She did remember. He'd called her a sugar junkie, and she'd called him a sour puss. When they'd stopped dating, he'd accused her of dumping him because he wasn't sweet enough. Relaxing against the sofa cushions, she shot a glance at him.

"You're not still annoyed with me for that, are you? You're really a sweet guy, aren't you?"

As she watched, Don slowly shook his head. A lock of hair fell across his forehead in a boyish fashion. For some reason, watching him made her dizzy. She propped herself more firmly in the corner of the sofa but began to feel strange.

With a panicked glance at Don, she watched his head shift back and forth, back and forth, in a mesmerizing movement. When she tried to blink and stop looking, she couldn't make her eyelids drop. She tried lifting her hand to her face, but had no control of her arms, either. A flutter of panic squeezed her chest as she continued to stare at Don.

"No sense in fighting it, Ker," he said softly. "I slipped a little something in your tea. Nothing personal, mind you. It's fast acting, but it shouldn't kill you. Just keep you paralyzed for a while. I need your cooperation and you're not always the most cooperative individual."

A slow, all-encompassing numbness spread through her body. Her arms dropped to her lap, useless, and her legs felt like lead. Without the support of the sofa cushions, she'd have slumped into a heap.

Keri frantically racked her brain for a drug that caused such an effect. Had he given her some sort of nerve toxin? A neuromuscular blockade would eventually stop her heart and lungs, but he'd said this wouldn't kill her. How could she have drunk it without noticing the taste?

Too late she realized she'd welcomed the enemy into her home, putting everyone she loved in more danger. She stared at him, frozen in place, unable to move or speak yet awake and aware.

"Since the bomb exploded prematurely, it's my guess most of the militia got wiped out with it," said Don, his tone and expression bland as though discussing the weather. "Anyone who survived will be under arrest, and the feds will be trying to clean up all the loose ends."

Loose ends? Is that what he considered himself? He'd been a part of it? A terrorist? For how long? Had he known about her mother's murder? Had he worked every day with her family while betraying everything they stood for? Why? Now what?

He'd poisoned her and sat there looking all calm and rational? He had to be insane! She'd opened her home and offered hospitality to a crazy man. How did you protect yourself from that kind of insanity?

"Are you feeling totally paralyzed yet?" he continued. "I need to load you into my car. You're my bargaining chip if anyone tries to stop me from leaving the county. I figured I'd better have some insurance until I'm out of Tennessee. After that, I can disappear and change identities. I had prepared for that possibility."

As he rose from his chair, they heard the screech of tires outside followed by the slam of a car door. He went still and slowly pulled a handgun from the back of his waist.

The action reminded her of Nick, and she said a silent plea for forgiveness. What if she never saw him again? It made her heart ache. What if she'd put him, her dad and brother at risk due to her lapse in judgment? It grated to know Don would use her as a pawn in his sick game, use her family's love and loyalty as a weapon. How long before the effects of the drug wore off?

They heard the key in the front door and the sound of it opening. Keri silently screamed a warning but couldn't force any sound from her throat. Jack called her name and then he stepped through the arched doorway to the living room. He flashed a glance at her but quickly faced Don, gun drawn. The two men glared at each other for a long minute.

"Give it up, Monroe," said Jack as he slowly sidled closer to the sofa and her.

"You're the one who'd better give it up, Jack. You've got a whole lot more to lose than I do at this point."

"What's wrong with Keri? What have you done to her?"

"Nothing she won't survive, and I promise she won't feel any pain if I have to shoot her to get your cooperation." Don issued the chilling threat with little inflection.

"What do you expect to accomplish by hurting her?" Jack demanded. "You don't want assault and kidnapping charges on your head. At this point you're only under suspicion for conspiracy."

"Ah, but it's conspiracy to commit a terrorist act. We both know that's the end of my career in law enforcement even if I don't do time. I need a fresh start and your sister is going to help me get it. So are you. You're gonna drop your gun and pick up Keri. You can carry her outside and strap her into your cruiser. That'll give me another edge."

The two men stared at each other, neither blinking nor moving a muscle. When Jack didn't follow his orders, Don slowly turned his gun until it pointed at Keri.

"Where should I start?" he asked in the emotionless tone of a madman. "You want me to blow out her knee cap? It might cost her a career, but she'd live. Or maybe put one in her abdomen? From what I've been told, there's not much left there to damage."

Her stomach rolled. Even though her nerves had frozen, she still felt nausea rising in her throat. Before Jack could react, they heard another vehicle brake to a stop out front. The phone had stopped ringing and the house grew deathly quiet. Then Nick shouted her name as he came through the door.

"Keri!" His tone sounded calm until he didn't get a response. He moved closer and he yelled in a louder voice, this time demanding a response. "Keri! Where the hell are you?"

"And the plot thickens," whispered Don.

He appeared to be enjoying himself, which cemented Keri's belief the man was certifiable. Her heart thudded as Nick finally stepped through the doorway. His gaze swept the surreal scene. Her heart pounded harder when he stopped beside Don, aligning with the enemy.

"*No!*" she silently screamed. "*Please, Nick!*" Their eyes met briefly, but her facial muscles were frozen. She could only hope the panic she felt was reflected in her eyes.

"Hey, buddy, what's happening?" Nick asked Don with curiosity and concern. "Why the guns?"

"It's just as we suspected," Don told him in a steady, genial tone. If Keri hadn't been in such a panic, she'd have admired his cool. "The Merritts are up to their eyeballs in the terrorist plot. I asked Jack to surrender his weapon, but he refused."

Keri watched in horror as Nick stepped closer to Don, facing Jack more squarely. He didn't reach for his own gun or contradict Don's accusation. A look flashed between him and Jack. Her brother stood between the coffee table and the sofa with his back to her. She couldn't read his expression.

"Listen, Merritt," said Nick in the same reasonable tone Don had used. "Why don't you lower your weapon until we get this situation resolved? None of us want Keri to get caught in crossfire."

No! No! No! she strained to scream at him but the only made a whimpering sound. *Please, Nick! Trust me, trust my brother!*

Chapter Eighteen

After another long, pulse-pounding pause, Jack agreed. "Okay, you're right. I don't want Keri hurt."

"Just put your weapon on the table," continued Nick, his head dipping in the direction he wanted Jack to move. "Lock the safety and lower it to the table."

She heard the click of Jack's safety, and then her brother slowly bent to place the gun on the coffee table. In doing so, he shifted his body fully in front of her, effectively becoming a human shield.

At the same instant, Nick lunged for Don's gun hand, catching the other man off-guard. A wild bullet slammed into the wall over her head before Nick was able to knock him to the floor. The two of them wrestled briefly before Jack stomped on Don's hand and retrieved the pistol. Then he and Nick subdued a screaming, flailing crazy man.

"You stupid sonofabitch!" Don yelled at Nick. "You don't know what you're doing! You're letting your feelings for a woman screw with your thinking? What kind of man are you? What kind of friend?"

"Shut up, Monroe," yelled Jack as they rolled him onto his stomach and slapped handcuffs around his wrists. To Nick, he added, "I'll take care of him. Get Keri to the hospital. I'll call the ER and let 'em know you're on the way. This bastard poisoned her with something."

Nick came to her quickly and gathered her in his arms. "It's okay, baby," he whispered gruffly.

Even hot, sweaty and breathless, he looked better to her than any man she'd ever known. She wanted to thank him for trusting Jack instead of Don. She had so much to say to him, but she couldn't even lift her arms around his neck. Tears filled her eyes and overflowed. Nick brushed them away with soft kisses as he carried her from the room.

"Take the cruiser. Keys are in it," Jack called to them. "I'll get some backup here as soon as possible."

Don had quit yelling at Nick and started cursing the Merritts and local government. The hatred in his voice shocked her when he raged against every race and religion besides his own. He sounded totally demented. Keri had no sympathy for his mental illness. She never wanted to see him again.

With some juggling, Nick managed to get her into the passenger side of the cruiser and fasten her seat belt. He ran back into the house and returned with her iced tea glass. Then he jumped behind the wheel, turned on the ignition, lights and siren before racing her to the hospital.

The trauma team met them a few minutes later at the entrance to the emergency room. They lifted her onto a gurney. She looked up at the familiar faces and wondered at the weirdness of being the victim rather than the nurse. The familiar walls and hallways looked strange from this angle, with blinding overhead lights and steady movement as they wheeled her to an exam room.

Nick explained the situation and the unknown cause of her paralysis. Jamie Tolman, the resident on duty, came to the same conclusion she had. She'd often teased him about being arrogant, but she welcomed his confidence now.

"It must be some sort of nerve drug, otherwise she'd be struggling to breathe. I've heard rumors about experimental testing, but there's no data on treatment or long-term effects. Her heart and lungs would have shutdown by now if he'd used a neuromuscular drug."

Nick handed him a glass. "I don't know if there's any residue in here, but I brought it just in case."

Edie Morgan, a veteran trauma nurse who often got paired with the young resident, took the glass and handed it to a nurse tech. "Get this to the lab and tell them it needs priority processing."

To the others, the buxom redhead added, "Even if they can identify the contents, it might take days."

Keri didn't care much for Edie's bedside manner. She made it sound like anything they learned would be too late to help.

"Tell 'em to put a rush on it!" snapped Nick as he picked up her left hand and held it in both his hands. She couldn't feel his touch, but it soothed her to have him close. When he looked into her eyes, she tried to let him see how much it meant to her.

"I'm sorry, sir, you'll have to leave," said Tolman. "Only immediate family is allowed in this area."

"The hell," said Nick.

Tolman puffed up like a banty rooster. He always wanted to be the big man in charge, so he got defensive. "It's the rule."

"I'm her husband."

The two men stared at each other for a long, charged moment. Tolman looked surprised and then suspicious. He glanced at their hands for rings and then demanded, "Prove it."

"Disprove it," countered Nick in his macho cop tone. "I'm not leaving. Somebody she trusted already drugged her and shot at her. I don't trust anybody, and I'm not letting her out of my sight."

During their little testosterone battle, Keri watched Edie start filling out a chart while Joy Rice took her vitals. Joy came to them through a temp service and filled in for sick or vacationing staff. Though mousy and introverted, she was also hard-working and competent. The regular staff didn't know her well but generally liked her.

She stuck a thermometer in Keri's ear and then wrapped the blood pressure cuff around her arm. As she got numbers, she repeated them for Edie and Tolman. He quit arguing with Nick and placed the end of his stethoscope against Keri's chest. After listening intently, he gave her an encouraging smile.

"Lungs sound fine. Fever's a little elevated and your blood pressure is low, but that's to be expected. I'll have Joy start you on a saline drip and see if we can flush the toxin out of your system. Until we know exactly what we're dealing with, I don't want to take chances. There's not much more we can do safely right now."

His decision eased her worries. They'd had their share of professional disagreements, but she respected his knowledge and skill. She didn't want to risk worsening her condition or making it permanent.

A few seconds later, they heard the familiar sound of the emergency squad's sirens. Everyone listened intently until the electronic doors whirred and another gurney shoved through the entrance. The paramedic's voice could be heard throughout the small trauma area.

"Car crash victim. Had to use the jaws to free him. Lost him a couple times in route," he said. "The other passenger was dead at the scene."

Tolman and Edie hurried toward the new arrival.

Nick cringed when the younger nurse drove a needle into Keri's right hand, and none-to-gently. He hated needles and hoped she couldn't feel the sting. She'd had enough trauma for one day. For a lifetime. Part of it was due to the terrorist situation, but most of it could be blamed on him. He gotten her more tangled in the web of deceit.

When everyone had left the exam room, Nick brought Keri's left hand to his mouth and pressed a kiss on the palm. Her skin felt cool and lifeless, making his heart ache. He stared into her eyes with apology in his.

"I'm sorry you got caught up in this mess. And so sorry you're the one who's suffering."

Her eyes, her beautiful, bright eyes returned his steady gaze. She didn't look at him in anger or pain but steady, unfaltering trust. He didn't know if her eyes mirrored her feelings, but he hoped so. Her faith in him melted his heart.

"You were right," he whispered. "I should have trusted your instincts about your dad and Jack. I still don't know how Don fits into the bigger picture, but we'll have answers soon."

Keri's fingers twitched slightly and he brought her hand to his lips again. Had he imagined the movement or was the drug wearing off.

"Are you getting sensation back?"

She made a sound. Just a small puff of air, but it sent excitement racing through him. He swooped closer and dropped a kiss on her lips. His lips lingered, and he kissed her harder, needing the contact as much as his next breath.

"You'll be fine. Whatever he gave you, it'll wear off soon and you'll be able to yell all you want. I know you have lots of questions and you probably feel like throwing things, but that's okay."

The next huff she made sounded like a demand, so Nick figured she wanted answers. He caught her up to date on the conspiracy and investigation. He told her about the team coming to Thornsbury and how they'd trapped the militia. About the terrorist's agenda and how it had been curtailed.

"We avoided a firefight and the bomb took out two of the terrorists from Miami. Knifer McDowell at the wheel, but no identity on the other one yet. The agents closest to the blast got blown off the road. They'll probably have some nerve damage in their ears. Hopefully no loss of hearing.

"Your friend Russ was in that final crash out near the mountain road. He slammed into some trees at a high rate of speed and then rolled the jeep. I don't know if he died on the scene or if he's here in the ER, but it sounds like the place is filling up with agents."

She continued to search his face with a steady gaze, and he gave her a smile. "I brought your SUV home without a scratch," he teased. "You can thank Uncle Sam for the airline transfer."

Keri made another demanding sound.

"Oh, you worried about your dad?" This time she blinked her eyelids. His smile widened. The stuff had to be wearing off. It couldn't happen soon enough to please him. "He and Jack are handling the local arrests."

The younger of the two nurses, her nametag read J. Rice, returned to the room and stepped close to the bed. She drew a syringe out of her pocket, flipped of the cap and started to put the needle to Keri's IV tubing.

"This will help speed your recovery a little," she mumbled.

Nick glanced at Keri and saw her eyes widen with alarm. She made a tiny sound of protest. He reached across the bed and grabbed the nurse's wrist.

She reacted swiftly and violently, trying to pull from his grip. Then she caught him totally off-guard with a punch to his wounded shoulder. His grip loosened and she tried to pull her arm away, but he dove across the bed and grabbed her arm with his good hand.

"Let go of me, you stupid bastard!" she screamed, pounding him with her free hand. "She deserves to die! It's all her fault. All her fault!"

Nick tightened his grip and squeezed her wrist until she dropped the syringe on the floor. He saw it shatter but still didn't let go of her. He knew he had to be crushing Keri but he wouldn't give Rice another chance to hurt her.

"I need help in here!" he yelled.

In seconds, the doctor returned with Jack Merritt at his side. Rice broke free and shoved the doctor aside, but Jack wrapped both arms around her. "What the hell?" he yelled, trying to control the kicking, screaming woman.

"She tried to inject something into Keri's IV," he explained, pointing to the floor where the syringe had fallen.

"I didn't order anything," said Tolman, shouting for reinforcements.

Rice continued to flail her arms and legs, fighting to free herself from Jack. "Let go of me, you ignorant, traitorous scum," she yelled.

The ruckus brought more agents into the tiny space. In another few minutes, they had Rice cuffed and escorted from the room. "You'll pay! You're all going to hell for this!"

Nick collapsed on the bed but quickly shifted his weight off Keri and rolled to her side. He slipped his right arm around her and pulled her into the circle of his arms. His heart pounded wildly in his chest as he struggled to steady his breathing.

"Damn, the crazies are coming out of the woodwork. I feel like I'm in the middle of the twilight zone."

Tolman moved to Keri's side and glared at him for being in bed with her. "You're breaking more rules, Detective," he snapped. "If you don't be careful, I'll have *you* hauled out of here next."

Nick didn't argue, but the look he flashed the doctor dared him to try. When he'd caught his breath, he eased his legs to the floor again but held Keri's hand in his. Tolman shook his head, checking her IV and listening to her lung sounds.

"Much stronger. Are you regaining some feeling?"

Nick answered for her. "She's made a few sounds and can move her fingers a little."

"We'll continue the saline drip. It seems to be working as well as anything else I could give you." He spoke directly to Keri, and she managed a small nod. "I guess it's safe to leave you with your personal bodyguard and an army of law enforcement officers in the ER. I'll get you moved to a private room. My shift's over so I'm heading out, but I want you to stay overnight. Get some rest, and I'll see you in the morning."

He nodded to Nick and turned to Jack. "Do you want me to have someone clean up the syringe and collect what's left of the drug Rice tried to use on Keri?"

"Better leave it for the FBI's crime scene techs," he replied. "Would you mention it to one of the special agents in the waiting room? We need to get the evidence collected before it can be contaminated."

"Will do."

Jack offered Tolman a hand, thanking him for his help, and the doctor left the room.

"I just keep cleaning up your messes, Lamanto," said Jack.

He stepped around the spill on the floor and moved to the head of the bed. Then he leaned down and pressed a kiss on his sister's forehead.

"You two can't seem to stay out of trouble, can you?"

Keri made another small sound of protest, but her lips curved into a tight smile. Nick didn't think anything had ever looked sweeter to him.

"What's the nurse's issue? Is she part of the militia crowd too?" he asked.

Jack hesitated, glancing at Keri and then back to him. "She's dated Russ Carson on and off for a few years. I'm guessing she shares his anti-semantic, anti-government, anti-just-about-everything beliefs."

"Carson?" asked Nick, wondering if the militia leader had survived the crash.

Jack slowly shook his head. "He was rushed to surgery, but it doesn't look good."

That explained why Rice had gone ballistic and tried to kill Keri.

Ironically, if Carson had rammed Keri's SUV, he probably would have increased his chances of survival. By braking to avoid her car, he'd caused the certain death of his passenger and maybe his own fatality. He had to have reacted from gut instinct and concern for her. Much as Nick hated what the man stood for, he couldn't fault Carson's last ditch effort to protect his childhood friend.

Keri tugged on his hand, drawing Nick's attention back to her. He knew she needed more answers. Before he could say anything, a special agent accompanied a lab tech with a forensic kit. Once they'd finished collecting the syringe and drug residue, they left the room and her dad arrived.

She made a sound of protest at the sight of Walt Merritt. One side of his face looked bruised and swelling. His lip was cut and bleeding. Blood stains spattered his shirt and one of his sleeves had been ripped from the shoulder seams.

"I'm fine, baby girl," he said as he cupped her face with a battered hand. "I told myself I wouldn't beat Moville to a bloody pulp, but he had the nerve to call your mother's death an unfortunate casualty of war."

"Moville?" asked Nick.

"Charles Moville of the Moville Funeral Home. I knew the brothers had to be funding the militia, but I couldn't prove it until we made the connection with Cooper Caskets. Then Keri told me she'd remembered the details of the wreck. She recognized Charles as the man who stepped up to the car that night, and Elaine's relief at seeing him just before someone shoved the car over the railing."

"You think Moville could have prevented the wreck?"

"Maybe, maybe not, but he's damned sure responsible for it by conspiring with the men who committed the actual deed. He tried to lay the blame on some gangbanger on Cooper's payroll. Moville's the anonymous tipster who called me about the wreck but didn't do anything else to help Elaine. He ran like the rat he is and left her to die."

The sheriff's voice went hoarse and Jack draped an arm around his dad's shoulder. Keri squeezed Walt's fingers. Tears filled her eyes and it hurt Nick to see her hurting. He tightened his hold on her hand, wishing he could ease her pain. Hopefully knowing the truth and finding some justice would help the family's emotional wounds to heal.

He didn't blame the sheriff for wanting to beat someone to a pulp. He'd felt the same way when Don had his gun pointed at Keri. He wished he'd had more time to pummel Monroe, but getting her to the hospital had taken priority.

Walt had had two years of impotent rage bottled inside him. Moville might have fought back, but Nick didn't doubt that the sheriff had put a hurt on the other man. Now they just needed an airtight case against all the conspirators.

"Moville confessed?" asked Jack.

"Got it on tape," said Walt. "He'll lawyer up and deny it, but I've got it in his own twisted words. He even tried to enlist me into his hate campaign."

"What about his brother Terrance?"

"In the wind for now, but we'll find him."

"I remember meeting the brothers," said Nick. "Terrance grumbled about how bad business has been the last few years. How'd they finance the militia? Did Cooper supply all the funding?"

"Far as we can tell, it's a full partnership," explained Jack. "The Movilles funded the camp and paid the militia men. Cooper supplied the guns and fertilizer. He had a license to buy it for his farm in Florida, but he bought more than he used over the course of three years to ward off any suspicions. We've also found evidence the Movilles embezzled money from their pre-planned funeral funds."

Nick whistled softly. "Bad news for anyone who invested with them."

"Which includes a lot of our hard-working residents," Walt added grimly. He took off his hat, ran a hand through his hair and put the hat back in place.

"So where does Don Monroe fit into the scheme of things? Was he in on it from the beginning?"

Jack shook his head. "We're still piecing it all together. We think it was all about the money for Don. They bribed him to turn a blind eye when the illegal shipments passed through the county." To Nick, he added, "When you started asking questions, he must have panicked and faked an attack."

Nick shrugged his bad shoulder, wondering if Don had intended to kill him or just scare him away. He glanced at Keri and knew she was thinking the same thing. Then her gaze shifted to her brother.

"Dad," she managed a whisper. "Nurse."

Jack smiled. "She's such a bossy butt even when she can barely talk," he touched her hair gently and affectionately then turned to Walt. "She's right, Dad. You look like you might need a couple stitches. I think it's safe to leave her in Lamanto's care."

The sheriff looked directly at him for the first time, their gazes locking. "You goin' anywhere?"

"They'll be moving Keri to a room soon," he told the older man, "but I go where she goes."

Walt slowly nodded. He leaned over to kiss Keri's cheek. "You get some rest, and I'll stop by again before I leave. I've got a mess of federal agents at my office and a lot of details to iron out about prisoners."

"Love you," she whispered softly.

"Love you back."

When Walt and Jack left the room, a hospital tech came in with an agent escort. They wheeled Keri down a couple of hallways and put her in a room directly across from the nurse's station.

Nurse E. Morgan bustled in behind them and glared at Nick. "You'll need to step outside while I get Keri settled."

"I'm not going anywhere."

She crossed her arms on her chest and peered at him over her bifocals. "Well, knowing our patient, her drinking habit and the addition of IV fluids, I'm guessing her bladder's about to rupture. She might not want you in here while we take care of that little issue, husband or no husband."

Nick frowned and glanced at Keri. Their gazes met, and she gave him a steady, unblinking stare. "Go," she mouthed to him.

He turned back to Nurse Morgan. "She might trust you, but she trusted Rice too."

"Wanna frisk me?"

Glaring at her, he snapped, "I'll do more than frisk you if you hurt a hair on her head. Got it?"

Morgan surprised him with a chuckle. "Sorry, Detective, I know you've had a rough day. I shouldn't be harassing you. I promise on my life I won't do Keri any harm. You can stand at the door if you want. Just give us a little privacy."

Nick leaned over the bed to press a kiss on Keri's lips. "I'll be close." He flashed another warning look at Morgan and walked to the door, stepping outside but leaving it ajar.

Jack came walking down the hallway, spoke to the nurse at the desk and joined him.

"What's up?" he asked.

"Nurse Ratchet is getting Keri settled."

Jack laughed. "Edie's a tough one all right, but she's mothered Keri ever since the accident. She couldn't be in better hands."

Nick glanced into the room. Morgan had pulled a curtain around the bed, and he didn't like having Keri out of sight. Jack's faith in the older woman allowed him to relax his guard a little.

"Glad to hear it. How's your dad doing?"

"They're still patching him up in the ER, but he'll be okay. A lot better now that he's finally confronted Moville. It's been eating at him for a long time."

"That bites."

"Sure does."

"How long have you known about the militia plans? I heard your voice the morning Don and I got shot. What the hell went down out there?"

"Half the damn town must have been prowling the woods that day," Jack said in frustration. "I couldn't see anything. My best guess is Don did the shooting. He shot you and gave himself a flesh wound, but then somebody hammered him hard enough to knock him unconscious. Did you hit him?"

"No, and I didn't see anyone. The fog was too damned heavy. The gunshot knocked me to the ground, and I dove for cover."

"Don must have gotten caught in the middle. He started out supporting the militia activity. When he got cold feet and tried to derail their operation by calling you, it all blew up in his face. In the long run, he's just as guilty as the rest."

"I thought he was ATF until I saw him pointing a gun at

Keri."

"Cousin Dwayne is ATF," said Jack.

"No shit?"

"No shit. He and Russ used to be tight. They spent a lot of time in the old hunting cabin until Dwayne joined the army. While he did his tour and trained with the ATF, Russ joined forces with the Movilles. When Dwayne got home, he pretended to approve of their plans, but they were too paranoid to give him all the details."

"He gave you and the feds information, but not the specifics you needed?"

"We had intel, just couldn't act on it without more evidence."

"Dwayne wasn't in the jeep with Carson, was he?" asked Nick, hoping he hadn't been instrumental in the death of Keri's cousin.

"No. He stayed on the mountain. Since it's Merritt property, he was supposed to stay behind to clean up and destroy evidence after they'd gone."

They stepped aside as Nurse Morgan pushed through the door. She nodded to Jack but directed her words to Nick. "Keri's comfortable now. I don't think she'll want anything else until the drug is completely out of her system. She just needs to rest. Why don't you go home and let her sleep?"

"My home is several hundred miles away," he declared flatly. At least it used to be, he added to himself. "Keri's my top priority right now, and I'm not leaving until she does."

The nurse sighed, but her expression softened. "Suit yourself. Just let her get some rest. Use the call button if her condition changes for the worse."

Chapter Nineteen

Keri heard someone approaching her bed, but she couldn't turn her head far enough to see. Edie had removed her clothes, bathed her face and dressed her in a hospital gown. She hadn't propped her up on pillows because she'd been ordered to rest.

Finding herself flat on her back and helpless was another recurring nightmare. She'd spent weeks like this after the car wreck and the succession of surgeries. She hated feeling so weak and vulnerable, hated being dependent on others for every basic need. At least this time she didn't have the constant, sometimes debilitating pain.

More of her body had begun to tingle to awareness, the feeling slowly returning to her nerve endings. Her hearing had returned to normal and the cloudiness cleared from her vision. Whatever drug Don had given her, it affected every inch of her body. He'd said it wouldn't kill her but he couldn't have known for sure. He'd taken a stupid, dangerous gamble with an unproven drug. She had no doubt Jack and Nick had saved her life. If Don had succeeded in using her as a hostage, they'd probably both be dead by now.

"Hey, Sis, feeling stronger now?" Jack asked as he stepped to her right side.

As much as she loved her brother, her attention focused on Nick as he rounded the bed and took up his spot at her left side. He looked tired, his clothes and hair rumpled, but still the most gorgeous man she'd ever known. He lifted her hand and kissed it. The touch of his lips sent thrilling warmth along her arm and straight to her heart. It went a long way toward reassuring her that all was well in her world.

"Hello? Earth to Keri? What am I, chopped liver?" Jack

teased her attention back to his side of the bed. She tried to give him a smile but wasn't sure how well her facial muscles followed mental orders.

"Bro," she whispered throatily. "Dad?"

"He's fine, minor scrapes and bruising. He didn't need stitches, just some bandages and a tetanus shot, but he's impatient to get back to the office. He doesn't like all the outsiders invading his territory."

"The FBI has jurisdiction at this point," reminded Nick. "They'll be taking the prisoners to a federal prison."

Jack nodded. "Can't say I'll be sorry to see any of them go. We'll have a lot of cleaning up to do in the county and we'll have to recount the details a couple hundred times for all our tax-paying citizens, but I'm sure glad it's done."

Keri knew what he meant. The excitement would fade in a few days, but the events would be rehashed for weeks, months and maybe years. Thornsbury had never been the source of so much newsworthy drama. She imagined their home answering machine had maxed out by now.

The Movilles, Don and Russ were long-time residents. It saddened her to learn of Russ's near-fatal crash, but he'd gone off the deep end with his fanaticism. His life, if he lived, would become his worst nightmare. He'd likely be sentenced to a lot of years in a maximum-security federal prison. She shuddered at the thought of what he'd already done and what he'd intended to do.

"Try not to dwell on it," Jack told her, patting her shoulder. "I'm gonna head on down to the office now and help Dad. We'll stop back before we call it a night, but Nick's staying. He can let us know if you need anything."

"Will do," agreed Nick.

Keri glanced back at him, wondering why he wanted to stay. He needn't feel responsible for her safety, and she didn't want him staying out of some misguided sense of duty. He didn't look as though he'd slept since the last time they'd shared a bed. Or shaved. Or eaten. Or even combed his hair.

She made a sound to get her brother's attention. "Food?" she whispered past a too-tight throat.

"You're hungry?" asked Jack. "Edie didn't think you'd want anything this evening."

She rolled her eyes toward Nick.

"Gotcha," he said after a brief pause. "Lamanto, you want me to have them bring you a sandwich or something?"

Nick gave her a smile. "Always the caregiver, huh?" To Jack, he said, "Yes, I'd like some food and a chance to hit the head before you go."

Jack nodded and Nick left her side for a few minutes. She watched him disappear and then looked back at her brother. He was giving her that all-knowing grin she'd grown up hating.

"Got it bad for the guy, huh, Sis? You had to pick a detective from the big, bad city?" he mocked, shaking his head. "All those years you've shunned law enforcement officers and then you fall head over heels for this one."

She tried to frown but couldn't feel her brows puckering. What she managed was a grunt of displeasure at his teasing.

"I'll have to give him extra points for coming to the rescue, though. He's smart and on the right side of the law. His superiors had nothing but good things to say about him, and the task force commander credits him for rounding up the last of the terrorists. You could do worse."

Keri glared at him, knowing he enjoyed teasing her while she couldn't respond. She wanted to warn him that payback was hell, but she had to settle for another grunt. Jack just smiled and kept up the banter until Nick returned to her bedside.

He'd splashed water on his face and combed his hair. She'd gotten used to the five o'clock shadow that always darkened his chin. The smile he gave her made her feel incredibly special. With him nearby, all felt right in her world again.

"Guess I'll be going now," said Jack, his tone still heavy with amusement. He patted her shoulder again. "Nice chatting with you."

Such a tease, thought Keri. She loved her brother dearly but sometimes he deserved a slap upside the head. When the door closed behind him, Nick leaned over the bed and kissed her softly. Then he drew back and held her gaze.

"You scared the hell out of me today," he told her in a low, deep tone that echoed throughout her body and resounded in her heart. His dark eyes glittered with emotion as he continued. "You've given me a few scares since we met, but nothing like today. I died a thousand deaths while Don had that gun pointed at you. I didn't know what he'd done to you or what he might still do, but I never want to be that scared again as long as I live. You got that, Miss Merritt?"

Keri never wanted to be that scared again, either, or feel so utterly helpless. She never wanted another madman waving a gun in her home or threatening the men she loved. Unfortunately, she tended to love men who regularly dealt with madmen. The thought distressed her to the point of agitation as she tried, but failed, to communicate her own feelings. Sounds got trapped in her throat and her hands refused her efforts to reach out to him.

Nick swiftly apologized. "Sorry, sweetheart, I shouldn't be laying this on you right now. I promised Nurse E. Morgan I'd let you get some rest. We can talk when you're better. Why don't you close your beautiful eyes and try to get some sleep?"

Keri forced herself to calm down. She knew she needed more time to cleanse her body of the toxin. Reluctant as she was to sleep, she was equally impatient to recover from the effects of the drug. Nick brushed a hand over her eyes. She closed them briefly but reopened them to watch him move around the room.

He shed his jacket and tossed it over the lone visitor's chair. Then he moved to the window and closed the blinds, blocking the afternoon sun. In her peripheral vision, she saw someone enter, and then realized one of the aides had brought him a tray of food. Nick took a seat beside her again, and she slowly drifted to sleep while he ate.

Hours later, Keri woke to the feel of the IV being taken from her hand. She felt a jolt of panic until she heard Nick's soothing voice.

"The night shift doc said you don't need any more saline," he told her from his position at her side.

After removing the needle and taping her hand, co-worker Liz Hart took her vitals and ordered her to sleep tight. He echoed the order, and she obeyed.

The next time Keri woke, it took her a minute to orient herself. The wall clock opposite her bed said three thirty. The room looked familiar, but not from her position. Then the events of the day rushed back, and she felt a surge or alarm until she lifted her arms.

Relief washed over her when she could feel her hands and feet again. She shifted her legs and twisted her head from side to side. Her gaze settled on Nick. Asleep in the straight-back chair, he looked horribly uncomfortable and indescribably beautiful. His right hand rested on the side rail of her bed as if he'd fallen asleep touching her.

She turned on her side, grasped his hand and tugged. His lashes flew up, gaze trained on her. Sleep cleared his expression, and he flashed her a smile.

"Hey there, pretty lady."

"Hey there, pretty guy," she replied, her voice hoarse but stronger. His soft chuckle made her smile and she actually felt her muscles responding. "That chair doesn't look very comfortable."

"Because it's not," he said, standing and stretching.

"How's your shoulder? I wanted to pound Joy for pounding on it. She must have heard about the gunshot wound."

"It's fine."

She locked gazes with him. "Would you tell me if it wasn't?"

"No," he said with a sleepy grin. Her heart did a little

somersault. She badly needed to touch him and hold him, to feel him as close as he could get.

"Why don't you put down this rail and climb in with me?"

She could tell the idea intrigued him. He gave it some thought and then reached behind his back and pulled his gun. He slid the clip out of it and laid it on the bedside stand. Next he crossed the room to make sure her door was closed, and he pulled a curtain around her for more privacy.

After dropping the bedrail, he kicked off his shoes and slid in beside her. Keri scooted against the opposite rail to allow him space, but as soon as he lay down, he gathered her in his arms.

She slipped her arms around him and held him tightly. His grip on her was crushing, but she didn't complain. Feeling his body snug against hers proved that all her nerves had recovered from the poison. Her body came alive with sensation and pleasure. They held each other for a long few minutes, delighting in the contact.

"Damn, but I've missed you," he said when they finally drew far enough apart to look at each other.

"I missed you too," she said, lifting a hand to run her fingers through his hair. It felt as thick and silky as always. Next she ran her fingers over his beard stubble, thrilled by the fact that she could feel the bristly hair. "I think the drug has finally worn off."

"We still don't know what he used, but the doctors don't expect long-term damage."

"Did I miss anything while I slept?"

"Your dad and Jack stopped by on their way home. I think your dad will have a real shiner tomorrow. They stabilized Russ Carson and flew him to a bigger hospital in Knoxville. They caught the second Moville brother trying to cross the Mexican border. All the other terrorists will be transported to a federal lock up later today."

"What about that Cooper guy in Miami?"

Nick stroked her hair. "No word yet."

"Who'll be transporting the prisoners?"

"They're in FBI custody. Part of my team already headed back to Knoxville. They'll fly back to Miami in a few hours."

"Do you have to go with them?"

His hand stilled, and he stared into her eyes. "I should. The lieutenant wants a report filed as soon as possible. There's Cooper to deal with, the McDowell hearing and a dozen other issues I've neglected for too long."

She'd known he couldn't stay, but it still hurt to hear him say he had to leave.

"Not the least being the destruction of your home," she reminded.

He frowned. "That too. I'll have to file insurance claims. What a mess. I hope Jenson is swimming with the fishes."

Keri chuckled. "How wicked of you. My dad always said there's nothing worse than a dirty cop."

"I like your dad. And your brother. They're good men."

Her smile deepened. "I told you they could be trusted."

"Yes, you did," he agreed, nodding. "But we detectives like tangible proof."

"Some things you have to learn the hard way."

Nick didn't respond. He cradled her head in his hand and guided her mouth to his. The kiss started out soft and easy, but gradually grew stronger and harder and more passionate. They'd grown breathless by the time their lips parted again.

He pressed his forehead to hers as they dragged in air. "Maybe climbing in bed wasn't such a good idea."

"I don't have any complaints," she told him. Then she slid a leg between his legs and felt the full strength of his arousal. "Ever made love in a hospital bed?" she asked as she slipped her hands down to his very delectable tush.

A rakish grin split his face. "What if one of your coworkers finds you in a compromising position? You'd be the talk of the hospital."

"I'm sure I've already given the gossips a field day. First I'm brought to the ER after being drugged by a homicidal ex-boyfriend, and then you announce you're my husband. They've probably already realized we spent the past ten days together. I'm branded for life."

He dropped a kiss on her lips. "Branded. I like the thought of that."

"You would."

Nick pulled her close again and slipped his left hand into the opening at the back of her gown. Keri knew she'd totally recovered from the drug when his touch seared her bare skin.

"Not much under this gown, is there?"

"Just panties."

He made a rough sound in his throat. "Tell me it's not a purple thong."

"It's not a purple thong," she whispered in his ear. Nibbling on his earlobe, she added, "Red bikinis. So skimpy that Edie gave me a *tsk, tsk* followed by a big thumbs-up."

He groaned and squirmed. Then he pulled her onto his chest and slid to the middle of the bed. She settled on top of him and cupped his face in her hands. He ran his hands down her back to squeeze her buttocks. Then he massaged the back of her thighs until she moaned with pleasure.

He stared into her eyes. "Consider this physical therapy."

"You don't look or feel like any therapist I ever met," she teased, peppering his face with kisses. "But you sure have great hands."

He proved his prowess by sliding his hand between their bodies and dipping his fingers between her legs for a deeper, more intimate massage.

"Nick!" Her whisper was part shock, part plea as he continued his bold caresses. She squirmed and rubbed herself against him with increasing intensity. He lifted his head and captured her lips in a deep, wet kiss, his tongue mimicking the motions of his stroking fingers.

Keri locked her fingers in his hair and clung to him as he

made the rest of her body tremble with need. Then he tugged at the neckline of her gown until it loosened and fell, baring her breasts to his hungry eyes and mouth. He moaned and caught her left nipple between his lips, sucking deeply. Keri clutched him tighter. When he shifted his attention to her other nipple, she felt the pull of desire deep in the core of her body.

"Nick, please!" she finally pleaded.

"Anything you want," he swore hoarsely. His dark eyes gleamed with passion as he stared into her equally hungry eyes.

She reached between them and stroked the length of his erection. Just the feel of his thick, hard shaft made her body weep and her muscles clench with desire.

"I want this," she whispered gruffly then amended. "I need this!"

"Anything else," he corrected, dipping his fingers deeper and stroking her until she shuddered with desire. "There's no lock on the door and no condom."

Keri considered his objections, but nothing compared with her need to connect with him in the most elemental fashion. She desperately wanted the intimacy, but the mention of protection stirred a whole hornet's nest of trouble.

"Are you diseased?" she finally asked him, staring deeply into his eyes.

He grasped her train of thought in an instant. "No. You?"

"Nope." She hesitated, and added, "Pregnancy isn't an issue."

He stilled his caresses for a minute and just stared at her. "Why wouldn't pregnancy be an issue? You want a baby? Our baby?"

Keri studied his features for a long minute. His rapt expression and hopeful tone meant he'd be happy if she wanted to get pregnant. His desire to create a child came as a chilling reminder that she couldn't conceive one.

She rolled off his body until she felt the press of the steel rail at her back. "I can't have children, Nick," she told him in a flat, defeated tone.

"Whoa there, come back to me," he reached for her, but she held him off. "What do you mean? You don't want kids yet? Or you just don't want them with me?"

"I like children, and I'd like a family. That's not the issue. The wreck destroyed my reproductive organs. I had a hysterectomy two years ago."

She could tell her admission shocked him, but then he quickly suppressed his reaction. He came from a big, loving family and wanted one of his own. Keri understood his desire to have children and mourned the loss for both of them. She might be his current heart's desire, but she wanted him to have everything he wanted in life.

Unable to bear his pity or his gradual withdrawal from their relationship, she decided to make a clean break of it. When he tried to pull her into his arms, she struggled and shoved him away.

"Keri, please."

"Drop it, Lamanto, or I'll ring for a nurse," she reached for the call button to back her threat with action.

"Don't shut me out," he argued. He gave her what little space he could and dropped his hands. "We can discuss it later or never discuss it again. There's no need to push me away. You're just feeling especially raw right now."

"You have to leave soon. You admitted as much. Now's as good a time as any to break things off. There's no sense prolonging the inevitable."

His eyes narrowed. "You don't mean that. You've had a rough couple days and we hit a snag, but we can work it out. Just like the trust issues."

"We can't work out the fact that you hate my home and everything about my life. I'd hate living in your concrete jungle." Tears filled her eyes, but she refused to let them fall. "Long distance relationships suck, and I can't give you the family you badly want, so there's really nothing left to discuss."

Nick slowly climbed out of bed but continued to stare at her with unflinching regard. "You're tired, battered and under a lot of stress. I'm going to leave before we say something that can't be forgiven, but I won't be gone long. When this terrorist mess is cleared up and you're back to normal, we'll finish the discussion."

"There's nothing more to discuss," she insisted, fighting to keep her voice steady. She'd never convince him to leave if she got all female and weepy. "It was good while it lasted. Great, even, if you discount all the violence. I couldn't have asked for a more exciting vacation fling, but I want my real life back."

"Vacation fling?"

His tone went low and angry. Keri didn't know if she'd hurt him with her careless words, but she'd definitely pissed him off. He glared at her for a long time.

When she didn't flinch or rescind the insult, he turned his back and reached for his gun. In slow, controlled motions, he slid the clip in place, tucked the gun into his waistband and reached for his jacket. She held her breath until he turned to her again.

With a blank expression and bland tone, he said, "Get some rest. I'll catch a ride to Knoxville and go home."

He started around the bed and pinned her with another tough-guy stare. "But I will be back," his tone deepened into a growl. "By then you should be fully recovered and ready to listen to reason."

Keri didn't turn to watch him go. She heard him speak to someone outside the door and assumed her dad had posted a guard. When the sound of his footsteps disappeared down the corridor, tears flowed over her cheeks. She didn't even try to swipe them off her face.

"Goodbye, my love," she whispered. A sob caught at her throat and then another and another. She curled into a fetal position and smothered the sobs with a pillow.

He wouldn't be back. She knew with all her heart he'd just walked out of her life forever. Gorgeous, filthy-rich, playboy-type city guys didn't settle down with backwoods, barren, country girls. Mismatched, star-crossed lovers only found their happily ever-afters in fiction, not real life. And it hurt so much.

Keri had to believe the hurting would stop in time. Nick had helped her heal the emotional wounds caused by her mother's death. Who'd help her heal all the new scars on her heart? Maybe she just cared too much, loved too deeply. Maybe she needed a whole new attitude about relationships.

Chapter Twenty

Keri finished her second week of vacation helping the hospital and the sheriff's department tie up all the loose ends of the failed terrorist attack. For the most part, she dodged the national media that swooped into their small community. Friends, family and coworkers diligently protected her from probing questions and hurtful reminders of the frightening events.

Nick called her repeatedly, both on her cell and at home. She let his calls go to voice mail. At first, he quietly explained what was happening in Miami, how he spent his days and that he badly wanted to talk to her. She didn't respond, but she listened to the messages over and over again. The sound of his voice was all that kept her from losing her mind at the thought of never seeing him again.

She went back to work and took on extra shifts to avoid dwelling on their relationship. Over the next two weeks, Nick's calls grew shorter, his tone increasingly frustrated when she failed to reply. Keri wondered how long he'd put up with her attitude before giving up on her altogether. She felt it best to alienate him, yet the soul-deep longing for him didn't ease.

On a Saturday evening three weeks after he'd left, Nick called her again. Alone in her bedroom and feeling miserable, she picked up her cell just before it rolled into voice mail.

"Hello, Nick." She greeted him quietly, sat down on her bed and pulled a pillow against her chest. It didn't fill the emptiness inside her, but she needed to cling to something.

"Keri." Her name sounded like a benediction. Relief mingled with pleasure in his voice, melting her heart and easing the ache that settled there when he left.

"The last time you called, you threatened to stop," she reminded. Even though she'd known it was best, the idea had nearly devastated her.

"I was tired and royally pissed that night, but I meant it at the time."

"So why call tonight?"

He went quiet for a minute. "Ever just have a bad need to hear a voice?" he asked softly.

Keri closed her eyes and sighed. She knew the feeling all too well. For the longest time, she'd desperately wanted to hear her mother's voice beyond her nightmares. Lately, she couldn't think of anyone or anything but Nick.

"I have," she told him noncommittally.

"I programmed my new cell number into your phone before I left Thornsbury," he said. "It's number one on your speed dial in case you haven't noticed. You could have given me a couple of minutes of time these past few weeks."

"I told you long-distance relationships suck."

"Especially if only one party is trying," he shot back.

She couldn't dispute that. She just hadn't realized how hard it would be to let go.

"So how are you feeling? Totally recovered from the nerve drug? Your dad said you canceled your final week of vacation and went back to work."

"You talked to my dad?"

"He doesn't refuse my calls."

"He didn't mention it."

"No surprise there. He said you're working too long and hard. He's worried about you."

"He's always worried about me."

"With good reason, I'm learning."

She made a rude sound. He ignored it and continued. "No other problems from the drug? No more crazies?"

"No problems and no crazy people, thank goodness," she replied and then added, "I heard on a network broadcast that

Cooper committed suicide."

"That's how the coroner ruled it," he said.

"You don't sound convinced."

"I'm not, but it makes a perverted kind of sense. He allegedly shot himself on the anniversary of his wife's death. And after he'd learned of the botched attack."

"She was killed on 9-11? At the towers?"

"Natural causes, but he still blamed her death on the attacks. That's why he planned his own form of revenge."

"And he killed himself on September 11?"

"It looks that way. The FBI agents found him dead when they went to pick him up for questioning."

"For a radical racist, the thought of prison might seem worse than death."

"Speaking of that, how's Russ Carson doing?"

"Okay, I guess. The feds aren't very forthcoming with information even though I've tried to get answers ever since I came back to work."

"You've been working a lot of hours?" he asked

"Yes."

"It won't help."

"Help what?"

"Trying to bury yourself in work and bottle up all the emotion. It didn't help you deal with your mom's loss, did it?"

She caught her breath. "Low blow, Lamanto."

"The truth hurts," he snapped back at her. "The lieutenant ordered me to do a few sessions with a shrink, so I'm all up to date on the psychological babble."

"What has the psychologist told you?"

"Not a damned, useful thing," he grumbled. "I told him the whole terrorist, wounded-on-the-run issue is past history. My only real problem is celibacy and a reluctant lover."

Keri smiled at his totally indignant, totally male attitude. His confession of celibacy lifted another weight from her heart. The thought of him sleeping with other women made her insane with jealousy. She'd never been the possessive type, so she had no idea how to deal with the emotion. But then, she'd never loved anyone as much as she loved Nick.

"What are you thinking? I can hear your thoughts spinning across the miles."

"You're altogether too full of yourself, Lamanto."

"Just another reason we're perfect together," he argued. "I have too much and you need more."

His reasoning made her smile again. He had an abundance of confidence. She had too much insecurity. Did that make them right for each other? Or did it guarantee failure? She couldn't risk choosing the wrong path.

"Did the shrink tell you that?"

His tone went flat. "The shrink told me to get laid."

Keri laughed out loud at his uncharacteristic crudity. She tossed the pillow aside and wrapped her free arm around her knees. "I've heard celibacy makes men surly. Your shrink might have a point."

"It's the only thing he's said that makes real sense," Nick claimed. "So what are we going to do about it?"

"We?"

"Have you slept with anyone since I left?"

"Of course not."

"Then why do you think I'd sleep with anyone but you? Like it or not, Merritt, we're in a committed relationship. I honor my commitments. Are you saying you don't?"

Trick question. Keri didn't respond. She wouldn't demean what they'd shared. She'd committed herself heart and soul, but weeks of trying to find an answer to their other issues had left her feeling hopeless.

"There's a big difference between emotional commitment and long-term practicalities."

"Talking is practical and a good start."

"Talk's cheap," she teased softly.

His tone dropped an octave, to a low, sexy timbre that sent

a shiver over her. "There's always phone sex."

Intrigued despite herself, she felt her body going all liquid and needy. How could he affect her so intensely with nothing more than a naughty suggestion?

"I doubt that's what your shrink had in mind."

"The hell with the shrink. All I want is you. Any way I can get you."

The bold declaration stole her breath. Keri hugged her knees tighter to her chest as her breasts prickled with arousal. It had been too long. Way too long since she'd felt his touch.

"Have I shocked you speechless, Nurse Merritt?"

"I've never had phone sex, Lamanto," she chided. "Are you an experienced phone sex guy?"

"Can't say that I am, but I'm willing to give it a shot."

She laughed at his candor. "Well, I'm in my bed. I guess that's a start. Where are you?"

"My bed at the villa. Since I've never been in your bedroom, we'll have to do it here."

She rolled onto her side and kept laughing. "Do it?" Typical male. "That's so romantic. I'm blushing with arousal."

His tone went low and serious. "Is your hair all mussed and your cheeks flushed? Are you wearing some skimpy, silky underwear? Or nothing at all? Give me a little visual here."

"My hair is a mess and my cheeks feel warm," she lowered her tone to match his. "I'm wearing an old, thin T-shirt and cotton pajama bottoms."

"Are your nipples hard?"

How could they not be, she wondered, when he said the words aloud? The sound whispered along her nerves and spread heat throughout her body.

"They are now."

"Damn."

The hunger in his lone word made her breath catch again and her breasts tighten. Keri had to clear her throat before she could respond. "What are you wearing?"

"Not a thing."

"Are you hard?" she whispered huskily.

His voice roughened. "Hell yeah. Since I left you."

She almost choked as she envisioned him naked and aroused. Her whole body throbbed with matching need. "Then I guess this is how you do phone sex."

"The easy part," he challenged, "but I'm a sensualist. Satisfaction comes with touching, tasting and feeling. Nothing compares to being together."

"Long distance relationships suck."

"So come to Miami."

His demand hung in the air between them. He knew she didn't want to come to Miami. She knew he didn't want to come to Thornsbury. They lived totally separate lives. It wasn't just a matter of distances but cultures and lifestyles.

"Square one again," she replied quietly. "We can't fly back and forth indefinitely. The nearest airport is a long way from Thornton. We'd spend more time traveling than being together. How long before that causes guilt, hard feelings and finger pointing? Will we end up hating each other?"

"I don't have any easy answers."

"I'm not looking for easy, Nick, but I can't see any way past the major obstacles."

"And what we have isn't worth the effort? Is that what you're really saying?"

The statement took her by surprise. Before she could formulate a response, he told her good night and broke the connection. She stared at the phone, heart pounding.

It had started already, just as she'd known it would. Discussing the issues keeping them apart could only lead to anger and resentment. Soon the resentment would turn to bitterness and they'd destroy the love they shared. That's what she'd hoped to avoid by not taking his calls.

Nick's shrink might think sex would solve the problem, but Keri knew better. As much as she wanted to prolong their relationship, it would be cruel and selfish. He hadn't mentioned her inability to have children, but she knew it would put an additional, possibly paralyzing, strain on their relationship. She needed to be strong and resist his charm. She couldn't bear to fall deeper in love and then lose him.

Lost in thought, Keri didn't hear the knock on her bedroom door until the second one was accompanied by her dad's voice.

"Keri?"

She turned to sit on the edge of her bed and told him to come in.

"What's up?"

Walt stood in the doorway and gave her a smile. "I heard laughter from in here and wondered if you had company. It's been a long time since I heard you laugh."

She frowned. "Have I been such a sour puss lately?"

"You have," he said, grinning. "So who or what made you happy this evening?"

"Nick, I talked to him on the phone."

"He makes you happy, yet you refuse most of his calls. I didn't think I raised such a dense daughter."

She made a face at him. "I'm not dense, thank you very much," she responded lightly. "You taught me to be sensible, logical and face my problems head-on."

"But not in a cowardly fashion," he inserted firmly. "You're trying to solve a problem by avoiding it. Nothing gets fixed if you don't try."

"There's nothing to fix!" she insisted, frowning at him in frustration. "We're totally unfit for each other. Our worlds are light-years apart. You have no idea."

When her dad returned her steady regard, she qualified. "You do know, don't you?"

He nodded. "I did a background search, just like I have for every other man you've shown an interest in over the years," he declared without apology. "It wasn't easy because Lamanto protects his private life. With the help of his lieutenant, I finally learned more about his background."

"Incredible wealth, Dad. Not just well-to-do but centuries-old wealth and influence. Totally not my thing."

He shook his head at her reasoning. "I also learned what others think of his character and values. He's a good man. He's proved that more than once. The fact that you trusted him with your life was a pretty strong point in his favor too. You have good people instincts and you don't freely offer your trust."

"Maybe I'm just a foolish woman who succumbed to his charm. One of many, I'm sure."

"If he has so many, why bother with a reluctant one?"

She'd asked herself the same question numerous times. "Maybe it's the challenge or the thrill of the chase."

"You really believe that?"

Keri ran both hands through her hair. "No."

"You love him?"

She averted her gaze. "Yes, but..."

"There is no but, baby girl. It's not something you toss aside because you're afraid. You give it a lot of thought and then a lot of effort and then more effort. True love is worth a lifetime of nurturing."

"How in the world are you supposed to know if it's true love?"

"You feel it with all your heart and soul."

Toward the end of a twelve-hour shift the following Friday night, Keri stood at the nurse's desk checking patient charts. She heard the grind of the automatic doors as they opened but didn't look up until Edie nudged her with an elbow.

"Your husband's here."

Tired and distracted, Edie's words didn't register until Keri glanced toward the late arrival. She watched Nick Lamanto stride through the doors and forgot all about the day's frustrations and exhaustion. Her breath hitched as weariness gave way to excitement. The sight of him delighted and re-energized her. Happiness blossomed within her as their gazes met. She gave him a slow, wonderful-to-see-you smile.

Nick searched her features intently as he narrowed the distance between them. His perusal made her heart pound and her nerves jangle. His jeans, shirt and jacket looked rumpled, but he still oozed sex appeal.

Suddenly self-conscious about her stained uniform and disheveled appearance, she wiped the smile off her face and tried to appear more professional.

"Lamanto," she greeted him as he stepped up to the desk.

"Merritt," he replied with a nod.

His hair had grown, the thick waves more pronounced. His cheeks bore the end-of-the-day shadows. His dark eyes glittered as they locked with hers. For a long time they just stared at each other. Neither moved nor spoke but soaked in the sight of each other, cataloguing every minute detail until Edie broke the silence by clearing her throat.

She shot a glance at her friend.

"Take your time," said the older woman. "I can handle things for a while."

Keri motioned for Nick to move around the nurse's station. She stepped through the opening, and he took hold of her arm. Heat rushed through her body at his touch. Just being close to him brought her unimaginable pleasure.

Nick leaned close and whispered in her ear. "All the hospital shows on TV have a maintenance closet or boiler room where couples can make out. Got one of those?"

She didn't look at him but smiled at his impatience. "You want a little privacy?" she teased.

"I want a lot of things, but privacy's a good start."

The hospital had a tiny staff lounge with personnel lockers, an aging dinette set and a narrow bed. Keri led him there without another word and turned the knob of the door. He followed her inside the darkened room, quickly closed the door and leaned against it. Then he pulled her into his arms and gathered her close.

He studied her upturned face for several long heartbeats as she snaked her arms up his chest to his shoulders. She returned his steady gaze, wanting his kisses more than her next breath. He brushed his lips back and forth across hers, teasing and tasting.

"Damn, I've missed you," he whispered gruffly.

Impatient for more of him, she rose on tiptoe and captured his mouth with hers, sinking her fingers into his hair and kissing him with all the pent-up hunger simmering inside of her. Nick made a rough sound of matching hunger and thrust his tongue into her mouth. He tightened his hold. She wrapped her arms around his neck, leaning into the kiss, pressing her whole body against his.

They strained to get closer as one kiss led to another and another, deeper, hotter, harder. She sucked his tongue hungrily until his body bucked with desire. He gripped her hips and lifted her until their bodies aligned perfectly.

"Here. Now." His gruff command had her reaching for the snap of his jeans, but he stalled her by tugging her tunic over her head. While her trembling fingers worked at his zipper, Nick slid her bra straps off her shoulders, uncovering her breasts. She'd just freed his erection when he dipped his head and took a nipple into his mouth.

Her low moan echoed around the room. She grasped his head again as the pull of his mouth on her breasts echoed to the core of her body.

"Bed," she gasped.

"Too far," he replied, tugging her uniform pants and panties down her hips. Keri toed off her shoes and shimmied out of her the rest of her clothes.

"Now?" he coaxed roughly.

In response, she wrapped her arms around his shoulders and let him lift her onto his straining flesh. As they made the most intimate connection, they groaned in unison and locked gazes again.

"I've missed you like crazy," he declared with sexy, passionate sincerity.

The declaration thrilled and scared her. Instead of returning the words, she locked her mouth onto his and kissed him deep and hard. Her hungry impatience destroyed what little control he had on his desire. He thrust into her with urgency. They strained for harder, deeper contact.

Their breathing grew loud and rough as their bodies moved in rhythmic demand. His fingers dug into her hips, pulling her still closer, squeezing her harder. She rocked against him with urgent thrusts, matching his pace and fervor. In another few minutes, Keri stifled a cry of satisfaction. He found completion with one final thrust, and then muffled his triumphant howl in the curve of her neck.

The sound of their ragged panting reverberated in the otherwise silent room. For a long while afterward, they held each other as their bodies gradually calmed from the physical high. Nick nibbled on her neck until their breathing settled to a more comfortable level. Keri eventually unwound her legs from around his waist and dropped her feet to the floor.

"I so needed that. Needed you," he told her.

"Me too," she confessed, planting kisses on his whiskered jawline. "Thank you very much."

"You're very welcome. I could really get used to this bareback stuff," he teased, flashing a rakish grin. "It's a first for me."

Keri stroked a finger down his cheek, brushing her thumb over his lips. "A little messier on my end," she noted.

"Sorry, sweetheart. I didn't think of that."

"No need to apologize. I'm sure not complaining."

Nick's grin deepened. "Glad to hear it."

He reached for the light switch, but she stalled him, suddenly feeling too naked and exposed.

"First dibs on the bathroom," she said, bending to gather her clothes before darting toward the lavatory door. His wicked chuckle followed her.

"Hey, I don't mind. I like the rear view!"

"You're so bad!" she charged, laughing as she closed the door between them.

It only took her a few minutes in the bathroom and then Nick had a turn. She walked across the room, flipped the light switch and went to the refrigerator. When he came back into the lounge, she offered him a cold bottle of water. Keri started to take a seat at the table but he redirected her to the bed.

"I like you close," he explained as they sat side by side on the squeaky mattress. Grasping her free hand, he entwined their fingers as they drank thirstily. She loved that he was such a sensual man. Loved that he liked touching her.

Keri could hardly believe how much comfort and pleasure she found just holding his hand. The connection, any connection with him, made everything seem right in her world. What in the hell was she going to do about it?

"Am I keeping you from work? Do you have a limited break time? I don't want to cause any trouble here at the hospital."

"The staff already labeled you troublemaker of the year," she teased, but his thoughtfulness pleased her. "I'm fine. It's been a slow evening and my shift's over at midnight." She glanced at her watch. "Another few minutes. Edie said she'd cover for me, but I do need to go sign off on my charts."

"What then?"

"Normally, home to bed. What did you have in mind?"

Nick frowned. "I hoped to spend the weekend. It's the first free one I've had in weeks. But I got a call from Brice while I was renting a car in Knoxville. He needs some help tomorrow morning, and I couldn't say no. I owe him."

"He didn't know you'd flown up here?"

"No."

Keri wanted to argue. She wanted to tell him to let Brice find someone else to help him. But she knew the favors Nick owed were probably because of her.

"So you just have tonight?"

He glanced at his watch. "A couple hours. I scheduled a return flight for first thing in the morning."

She brought his hand up to her mouth and pressed a kiss on his fingers. "We can hang out on the couch at my house, but I have to be back here by noon tomorrow."

"And you need some rest."

"If I want to be able to function at all. It'll be the third of three twelve-hour shifts."

"Well hell," he said.

Keri finished her water and tossed the bottle in the recycle bin. Nick did the same. Then he turned to her again.

"Do you still have a week's vacation coming to you?"

She nodded, wondering what he had in mind.

"My sisters are planning a thirty-fifth wedding anniversary party for Mama and Pop. The last weekend in October. Can you come and spend a few days at the villa?"

Keri hesitated. Spending time with him was one thing. Meeting his extended family was a whole different kettle of fish. "You're living there now? Full-time?"

"At least 'til the end of the year. I'll pay airfare and expenses. You just have to show up."

Remembering her dad's lecture about cowardice, she gave him a smile and said, "I'll request vacation before I leave tonight."

Nick's obvious relief made her feel guilty. He gave her a heart-melting smile and dropped his head for a kiss. Their lips just touched as a sharp knock came on the door accompanied by Edie's voice.

"Squad just called. Car wreck with multiple victims. Five minutes out."

"I'll be right there," said Keri. She sighed and gave Nick an apologetic smile. "Duty calls and it doesn't sound like I'll be getting out of here anytime soon."

"No problem," he brushed a finger down her cheek. "You'll

need sleep after that. I can head back to Knoxville and catch a few zees at the airport."

"I hate that we don't have more time. You should have let me know you were coming. I could have juggled my schedule."

"I didn't have enough time, but I got what I needed."

The comment annoyed her. She'd needed him too, but it irritated her to think he'd wanted her body more than spending time with her. "Pretty expensive sex."

"That sex was great, but not what I came for."

That gave her pause. She studied his features. Nick gave her a slow, sexy smile, his eyes glittering with intensity.

"Then what did you want?"

"I needed to see your gut reaction when I showed up unannounced."

Keri didn't blink. "And?" she prodded, remembering the thrill she'd felt at the sight of him.

"And your face lit up like a woman in love," he said, cupping her head in his hand and drawing her close for another long, deep kiss. His tone went husky when he continued. "The sex was a bonus, *la mia infermiera d'angelo.*"

Chapter Twenty-One

After a week of cold, dreary fall weather in Thornsbury, Keri welcomed Miami's sunshine. According to her pilot, the heat and humidity of the summer had given way to near-perfect temperatures and perfect blue skies. Keri stepped off the terminal ramp and into the clusters of people awaiting friends and family, wondering if he said that every time he landed.

Then the sight of Nick stripped all other thought from her mind. She dropped her carryon case and pocketbook to the floor as he swept her into his arms. They hugged tightly and kissed deeply despite the beehive of activity moving all around them. Phone sex and regular conversations just didn't compare to the feel and scent and taste of the man.

"I've missed you so much!" she confessed on a laugh when he finally allowed her feet to touch the floor again. She stroked his cheeks, smoothly shaven for once, and stole another kiss.

"I've missed you more," he declared, his gaze scouring every inch of her face. "I've spent the better part of the month sitting in court rooms, bored out of my mind. The image of you is all that kept me from going ballistic."

"So did the gangbanger brother get a life sentence?"

"He did," Nick said with satisfaction. "Along with a couple of his cousins. The McDowell gang is permanently retired."

"Glad to hear it."

"Glad to be done with the legal end," he said. "Do you have bags to claim?"

"One big one," she said, grabbing her pocket book as he shouldered her carryon. "Are we heading straight to the villa?"

He gave her a wicked grin. "I thought about renting a motel room and having my way with you for the rest of the day."

She squeezed his arm. "Hmm...I like the sound of that."

"But Brice just called to let me know he brought the 'copter to the city. He's loading groceries on the other side of the airport, and we can hitch a ride with him in an hour or so. We only have time for lunch if you want."

"Lunch sounds good. I'm hungry, but please tell me we'll have a little privacy once we get to the villa."

He gave her a wink and another kiss. "The folks won't be home until this evening. We'll have the place to ourselves all afternoon."

"And then I'll get shifted to the guest side of the villa?" She didn't like the idea of sleeping so far from him in that great big old mansion.

"Nah, I did some bargaining with Maria. She and her brood will be using another suite so you'll have the room next to mine. The one you used last time."

"Your family's okay with that?"

"The family is so happy to have me living at home they don't argue about anything I want."

"You are so spoiled!" she teased, bumping shoulders with him as they made their way to the baggage claim. It felt good to be near him, close enough to touch him and see his amazing smile instead of just hearing it.

"Well loved, not spoiled, big difference."

Keri chose a sleeveless turquoise blouse paired with a wildly patterned multi-colored skirt for dinner that evening. Shopping for a week with Nick's family had involved more time and consideration than she'd given to her wardrobe in years. She'd aimed for casual elegance and hoped she'd succeeded.

The silky, tailored style of her blouse accented her breasts without being too tight or suggestive. It tucked into the waistband of the skirt, which, thankfully, had a slimming affect on her hips.

Unaccustomed to wearing high heels, she'd limited her

shoe choices to low-heeled sandals. A curling iron had enhanced the femininity of her normal hair style. Her jewelry included a matching set of yellow gold necklace, earrings and bracelet. She'd just finished applying a light coat of lip gloss when Nick knocked at the bedroom door.

His eyes widened at the sight of her, and he gave her a low whistle of appreciation. It went a long way to settling the butterflies in her stomach. The thought of meeting his parents put her in a state of panic every time she allowed herself to dwell on it.

"At the risk of boring you with an old cliché, you look good enough to eat," he said as he reached out a hand for one of hers.

Keri locked her fingers with his and felt the now-familiar zing of electricity ripple through her body. They'd spent an incredible few hours in bed this afternoon, making up for lost time and loving each other with new depth and intimacy. She blushed at the memories.

Nick laughed. "Don't even let your mind wander back to bed, sweetheart, or we really will be in trouble with the family. I'm this close," he rubbed noses with her, "to hauling you back to my room."

She laughed softly, brushing her lips over his. "I never wanted to leave it in the first place," she teased.

He grumbled, "It was your idea to shower separately. We could have saved time and water." He slipped his arms around her waist and drew her close enough for her to feel his very male reaction to the conversation.

Heat suffused her body at the evidence of his renewed arousal. Her body still hummed from earlier loving. They couldn't get enough of each other. She didn't know if they'd ever get enough.

"Dinner, your parents," she reminded when Nick started pressing kisses at the curve of her neck. The moist heat of his mouth sent a shiver of desire over her. The hours of loving made her putty in his hands.

"Dinner, parents," he mimicked, nuzzling the tender spot beneath her right ear. "All I want is more of you—days, weeks, months of you."

A clock chiming in the hallway drew their attention to the passing of time. He straightened and stepped aside so she could precede him out the door, but the look he gave her sizzled with hunger.

"Later, big boy, later," she promised, flashing him a sultry smile. "Just use the time to think of all the ways you want me to pleasure you. Then I'll see about bringing your fantasies to life."

His moan was low and long and heartfelt as they headed down the flight of stairs to the main floor. He scolded her for putting that thought in his mind as he led her to a small sitting room where his parents waited. His X-rated promise of retribution had her blushing wildly.

Keri hoped their expressions didn't advertise their thoughts as his mother and dad rose to meet them. They looked older than the picture she'd seen of them, but very cool and distinguished. His dad wore dark slacks and a cotton dress shirt. He looked like an older version of his son, but with silvery white hair. Nick's mother looked a little heavier than in the photo but very chic and sophisticated in her black cocktail dress.

Keri reached out a hand to each as Nick introduced them by their first names, Paul and Bethany. She politely commented on the beauty of their home and thanked them for their hospitality.

"Nick's friends are always welcome," said Paul. "For too many years, he's been remiss in bringing them."

Nick had warned her that his parents would chastise him first, ply them both with wine and then do some serious prying into her life. Keri knew the parental routine all too well. Except for the wine, she'd lived it most of her life. Apparently, you never outgrew it.

Bethany returned to her seat on the sofa and crossed her

legs. "Please sit down. Teresa said she'd call when dinner is ready. We have a few minutes to relax and chat."

"How about some wine while we wait?" asked Paul, moving toward a beautiful, built-in bar of the light, airy room. The Mediterranean décor boasted a wall of windows with the sun dipping in toward the ocean. A cluster of furniture sat on a beautiful oriental rug. Nick guided Keri to a chair and then took a seat in a matching one, facing his parents.

After serving them each a glass of wine, Paul sat down beside Bethany. Nick shot Keri a warning glance. After the wine and pleasantries, the real interrogation would begin.

"Nick tells us you're a trauma nurse, Keri."

"Yes, in a small county hospital near my home."

"In Tennessee," said his dad.

"Thornsbury. It's on the northeast corner. The closest city is Knoxville."

"We've visited Nashville, but never Knoxville. A beautiful state, though, from what we've seen," added Bethany. "Has your family always lived in Thornsbury?"

"Several generations of my dad's family."

Nick's parents both nodded. Keri didn't know if it was an acceptance of the generational commitment or just a verification of what they already knew. She didn't doubt they'd had her investigated. It's what her dad would do.

"Are you Catholic?" asked Paul.

Nick made a sound of displeasure. "Pop."

"Protestant," she said, trying to keep Nick from getting all defensive on her behalf. "I was raised in the Baptist church."

"And your father is in law enforcement?" asked Paul, shooting an unapologetic glance at his son.

"Yes, as well as my brother and various other family members over the years."

"You must have been very worried for them during the terrorist activity last month," said Bethany. "Such a frightening event."

"Yes, I was and it was," she replied, wondering at their line of questioning. It didn't seem like the usual "Who are you and what do you want from our son?" questions.

"Nicholas said he'd been visiting in the area just days before the trouble erupted."

Keri nodded and took a sip of wine. She didn't look at Nick, and she wasn't about to comment. Now she knew exactly what details they wanted. Did they blame her and her family for their son's involvement? Were they even aware of Nick's role in averting the terrorist plot?

"Did you know any of the people involved?" asked Paul. "Were they from your hometown?"

"Several," she said, deciding to reply without volunteering any information. In her teenage years, she'd advised boyfriends to do the same during her dad's inevitable interrogations.

A peripheral glance at Nick had him crossing his arms over his chest, his expression hardening.

"Stop with the third degree," he told his parents with respectful firmness. "I told you Keri and I played very minor roles in the terrorist incident. Right, Keri?"

She took another sip of wine and then stared into the crystal goblet, contemplating the sparkling liquid. The Lamantos wanted the truth. Nick wanted her to give them empty reassurances. She didn't want to reply at all.

After a brief, pregnant silence, Nick prodded. "Back me up here, Keri. What's the problem?"

"Well," she drawled slowly. "I'm thinking there's a fine line between backing you up and deliberately deceiving your parents. I'm trying to choose my words very carefully so I don't cross any lines that can't be uncrossed."

Nick reached across the small table between them and touched her arm, nudging her to look directly at him. "When it comes to fine lines, you're supposed to stay on my side of it," he declared. "Of that, I'm sure."

"But, Nico, I'm so interested in Keri's take," said Bethany.

And to her, "Nick led us to believe he'd stayed out of harm's way. Did he give us a whitewashed version, as usual?"

"I don't whitewash," he groused.

"Then why don't you let the young woman explain in her own words."

Keri finished off her wine and set the glass on the table. Her head spun a little from drinking the wine too quickly on an empty stomach. She gave Paul a smile.

"My words would have to include a GSW, APB, mercenaries with machine guns and vicious dogs. You probably know his home got blown to bits. He was shot at by a dirty cop and tackled a madman with a gun pointed at me. Then he helped round up all the terrorists so they couldn't blow up innocent people. I'll leave it to you to decide how minor his involvement."

His parents stared at her, speechless for a second. Nick dismissed her words with a wave of his hand. "The FBI and Homeland team rounded up all the terrorists, I just gave them directions."

His dad's bushy white eyebrows rose in concern. "Just a traffic cop, Son?"

Keri smiled at Paul's expression, so like the one his son used to chastise her on occasion.

"Oh, and I forgot the crazed nurse with a hypodermic he wrestled to save my life the second time."

"Crazed nurse?" his mother said in a choked voice. Keri could tell she was finding it difficult to process the extent of Nick's participation.

"Don't mention that homicidal maniac," Nick said with a snap in his voice. He stood and stared down at her. "I get furious just thinking about her and that needle. In another few seconds, she'd have killed you. Killed you with me standing over your bed! I have nightmares! Another few seconds! Too damned close for comfort."

Keri looked into his eyes and saw a resurgence of turbulent emotion. The memories of that night surfaced rapidly, engulfing her. She knew he felt the same pain, fear and uncertainty. Despite therapy, they'd suffered more emotional trauma than most couples experienced in a lifetime.

The parental inquisition forgotten, she rose and took his hand as a wave of remembered terror swept through her. If not for him, she would be dead. He'd healed her and saved her in so many ways. She gave him a smile and lifted his hand to her lips.

"My hero," she mouthed.

He shook his head, denying the credit.

"You're mine," he replied softly, dropping a hand to her waist and pulling her closer. They'd gone through a lot together and become stronger in the process. The love and respect they shared had a rock-solid foundation.

Keri didn't know if it was the wine or Nick, but her head and heart felt lighter. He stared at her lips for a long minute. They didn't kiss but she still felt the impact of his caress. He only had to look at her with his beautiful eyes and she knew what he wanted.

After another long minute, his mother interrupted them with a hoarse question. "GSW stands for gunshot wound in medical terminology, doesn't it?"

Nick and Keri stepped apart. She glanced guiltily toward his parents, embarrassed to have ignored their presence.

"Just a flesh wound," Nick told her in a soothing tone.

"Twelve stitches," added Keri.

Nick frowned at her. "You know, there is such a thing as too much information."

"Sorry," she said, sounding anything but apologetic. "Should I apologize for being naturally honest? I'm not used to undercover secrecy and deception."

His parents sudden burst of laughter dispersed the growing tension in the room.

Bethany rose from her seat and stepped close enough to hug Keri. She said, "A very warm welcome to our home, my dear. Anyone who can hold their own with our difficult, argumentative son, will always be welcome here."

"The hell," Nick protested.

"I'd like a little more information about the gunshot wound," said his dad. "Nick's never been very forthcoming with details. His mother and I had to pry information out of him as a child. I don't know how he got so secretive."

"I'm fine. I had an awesome nurse."

The intercom beeped, and Teresa announced dinner. Nick made his parents swear they wouldn't drill Keri anymore. For that, she gave him her sweetest smile.

The following evening, Nick stole her breath when he came to her bedroom door dressed in a tuxedo. She'd never imagined herself with a man so incredibly gorgeous, who wore the formal attire as comfortably as jeans. A huge wave of insecurity hit her at a reminder of the differences in their upbringing and lifestyles. Already nervous about the anniversary party, she felt nausea swirling in her stomach.

"Hey, it's not that bad," he insisted. "I only wore it to please the folks. If you hate the monkey suit, I'll get rid of it in a couple hours."

"You think I hate it?"

"Your expression went pretty sour."

She tried to fend off his probing with flattery. "It's not the suit. You look too yummy for words." Moving closer, she pressed her hands flat on his chest and leaned in for a kiss. He dropped one on her lips.

"The wealth again?" he guessed at her concern. "That's one dragon I can't slay for you," he said, dropping a second, harder kiss on her mouth. "It is what it is. It's part of my life, but it does not define me."

Keri gave him a smile. She didn't want to be defined by her family or finances, either. But understanding and accepting it in her heart were two different things.

"I'm glad," she replied softly.

Nick slipped his arms around her waist and drew her close. All the party preparations and the arrival of family had kept them too busy for alone time. Her body instantly responded to his touch.

"You look beautiful tonight," he told her as their gazes locked. "You should wear red more often. It suits your coloring and your personality."

"That so?"

"Red-hot," he teased, running his hands up and down her back. "And I like the feel of it."

The gown she'd chosen for the party had a draped bodice and figure-hugging fit with a calf-length, handkerchief hem. The softness came from polyester, not silk or satin.

"Edie labeled it my slinky red number."

"Edie's right on. I'd like to take it right off." He dropped a kiss at the top of her chest, where the fabric dipped to show a hint of cleavage.

Keri laughed at his tone and expression. Then her breath hitched as his kiss turned into a gentle sucking. "I'd be happy to let you, but we're expected at the party. I don't doubt for one minute that we'd have a search party after us if we don't show."

Nick drew back until they could look into each other's eyes again. "As soon as it's polite to leave, we're sneaking out to the cabin cruiser and getting lost at sea for a few hours. I need my Keri Merritt fix to make it through the rest of the weekend. My bedroom's off-limits since the munchkins don't understand the concept of privacy."

She smiled at his nickname for the nieces and nephews, envisioning them pouncing on him in the early hours. "Speaking of which, I heard lots of giggling downstairs."

Nick pulled her close for another long kiss, his mouth a warm, moist, consuming reminder of the intimacy they shared. When they finally drew apart, his eyes held a possessive gleam. A fine tremor shot through her and she knew her expression mirrored his. The bond between them continued to strengthen and consume her thoughts.

He offered his arm and escorted her to the first floor where guests had started gathering. Neither of them spoke, both preoccupied by the intensity of their emotional connection.

The ballroom glittered with chandeliers and smelled of roses, Bethany's favorite flower. On tables throughout, champagne fountains sparkled, ice sculptures glittered and caterers kept trays piled high with food. Music played softly in the background, but the increasing level of conversation quickly drowned the melody.

They hugged his parents and wished them many more happy years of marriage. Then Nick started introducing her to his relatives. Her earlier visit to the villa had paved the way to remembering names and matching them to faces of his siblings. Only family and closest friends had been invited to the anniversary party, yet people poured in by yachts-full, filling the huge ballroom and overflowing to the balconies.

The Lamantos had six grandchildren but dozens of nieces and nephews, great-nieces and nephews, as well. All had dressed in their party finery and were on their best behavior. Keri tried to mentally log the additional names, but lost track. Nick told her not to worry, just smile and nod a lot.

She quickly learned how much they all loved him. His siblings, nieces and nephews demanded individual attention, vying for hugs, kisses and a minute of undivided time. Keri enjoyed watching him interact with them as the hours slipped by with surprising speed.

"I wouldn't have imagined you being so patient," she said a good while later when all the parents had herded their children off to bed.

"I'm a doting uncle and a godfather. I have to keep up with what's important in their lives. Konor's into monsters, superheroes and anything ghoulish. Emily loves monkeys, baseball and everything blue. Jadyn's a miniature fashionista who follows the teen movie stars. Allison likes princesses and gymnastics. Aaron and Aidan aren't very verbal yet, they like guitars, rocks and worms."

She laughed and took his proffered arm. "I'll take your word for it, *Zio* Niko. I had a hard time deciphering some of the chatter."

"You get used to it, but all that chatter made me thirsty."

"And hungry."

He shot her an apologetic grin. "Damn, I'm sorry, I'm a terrible host. You're probably starved."

"That's okay. No afternoon delight to work up an appetite today," she drawled, batting her eyes but quickly dissolving into laughter. Nick laughed too, and then dropped a kiss on her mouth and led her toward the food.

They ate and drank champagne and ate some more, always chatting, always catching up on someone's news. Keri knew she was the focus of conversation with many of the guests. Only a couple of women glared at her, but she wrote that off as jealousy since they didn't even know her. Most everyone else welcomed her with smiles and genuine warmth.

Halfway through the evening, she found herself separated from Nick but sharing a quiet moment with his mother. The two women stood near a wall and watched everyone else mingle.

"You have a beautiful family," she told Bethany.

"Thank you. I think so too. We're very fortunate and very proud of them."

"They obviously adore you and Paul."

"And we adore every one of them."

Keri didn't know why, but she felt compelled to confide her worst fear to Nick's mom, maybe because it had preyed on her mind all evening, maybe because she couldn't discuss it with her own mother or maybe because she simply needed to get it off her chest.

"I can't have children."

Bethany turned to her with a frown. "You can't because you don't want to? You're afraid of childbirth? Or just more interested in your career?"

"I'm not afraid or unwilling. I always wanted children, but I had a hysterectomy as a result of a car wreck. I'm not physically capable of bearing a child."

Bethany moved closer and slid an arm around her waist. Though she barely knew Nick's mother, Keri suddenly felt overwhelmed with emotion. She felt a warmth for and connection with the wealthy, successful executive she'd never expected.

"I totally understand, dear. I'm not just saying that, I honestly do. My reproductive system never developed properly when I went through puberty, so I couldn't bear children either. It can be a burden on your heart, but it doesn't have to stop you from having a family."

Bethany's gentle tone and affectionate hug brought tears to Keri's eyes. She blinked them in confusion. "I'm not sure I understand."

"It's not a secret. All of our children are adopted."

Keri's eyes widened in amazement. She glanced around the room again. Each member of the Lamanto family bore a striking resemblance. "How?"

"We adopted the children through Catholic services and with a preference for Italian heritage. The twins are actually blood relation of mine. I had a cousin in Italy with eight children. When they learned she was carrying twins, they knew they couldn't handle two more, so they agreed to let us adopt them. Sonia and Sofie visit their biological parents and siblings as often as possible, but they're our family too."

"So they've always known?"

"Our children have always known the circumstances of their birth, as much as we knew to tell them. But, as you said, we adore them and we're a close-knit family despite the biological issues."

"Nick? He looks so much like Paul."

"He's never mentioned his adoption?"

Keri shook her head, trying to absorb the information and reconcile it with the abundance of love and respect she'd witnessed all evening. Why hadn't Nick told her? He'd had plenty of opportunities to discuss the issue, and he knew it bothered her.

"Hey, why are my two favorite girls standing here like wallflowers?" Both women looked at Nick in surprise. Deep in conversation, they hadn't noticed his approach.

"I was telling Keri how your papa and me created our family," said Bethany.

Nick studied Keri's face. "Happy tears? Sad tears? I don't like any kind of tears." He reached out to brush a teardrop from her cheek. "Or are you upset because you learned my biological father was the reprobate of the Lamanto clan?"

"He wasn't a reprobate," Bethany defended, and Keri could tell by the tone it was a long-standing issue of disagreement. "He just wasn't a family man, and he got mixed up with a bad crowd."

"You know him?" Keri asked Nick.

"Only through family gossip. He died a violent death while I was a youngster. He leaned toward the wrong side of the law."

"Nicholas!" admonished Bethany. She started to say more, but Paul approached and interrupted them.

"Our guests want to dance and insist we do the honors," he said, reaching a hand to his wife.

They shared a special smile, and he led her into the center of the room. A space had been cleared for dancing and applause rose when they moved to the center of the floor. The music rose, a slow ballad and favorite love song. They watched as Paul and Bethany moved gracefully around the room. Other couples soon joined them.

Nick wrapped his arms around Keri's waist and drew her close. She slipped her hands over his shoulders and locked her fingers behind his neck. As soon as their bodies touched, the familiar thrill of excitement sung between them. She inhaled the scent of him and felt the powerful flow of muscle, losing herself in the sensuality of the dance.

Her thoughts drifted to the conversation with his mother and his comment about his dad.

"You told me not to judge you by your family's money," she whispered softly.

Nick drew back to look into her eyes and responded in a cautious tone. "Yeah?"

Keri gave him a slow smile. "So why do you judge yourself by your biological father's flaws?"

Nick went utterly still for a minute, eyes narrowing. "Don't you start psychoanalyzing me," he grumbled. "I already heard enough of that from the department's shrink."

He pressed her head against his shoulder and began dancing again, effectively ending the subject. Keri just smiled against his jacket. The news of his genetic concerns helped her understand what drove him to prove himself one of the good guys. Given his normal air of self-assurance, she'd never have suspected he had confidence issues. Hopefully the police department's shrink had made headway in his hard head.

Before long, Nick began to glide toward the balcony doors. Once there, he kissed her gently and continued toward the staircase leading in the direction of the boathouse.

"Time for us to escape."

"Your parents?"

"I told them we'd be ditching early."

Outside, the air felt balmy on her skin, the breeze smelled like a floral garden and stars studded the midnight sky. The entire island sparkled with lanterns. A few party goers sat in chairs along the railing, but Nick ignored them and led her to the far end of the balcony.

He stopped a minute to kiss her breathless then turned and went down the ladder first. She followed. He grasped her waist and turned her in his arms when she neared the bottom. Turning, she slowly slid down his body, and they shared another hungry kiss.

"Now isn't that sweet?" The gruff voice accompanied the shadowy figure of a man leveling a gun at them.

Chapter Twenty-Two

The grating voice startled them out of their sensual bliss. Nick adroitly twisted to shield her body with his. From behind his shoulder, Keri watched as a gaunt, unkempt man stared at them with a malevolent expression.

"Jenson," Nick identified the dirty cop. "I hoped you were fish bait."

The other man's bark of laughter held no humor. "I'll bet you did. I'm a hard man to kill," he boasted. "So are you, Lamanto. I thought I'd eliminated you when the boat blew, but no such luck."

Keri felt Nick stiffen even more as the man's jibe about his boat infuriated him.

"I never thought you'd be stupid enough to trespass on this island, Jenson. Don't you have sense enough to know our security is the best in the world?"

"I got here, didn't I?" came the smug reply. "I didn't exactly blend with the tuxedo crowd, but I slipped past security without a hitch."

"You won't be so lucky leaving," Nick swore darkly.

Jenson continued, undaunted. "I need some serious money to retire to Mexico. I figure your parents are good for a couple million in ransom. I'll just kill the girlfriend to prove I'm serious. Then I'll still get the pleasure of killing you but I'll be a whole lot richer."

"Bold plan," said Nick, his tone flat and hard.

"I don't have anything to lose," Jenson reminded. "You know the profile—the most dangerous ones are the ones with nothing to lose."

"Or the ones with the most on the line," Nick replied in subtle warning.

Jenson started to laugh again, but a low, aggressive howl cut off the sound. A second warning growl sliced the air. Nick whistled sharply and the next thing Keri saw was a dark brown dog leaping in the air and catching Jenson's gun hand in his teeth. The force of the hundred-pound canine's attack knocked Jenson flat on the ground. He got off two wild gunshots, quiet thuds from a silencer, but the bullets flew in the opposite direction.

Keri's hoarse scream sounded louder in her head than the heavy night air. Nick jerked from her grasp and hurled himself on the gunman. The dog held on to Jenson's wrist despite the frantic man's attempt to dislodge him. He swung his other fist at Nick and the two exchanged some punches before Nick managed to grab the barrel of the gun.

Keri searched the ground for a weapon, but the pristine yard didn't offer anything useful, not even a stick or stone. With the two men and dog thrashing on the ground, she couldn't risk kicking at one without hurting the other.

Frantic to help, she bent down and grabbed a hand full of Jenson's hair, pulling hard. He yelped, tried to jerk from her grasp and knocked her on her rear. Then he swung wildly and hit Nick's weak shoulder. When she heard his grunt of pain, she dug in her heels, sank the fingers of her other hand into his hair and pulled with every ounce of strength she possessed.

She focused all her pent-up rage on Jenson, channeling years of anger, frustration and injustice into subduing him—the needless loss of her mother, her own infertility and the untold damage caused by greed and hatred.

With Jenson's neck stretched unnaturally, Nick landed a debilitating uppercut to his jaw. Keri actually heard the crunch of bone. Jenson went limp and Nick fell to the ground beside him, winded and struggling to catch his breath.

Then Brice and a man she'd never met showed up to call off the dog. They quickly bound Jenson's hands and ankles. Keri relaxed the strain on her arms but didn't let go. Jenson's hair felt greasy and disgusting, yet she couldn't get a message from her brain to her fingers. They remained locked in a vicious battle with right and wrong.

Nick rose to his knees and emptied the remaining bullets from the gun before handing it to the security guard. Next he rested his hand on hers. "You can let go now, baby," he whispered gruffly. She'd never heard his voice go so soft and tender. It made her heart ache.

"My fingers won't work," she said through a tear-clogged throat. Tears rolled down her cheeks, blinding her. Her whole body trembled with the aftermath of so much negative emotion.

Nick gently pried her fists open. She had handfuls of Jenson's hair tangled in her fingers. Nausea threatened as she wailed in disgust, shaking her hands violently to rid them of the dirty stuff. Nick grabbed her by her elbows and lifted her to her feet, helping her brush away the last of Jenson's hair. He hugged her fiercely, but then the would-be kidnapper woke and found himself bound. He began to fight again, swearing viciously, but the guard quickly dragged him to his feet.

"Shut your foul mouth, Jenson, or I'll have Brice gag you too," Nick warned angrily. Then he looked toward the balcony, but nobody seemed to have heard the ruckus.

"You're lucky you didn't disrupt my parents' party or I'd have to beat you senseless again."

At a small woof from the dog, now sitting obediently at his side, he reached out to stroke its head. His tone changed to one of proud affection. "Damnedest guard dog in the world."

To her, he explained in a still-gentle voice. "Luther can smell the bad guys a mile away. His hearing's almost as keen as his sense of smell, and he's trained to go for the gun hand."

Keri knew Nick wanted to distract her. She struggled to regain her composure, embarrassed by her own loss of control.

"He has my undying gratitude," she managed, still trying to regulate her breathing and collect her wits.

Nick tugged at his disheveled tuxedo and pulled her back

into his arms. He held her close.

"I'm sorry," he whispered near her ear.

Her throat closed again, making speech difficult, but she asked, "Sorry for saving my life again?"

"Sorry for endangering it again."

"You didn't," she said. His job had. Could she bear this paralyzing terror on a regular basis? Could she kiss him goodbye every morning wondering what maniac he'd encounter that day? She loved him so much, but could she bear a long-term relationship? Could she bear to lose him permanently?

"You'd better go with Jenson," she finally told him, withdrawing from his embrace. "I know there will be reports to file and other police stuff to take care of."

He stared at her for a long, pregnant minute. "You're sure?"

"Go," she said, "All I want is a shower and bed."

"I'll be back as soon as possible," he promised with another brief kiss. He walked her to a private entrance that would help her bypass the party and then he was gone.

He returned several hours later. Keri had showered and gone to bed, but not to sleep. She heard him enter the room and walk quietly to her bedside. Breathing soft and easy, she pretended to be asleep. Nick brushed a lock of her hair from her face and stroked her cheek. When she didn't respond, he finally left the room.

Coward. Keri remembered her dad's words. She'd never thought herself a coward, but she felt like one tonight. Nick embodied everything she'd ever wanted in a man—bravery, loyalty, passion. She trusted him with her life, but could she find the courage to trust him with her heart?

A tear slipped from beneath closed eyelids.

On Sunday, they left the villa shortly after breakfast even though Keri's plane didn't leave until late in the day. Nick's plans for a night of loving hadn't materialized. The bruises on his face and hands had alarmed his family, so he'd given them a watered down version of events. Keri hadn't contradicted him.

They took the speedboat back to the marina with him at the wheel and her in the passenger seat. The rumble of the engines made up for the lack of conversation. Once there, they docked and dropped anchor. Nick led Keri to a sporty red Mustang convertible and popped the trunk.

"Why am I not surprised you drive a hot, fast car?" she teased in an attempt to lighten the heavy tension between them. Already dreading the inevitable parting, she didn't want to make it worse by silence and brooding.

Nick responded in kind. "Because I'm a hot, fast guy?" he tossed back at her. After loading her bag in the trunk, he helped her into the passenger seat. With a quick kiss, he closed the door and rounded the front of the car. Once behind the wheel, he revved the engine and left the marina with a squeal of tires.

"In a hurry to be rid of me?" she asked. "Or need to get rid of some pent-up anger?"

Nick took a deep breath and gave her a smile. His left cheek bore a purple bruise. His eye was swollen, his lip cut, but he still looked gorgeous to her. Gorgeous and wounded.

"A little leftover tension, I guess, combined with a whole bunch of new tension."

Keri assumed he meant the tension of parting ways again. As the time for her to leave grew closer, he'd grown more distant.

"Mind if I put the top down?"

"Not at all," she said, knowing she should soak up as much sunshine and warmth as possible.

Just the thought of returning to Thornsbury gave her a chill. And that made her frown. She'd never really liked the fall of the year. For some, it meant crisp air, clear skies and brilliant color. For her, it had just meant the end of summer and she'd never welcomed that time of year.

"Do we have a destination or are we just sightseeing until I have to get to the airport?" He'd gone all secretive when she'd prodded him for details earlier.

"We have a destination. Just relax and enjoy the scenery while I blow some cobwebs from my brain. I'll do the tour guide thing if you want to know anything specific."

Once on the open road, the wind roaring around the car prevented small talk, but Keri found it exhilarating. The warmth and wonderful mixture of scents soothed her frayed nerves. She enjoyed the wind tangling her hair and the sun on her face. Neither of them had gotten much sleep, so it did help clear her head.

Nick slowed the car when they reached more densely populated residential areas. They passed by expensive-looking gated communities and moved farther into the suburbs before he finally turned into a small community of older houses and tree-lined streets. The homes had mature landscapes with flowering shrubs and well-tended gardens.

He drove past a small park where families strolled and skateboarders zipped along a special path. A pool glistened in the sunlight, empty now because of the early hour. Keri heard the chime of nearby church bells as Nick pulled to a stop in front of a lovely, cream-colored split-level house.

"Are we visiting someone?" she asked when he switched off the ignition.

"No, there's something I want to show you."

He climbed from the car and moved around to open her door.

Keri unfastened her seat belt. "Here?" she asked, looking toward the house. It sat about twenty yards from the street with a flower-lined sidewalk.

"You don't like the looks of it?" he asked as he took her arm and ushered her up the walk.

"It's a lovely house."

"It has a front porch."

She noticed that. The wide porch had an old-fashioned

wood swing on one side and an assortment of wicker furniture on the opposite side. It looked a lot like their front porch back home.

"I want to sit on the swing and talk awhile."

"Do you know the owners? They might not appreciate us perching on their porch."

"Nobody lives here right now," he explained as they crossed the wood floor and took a seat on the swing.

"Then do you mind explaining why we're here?"

Nick didn't look at her but slipped an arm around her shoulders, pulled her close and put the swing in motion. "I hired a realtor and asked her to visit Thornsbury. I wanted her to check out the homes and then find something as close as possible in Miami. She found this community and this house."

"Oh, Nick!" Keri was lost for words, looking around them with new eyes.

"There are hospitals and a couple of urgent care facilities in driving distance. The neighbors are decent, family-oriented people and the crime rate is really low. It's like a small town in the concrete jungle."

"Nick!" she squeezed his hand and tried to interrupt, but he continued.

"Nonna Lamanto used to say, 'Don't just wish for it, make it happen.' With the insurance money from my boat, I could put a sizeable down payment on this place. I just need someone to share expenses."

Keri wondered what he wanted from her. Did he want a wife, a live-in lover, a roommate? How did he envision their future? They hadn't discussed the issue for weeks.

"Share expenses?" she repeated cautiously.

"Share expenses, share my bed, share my life," he expanded. Then he reached into his pocket and withdrew a small square box. Her eyes widened when he opened it to show her a beautiful solitaire diamond. The sunlight caught the stone and sparkled with brilliance.

"Oh, Nick!"

"Will you marry me?" he asked, his voice low and gruff with emotion.

Heart nearly pounding out of her chest, she reached toward the ring and touched the gemstone.

"If you don't like it, you can pick out something else."

"It's gorgeous. I love it."

"And I love you," he whispered softly. "I have since I stowed away in your car and my angel shoved a gun in my face."

She still had doubts. Still worried about his work and still didn't know if she could survive city life, but she also knew she couldn't live in Thornsbury when her heart lived in Miami. She didn't want to be a coward, didn't want to miss a chance to know true love.

"I'm old-fashioned," she whispered.

"You want me on my knees?" he asked lightly.

"No. Never," she quickly replied. "But I would like you to put the ring on my finger."

Nick's sigh of relief echoed around the porch. He pulled her close for a hug and kiss and then lifted the ring from its velvet bed.

As he slipped it on her finger, he added, "I already talked to your dad and brother. Jack is okay with us getting married. Your dad's not totally sold on the idea, but he's not against it, either. He wants you to be happy."

Tears filled her eyes at the thought of her dad, her friends, and the only home she'd ever known. Since meeting Nick and falling head over heels in love, the rest paled in comparison.

She watched as he slid the ring onto her finger. He lifted her hand to kiss it and she clutched his hand in return. Then they were wrapped in each other's arms, holding tight and kissing deeply. Keri knew this is where she belonged now. With this man, whatever the future might hold.

"Forever?" she asked softly.

"You bet. I don't make commitments lightly," he added,

stroking a curl off her cheek. "I've given our future a lot of thought, and I've decided to leave the police force."

"What?" She leaned back a little and stared into his eyes. "I thought you loved your job, and you're a great detective."

"The department shrink says I had some deep-seeded need to prove I was one of the good guys."

"But not anymore?"

He smiled. "Maybe not so much. I'm taking a job with the family security team. I may do some consulting work for the department, but no more undercover or street work."

"You're sure? I don't want you to regret the decision or grow to resent me because of it."

"I'm one hundred percent certain," he assured her, brushing his lips back and forth over hers. "With you in my life, I don't need the challenge or the risks. I want to be sharing this swing with you for the next fifty or so years."

Keri's eyes filled with tears as a rush of emotion blasted her. Her chest tightened along with her throat.

"You didn't think to tell me that before proposing?" she challenged.

He studied her intently. "I had to know if you wanted me for better or worse, richer or poorer, 'til death."

She looked into his beautiful, battered eyes. "That's how I want you." Cupping her hand on his un-bruised cheek, she drew him closer for a long, deep, commitment-rich kiss. When they finally drew apart, Nick wiped the tears from her cheeks.

"I have a key. Want to see the inside?"

She gave him a watery laugh. "Of course I do. Is it furnished?"

They moved to the door and he unlocked it. "Just appliances right now." Once he had it opened, he swung her into his arms. Holding her close to his heart, he carried her over the threshold.

Laughing, she chided, "You're not supposed to do that until we're married."

He kicked the door shut and slowly lowered her to her feet. Rubbing his body sensuously against hers, he said, "In my heart, we've been married since the first time I woke up in bed with *la mia infermiera d'angelo."*

Keri's smile deepened as happy tears rolled down her face. She grasped his face in both her hands and gave him a hard kiss. "I love you, Nicholas Lamanto."

"'Bout damned time you said so, Merritt."

About the Author

Becky Barker is an award-winning romance author whose novels have been translated into more than a dozen languages, published in electronic format, and re-issued in trade paperback as well as large print library editions.

Her personal hero is a former Marine who helped her create three wonderful children. Rachel and her husband, Jerramy; Amanda and her husband, Jay; Thad and his wife, Dara, all live within a few miles of Mom & Dad in rural Ohio.

Besides spending time with her family, Becky enjoys music, gardening, fishing and reading. She loves to hear from readers and can be reached through her website at BeckyBarker.com. Or find her on Facebook and Twitter with the name Becky.Barker.

She flew to him on broken wings...

On Wings of Love

© 2006 Becky Barker

Wounded and running for her life, photo-journalist Jillian Brandt turns to the only person in the world she feels she can trust—rancher Trey Langden—her former love, and the very same man she'd wronged more than once. Would he believe her tale? Would he even care? She gambled everything that he would.

It wasn't the phone call itself that rocked Trey's equilibrium, but the familiar voice on the other end. Why now? Just when he was coming to terms over the bitter break-up with the only woman he'd ever loved? Still, he couldn't turn Jillian away, not with the desperation he sensed in her cryptic utterings.

This time would be different and he'd be damned if he'd let her walk all over him again. He held the reins now.

Available now in ebook and print from Samhain Publishing.

Is he the real deal, or just another regret waiting to happen?

A Forever Kind of Guy

© 2011 Barbara Meyers

First on Hayley Christopher's list to get her train-wreck life back on track: stay away from men. Especially the ones who cause a ripple effect of bad decisions.

Still reeling from a high-profile divorce, the college dropout and former pro cheerleader is stumbling through yet another challenge—temporary custody of her nephew, Fletcher. No one knows better than Hayley that she's not mother material. When she opens the door to her new landlord and old flame, she wonders just how many more past mistakes she is destined to pay for.

After the death of his wife, Ray Braddock is still putting the pieces back together. Hayley—and the silent little boy at her side—both bristle with emotional barriers so high, it appears no one but him can see that together, three broken people just might make a whole family.

As she watches Fletcher respond to Ray's patient care, Hayley's determination to hold on to her heart begins to soften. But just when she begins to think that Ray is one opportunity she shouldn't let slip by, Fletcher's gang-connected father threatens to make her pay for the one good choice she ever made...

Warning: Touches on issues of death, child abandonment, neglectful parenting. Sensuous love scenes.

SAMHAIN
PUBLISHING
www.samhainpublishing.com
Green for the planet.
Great for your wallet.
OK

CPSIA information can be obtained at www.ICGtesting.com
Printed in the USA
LVOW081610180912

299307LV00004B/47/P

9 781609 288174